Clarity Bloom

KILLER BAIT

A Clarity Bloom Humorous Mystery Novel

MARTINA DALTON

Write as Rain Books

Book Formatting Template by Derek Murphy @Creativindie

Killer Bait : A Clarity Bloom Humorous Mystery

Copyright © 2019 by Martina Dalton.

For information contact :

Martina Dalton

http://www.martinadalton.com

Book and Cover design by Martina Dalton

ISBN: **978-1-7331168-2-4**

First Edition: September 2019

DEDICATION

This book is dedicated to our good dog, Comet, who we were blessed to have as a furry family member for only seven years. We miss you, buddy.

CHAPTER 1

TEXTING WHILE WALKING UP STAIRS is never a good idea. That thought hadn't crossed my mind until I tripped on the first step and sprawled face first on the short staircase to my house. Groceries hit the deck and tumbled out of the bag.

With a heavy sigh, I rubbed my bleeding shin and crawled to a sitting position at the top of the stoop. I glanced around to see if any of my neighbors had seen.

My phone was wedged between two slats of wood on the large wrap-around porch. I wiggled it out and checked the screen. Still intact.

I hit the send button again. It was the fifteenth time I'd sent the same text to my best friend, Janice. "Where are you?"

Like almost everyone at Opulent during the launch of a new product, I'd worked all morning—on a Saturday. Janice said she had something important to take care of and would be in later. But she never showed up.

I glanced at my screen again, waiting for a response.

Nothing.

It wasn't like her to ignore messages. Janice was a top-notch event planner. Her communication and organizational skills were bar none.

We were working together in preparation for the launch of our company's latest product, a high-tech wearable called the BFF Bangle. There'd been so many late-nighters with barely time to eat. Which was why I was now faced with gathering up the various items from my spilled grocery bags. I couldn't wait to restock my pantry and refrigerator. My stomach let out a loud grumble.

I stood up and dug the keys out of my pocket to unlock the door of my cozy Craftsman-style home. I shouldered it open and nearly fell over my cat. "Pumpkin, you scared the crap out of me." I kicked the door shut behind me with my three-inch Jimmy Choo heels.

Once inside, I took a deep breath. This house was my happy place. The warm wood floors and the stone fireplace instantly gave me a sense of peace.

At twenty-seven, I was fortunate to have a house in one of the more popular city neighborhoods in Seattle. I'd paid a pretty penny for an interior designer to pick soft earth tone colors for the walls and quality furniture to complement the layout of each room. It was my refuge.

Pumpkin meowed, twisting around my bruised legs as I attempted to carry the bags into the kitchen. He had just grown out of his kitten phase and was now a big cat with a full-grown appetite.

"I know, I know. It's six o'clock—time to eat. I'll feed you in just a second, okay?"

I set the bags on the counter and plunged my hand into the one containing the cans of cat food. I opened one, scraped the contents into a clean ceramic bowl, and set it next to the water dish. "Here you go."

My ravenous orange tabby made a beeline for the bowl and began wolfing down his food.

I frowned. Had I forgotten to feed Pumpkin yesterday? God, the entire week had been a blur. I wouldn't be surprised if I had.

My phone buzzed. Oh, good. Janice must finally be getting around to answering her texts. But the message wasn't from Janice. It was from Paul, the CEO of Opulent.

"Now what?" I said out loud. The cat momentarily looked up from his food, then dug back in.

The text from Paul read, "Where the hell is Janice?"

Good question, I thought. "I don't know. Been trying to reach her myself." I sent the message. This was bad. If Janice wasn't answering any of her texts, something had to be wrong. It wasn't like her to ignore messages.

"If she texts you first, tell her to call me. And tell her that if she doesn't get back to me ASAP, she's fired."

Nice. "It's Saturday. She deserves a break. We've been working hard," I texted back. Anger was bubbling up inside me. Janice and I had been working sixteen-hour days for the last couple of weeks in preparation for the product launch. Couldn't he be appreciative once in a while?

"It's my ass on the line, Clarity," Paul texted back. "I'll give you a break after the product launches. Find Janice. Now."

I sighed and set my phone down. Yes, I would find Janice. But first, I needed to eat. The cat food was starting to smell good to me.

Surveying my brand new remodeled kitchen with its dark granite countertops and cherry-stained cabinets, I was almost glad I hadn't had time to cook. There were no dirty dishes in the sink to fuss over. It gave me a feeling of luxury to see everything clean and in its place.

I unpacked the groceries and loaded a plate with hot, ready-made macaroni and cheese and a container of Caesar salad. After the first bite, I realized I really should have a nice glass of red wine to go with it because macaroni and cheese was pasta. And pasta deserved a decent glass of red wine. Once my wine was poured, I devoured the entire meal in less than five minutes.

I changed into my favorite sweat pants, a hoodie, and plush slippers. Ah, that was more like it. Much better. Those heels were killing me.

Now that my body had stopped shaking from hunger, my thoughts wandered back to Janice. I went into the living room and opened up my laptop. Sinking into the oversized couch, I launched Facebook. I sent Janice a personal message. "Are you there? I've been trying to reach you all day. Paul is pissed he can't get a hold of you. Is everything okay?"

While I waited for Janice to respond, I pulled up the spreadsheet of tasks left to do for the product launch. I still had to set up the series of Facebook and Instagram ads, schedule the radio interviews, and write the text for the Twitter posts. Being the company's social media maven was no easy task. We were releasing new products and apps at a rate of one every two months or so, a schedule that was frenetic and sometimes unrealistic. And the pace only seemed to be picking up.

I checked Facebook again to see if Janice had responded, but there was no indication my message had been read.

"Huh." Where could she be? I got out my phone again and scrolled down my list of contacts until I reached Janice's sister, Margaret. I touched the name on my screen.

"Hello?" Margaret had a rich, sultry voice. Janice was beautiful in her own way, but Margaret had cornered the market on sexy. No matter where that girl went, guys followed her like puppies drooling over a bone.

"Hi, Margaret, it's Clarity. Have you heard from Janice today? I can't seem to get a hold of her."

"She called me several hours ago. Before she went on her date," Margaret said. "And speaking of dates, I need to get back to mine."

"Janice has a date?"

"Yeah, didn't she tell you? Maybe I shouldn't have said anything. She was kind of embarrassed that she'd met the guy through an online dating service."

"Online dating service?" Janice didn't seem the type to sign up for something like that. She'd always preferred meeting people in person. Then again, she never had time to do so with the kind of hours she worked. Come to think of it, neither did I. Why hadn't she shared the news with me?

"Do you know where Janice and her date went? I need to find her. Our boss is angry he can't reach her."

"Your boss is a jerk," Margaret shot back. "The poor girl never gets a minute to herself. He's been working you two like mules."

I sighed. "I know. It's just that this product launch is a really big deal. If you hear from her, will you have her call me?"

"Of course."

After I ended the call, I got back on Janice's Facebook timeline. Had her status changed to "In a relationship"? No. It still said, "Single." Besides, Janice wasn't so impulsive as to change her status after just one date.

I scrolled through Janice's photos, looking for a picture of her with a guy that looked dateable. Aside from the photos of workplace parties showing Janice and some male coworker friends, there was no one.

Social media was a time-suck. I couldn't resist looking through my own photos, wondering if they'd be appealing to any member of the opposite sex. There were some dorky pics of me and my sisters. One of me and two of my brothers on the dock at sunset. That one wasn't bad—it showed off my long legs. However, it was taken at sunset, so it was hard to tell what I really looked like.

My profile photo was pretty good. It was a headshot taken for work, of course. My blue eyes and black hair made a nice contrast on the stark white, corporate background. Still, was I dateable? Was there a man out there who would like me enough to put up with my demanding work schedule?

I snapped out of my moment of self-doubt. I'd just wasted a half hour thinking about my non-existent love life. I closed the tabs on my browser and pulled up my to-do tasks again.

First thing was first—I needed to sort through the product photographs for the ads I was going to place. The images had to be engaging enough to catch a customer's attention within the first one or two seconds after they saw the ad.

My phone buzzed. It was my older brother, Zen. I accepted the call.

"Hey, sis."

"Big brother. What's up?"

Zen didn't often call me. Our lives were both so consumed by our careers, we didn't have much time to spend hanging out or even chatting on the phone.

"Have you talked to Mom and Dad yet this week?" He sounded slightly anxious.

"No. Why? Do they want us to come up and help with the hemp harvest again?" I rolled my eyes.

Zen chuckled. "Not this time. They want you to set up a website for their bed and breakfast."

"What bed and breakfast? They live out in the middle of nowhere."

"You know how they are. They're trying something new."

"Like the time they decided to have a goat farm?" I laughed. "Remember when the goats broke down the fence and we spent three days hunting them all down? Good times."

"I do remember." Zen hesitated. "Could you go out and check on them tomorrow? Maybe take some photos for their website? I'd do it, but I'm working on a big case, and I just don't have the time. Besides, this seems like it's more up your alley anyway."

I sighed. "You think I have time? I'm in the middle of a product launch. Why can't Harmony do it? She only lives an hour away from them."

"Harmony went to Vegas with her boyfriend."

"Oh." The good and bad forces were duking it out in my head. They were my parents. I had an obligation to help them out. On the other hand, they were always doing dumb stuff that required their kids' intervention. It was like they did it on purpose just so we would visit. I put my palm to my forehead. God, that was so sad. They just wanted to have a connection with us kids. The guilt kicked into overdrive. "All right, fine. Why can't you join me again?"

"I'm working on a homicide case," Zen said. "Several women have disappeared in the Seattle area in a short window of time. We found the body of one of the women an hour ago."

"That's awful! I guess that beats my product launch." I felt another stab of guilt. "I'm sorry—I didn't mean to trivialize a woman being killed."

"It's okay," Zen said. "I know that wasn't your intention."

I frowned. I stared hard at the unanswered Facebook message to my friend. Suddenly, I had a bad feeling in the pit of my stomach. "Zen? Have you identified the body of the woman?"

There was long pause before he answered. "Hang on. Swanson just confirmed the identification." There was another pause. "Shit."

"Who is she?" My heart beat faster.

His voice nearly broke. "I'm afraid I can't tell you. We haven't notified the next of kin."

"Zen?" My voice shook. "Can you tell me if the name of the woman is Janice Trudeau?"

There was a long pause before he answered. "How did you know?"

CHAPTER 2

Zen knocked on my door an hour later.

My cheeks were wet with tears and my eyes were so puffy I could barely see.

"How is this possible? How did she die?" I hitched in a sob and wiped the mucus from my nose with a crumpled tissue. "Her sister said she just talked to her a few hours ago."

He nodded. "One of my men already talked with Margaret. She told us the same thing."

I broke into a fresh round of sobs. "She must be devastated! Janice was her only sister. Her only sibling, as a matter of fact. I can't even imagine if I lost you or any of our other brothers or sisters."

Zen pulled a handkerchief out of his pocket and handed it to me. I mopped my face with it and blew my nose. It was drenched within a few minutes. "Here." I tried handing it back to him.

"Keep it." He waved the cloth away.

"Poor Janice." I started up again. "She was such a good person. She didn't deserve to die. Oh, God." I nearly fell over with the gut-wrenching, emotional pain. Zen caught me and led me to the couch.

"Sis, I hate to do this to you, but I've got to ask you some questions."

"What?" I looked up at him, trying to see him through the slits my eyes had become.

"Have you and Janice been friends a long time?"

I blinked. How could he not know this? "Not just friends, Zen. *Best* friends. For a couple of years now. Ever since we started working at Opulent."

He gave me a guilty look and wiped his brow. "Sorry. I have to know if she mentioned anything to you. Was there someone new in her life? Or anything unusual going on that raised a red flag with you?"

"Not that I know of." I thought about what Margaret had said. I was still wondering why Janice hadn't mentioned she'd had a date for this evening. "Margaret told me that Janice had a date tonight—through an online dating service."

Zen perked up. "Margaret didn't mention that. Did Janice tell you anything about the guy?"

I shook her head. "No. As a matter of fact, she didn't tell me about the date at all. I didn't know until Margaret told me."

Zen sat down next to her. "That's unusual. Don't best friends tell each other everything?"

More tears leaked out of my eyes. "I thought so. But I guess not."

Zen got up and went to the kitchen. He opened the freezer and took out an ice pack, wrapped it in a dish towel and brought it to me. "Here. Put this on your face—it'll reduce the swelling. It's going to be all right. It probably doesn't seem like it now, but you'll feel a little better eventually. Grief can sucker-punch you. It can cause an intense physical, as well as emotional, pain."

I sniffled. "Yes, it really does hurt. How did you get so smart?"

He gave me a sympathetic smile. "I deal with the effects of grief every day. I talk to families who are going through hell when their loved ones are killed. It's tough to watch, but I've become accustomed to it in a tragic sort of way."

"I don't know how you do it." I leaned my head back on the back of the couch and applied the ice pack to my eyes.

"Part of the job."

"Well, I would never want a job like that."

"It has its rewarding moments to balance out the bad ones." Zen sat down next to me and patted my leg.

I took the ice pack from my face and stared at Zen intently. "Where did you find her body?"

Zen shook his head. "I don't think you really want to know the details right now, do you? I mean, you've just had a terrible shock."

"No." I sat up straight. "I need to know what happened to her."

"Maybe a little later would be better." Zen gave me the look. The look that communicated that the truth would be too awful to hear right now.

I leaned forward. "No. I need to know."

Zen sighed. "You're so stubborn."

"It runs in the family."

"All right. But don't say I didn't warn you." He got up from the couch and went into the kitchen. He took a beer out of the fridge for himself and poured a glass of red wine for me.

"Here." He handed me the glass. "You're going to need this."

I took the wine from my brother and took a big gulp. "Tell me."

Zen cleared his throat. "Janice was found in an industrial park in South Seattle."

I frowned. "Where in the industrial park?"

"In a dumpster. She was beaten badly, strangled and…" Zen's voice broke. "And hacked into pieces with a large knife or axe."

I gasped. "What?"

Zen wiped his forehead with his sleeve. "I'm not gonna lie. It was a terrible sight."

I stood up on shaky legs. I felt the color drain from my face. "You're telling me that my friend was beaten, strangled, hacked to pieces," I hitched in a ragged breath, "and thrown in a dumpster?"

"Sis, you should sit down." Zen reached for my hand and gently tugged me back onto the couch.

I shot right back up to my feet. "What kind of a psycho would do something like that to Janice?" I began pacing around the room. "I mean, I don't understand. How could someone do that?"

Zen took a long swig of his beer and then stood up. "I've been asking myself that for the past couple of hours."

"Oh, God," I moaned. "This can't be happening."

"Maybe you should go lie down and rest."

"No! I want to do something! We need to find her killer and make sure he doesn't do this to anyone else." Purpose welled up inside me. "Lying down is not going to make me feel better."

"Tell you what, you get cleaned up—maybe take a hot bath. My new partner is waiting for me in the car outside. We have some paperwork to do and we need to confer with the higher-ups at the station. I'll call you if I think you can give us some insight about Janice and the type of guys she might've gone for."

I nodded and dabbed at my face with a tissue. "I'll do whatever it takes to catch whoever did this."

CHAPTER 3

My dream was a welcome escape from reality. In it, I was walking hand-in-hand with the quintessential tall-dark-and-handsome man on a white-sand beach. The gentle breeze carried the heavenly scent of gardenias and the briny smell of the ocean. The two aromas separated, intertwined, and became a new fragrance altogether.

The man scooped me up in his strong arms and carried me to where the surf met the sand. I laughed and held onto him tightly.

The sun was warm upon my—riiinnnnng!

I opened one eye.

Riiiingggg! My ringtone jarred me awake. I smacked my phone, as if that would make the infernal noise stop. Who was the man on the beach? I desperately tried to burrow myself back into my dream.

Riiiiingggg! Damn it. Why hadn't I set my phone to silent? I forced my eyes open, grabbed it, and hit the answer button. "Hello?"

"Clarity." It was my boss, Paul. "You promised me you'd get a hold of Janice. Why hasn't she called me?" His voice was terse, and it grated on my nerves.

I sat up and rubbed her face. "The police haven't told you?" I could barely see out of my puffy eyes.

"Police?" Paul sounded annoyed. "Why, what has she done? Is she in jail?"

I felt a twinge in my chest. "No, Paul. I'm so sorry to be the one to tell you…Janice is dead."

A pause. "Yeah, right. She better be dead. Because I'm going to kill her for not getting her butt to work when all hell is breaking loose!"

I winced. "I'm not kidding, Paul. Janice was killed. She was murdered."

"What the?" Paul's voice rose an octave. "Is this some kind of sick joke?"

"No, of course not. I wouldn't joke about something like this." I was on the verge of tears again. "She's dead." A sob escaped my lips, but I managed to force down the full extent of my emotions.

"What the hell? She was right in the middle of booking everything for the tech conference in Vegas. How am I going to replace her on such short notice? Not to mention having to train someone new. I can't believe she went and got herself killed!"

I held the phone away from my ear and stared at it. Was I still dreaming? I must've misunderstood him.

"Clarity!" Paul roared. "I'm talking to you."

"Are you serious? I just told you that Janice is dead. There are more important things than the tech conference. This was Janice."

"Yeah, I know." The irritation in Paul's voice was apparent. "And while we all liked Janice, we have work to do. And just because our event planner is… no longer living doesn't mean that the earth stops spinning on its axis. I want you to write up a job description for Janice's position immediately. Post it to our LinkedIn page, our Facebook page, and tweet it. Oh, and does anyone look at the monster job board thingy anymore? If you think they do, post it there too."

I could feel my blood pressure beginning to climb. "I can't believe…"

"When you're done with that, get to the office ASAP. I'll need you to take over her duties until we find a replacement. I'll send you a task list. You'll also need to access her email and go through that, so you can determine what got done and what didn't."

My blood pressure level popped the top of my head right off and a flood of anger blew out and splattered the ceiling. "No effing way am I coming in today! My good friend and colleague was murdered. And it's Sunday. I have family obligations. I'll see you on Monday morning." I jabbed the call end button and threw my phone on the bed, my heart pounding. "Of all the rotten people in the world, that one takes the cake."

Pumpkin, who'd been eyeing me from the foot of the bed, jumped off and ran out of the room.

I got up, anger still racing through my veins and marched into the kitchen. I banged open the cupboard, where my coffee-making supplies were organized neatly, and proceeded to make myself an industrial-strength Americano with cream. I was far too upset to eat, so I sat at the kitchen table and sipped my coffee until my breathing had slowed and the pounding in my ears had subsided.

When had the company gotten so fast-paced and out of control that my boss was willing to forego grief to launch a product? I needed to seriously re-evaluate my role there. No, I needed to calm down. I couldn't quit. Not now. There were too many bills to pay.

I took a deep breath and reminded myself that everyone handled grief differently. Some people went into a deep depression and hibernated while they were grieving. Others kept themselves really busy to delay the grief until they could handle it better. Maybe that's the kind of person Paul was. Maybe his way of dealing with Janice's death was to pretend it didn't happen and immerse himself in so much work that he didn't have to deal with the emotions.

Suddenly, I felt silly getting so upset with him. He wasn't such a bad guy. He just grieved differently from me.

Still, I wasn't going into the office.

I poured myself another cup of coffee. I'd told my parents I was going to take pictures of their new bed and breakfast and create a website for them. And on further reflection, keeping busy sounded a lot better than laying in bed and crying all day.

Maybe I was a little more like Paul than I'd like to admit.

CHAPTER 4

On the way to my parents' house in the Skagit valley, I watched the somewhat bland scenery go by. Evergreen trees, malls, and farmland seemed less exciting than the city. However, July had been a lovely month, and I found myself enjoying the blue skies and the natural surroundings of the Pacific Northwest landscape.

My cell phone rang. I pressed the answer button on my steering wheel. "Hello?"

"Hey, sis, I have some news." Zen's voice sounded a little garbled on the car's speakers.

My heart pounded. Had my brother found Janice's killer? "What is it?"

"You know that dating service Janice signed up with?"

"Yeah…" I bit my lip.

"Well," her brother continued, "she had twenty-three hits."

"Twenty-three men were interested in her profile? Is that a lot?" I pushed my sunglasses to the top of my head. I could think more clearly without them darkening my vision.

"Yep. These aren't just the ones who liked her profile, these are the ones who actually sent her a request for a date."

I drew in a deep breath. Maybe the man who murdered Janice would be arrested and brought to justice sooner than I'd imagined. "Can you find out which one of them she was with when she was killed?"

Zen sighed. "Not yet. We have to interview each and every one of those guys. This could take a while."

My mind raced. "What if the killer just packs up and leaves before you get a chance to interview him? You might be interviewing suspect number one while the killer, suspect number whatever, flies off to Mexico."

"We've got two teams out there tracking them all down. We just have to stay focused and get it done as quickly as possible."

"Sounds tedious and stressful. Hope it goes well." I passed an old lady doing fifty miles per hour on the freeway.

"Are you at Mom and Dad's yet?" he asked.

"I should be there in about fifteen minutes or so."

"Thanks for checking in on them. I know it drives you nuts to go out there."

My mind flashed back to when all nine of us were kids. My parents never seemed like adults. Ever. Just a couple of hippies who were figuring out life as it came along. Disorganization and chaos were their middle names.

"Well, you know how they are," I said. "They start a new business every other month. This one won't be any different. They get us involved, take up a bunch of our time, only to abandon the business a few weeks or months later. You're right. It does drive me crazy."

"You're preaching to the choir," he said. "But you never know, maybe this one will turn out differently."

"Always the eternal optimist." I laughed and noticed a Starbucks sign up ahead. "I need to end the call and tank up on caffeine. Thanks for the update on Janice. Will you call me if there's any news?"

"Sure. Hopefully Mom and Dad won't suck you into their drama. Good luck."

***

With coffee in hand, I opened my door and stepped out of the car. I grabbed the camera bag off the front seat and stepped back to survey my parents' home.

I was shocked. They'd actually built an addition onto the side of the house—and it was cute. They had repainted the entire house white and the once dull-gray shutters were now a rich black. Flower boxes hung from every window. Pink and purple blossoms cascaded out of them, creating a postcard-like image.

"Do you like it?" My mother's voice sounded behind me.

I nearly jumped out of my skin. "You scared me!" I turned to see my mom, whose long black braid was now streaked with gray. Her jeans were ripped at the knees and her tie-dye t-shirt was stretched tightly over her low-hanging bosom.

I hugged her, my nerves still on edge. I turned back to the house and nodded approvingly. "It's really nice, Mom. Fantastic."

Mom clapped her hands. "Oh, I'm so glad you like it! Darren! Come out here. Clarity just arrived."

I watched my father come around from the back of the house. He was covered in grime. His thinning pony tail was also losing its natural shade of chestnut and was fading to white. When had they gotten so old?

My dad grinned from ear to ear. "There's my girl!" He rushed in for a hug, nearly knocking me over and spilling my coffee. "Oops. Sorry."

I brushed the dark brown drops off my white shirt and was pleased to see they hadn't soaked in. It was a Neiman Marcus special, after all. "That's all right, Dad."

"What do you think?" He stood back and admired his work. "Not bad for an old man, eh?"

"And an old woman," Mom grumbled.

"I love it." I was surprised to realize that I meant it. "You two did an amazing job. So, you need pictures for your website?"

"As a matter of fact, we do." She gave my coffee a reproachful look. "Why don't you come inside and get some grub. I just whipped up some wheatgrass smoothies."

***

I had taken dozens of photos of the exterior of the bed and breakfast and was now headed into the garden. I stopped short and stared. "What happened to the goats?"

My mother and father's last idea had sent my siblings and me scouting for a special breed of goat that specialized in clearing brush from large, overgrown areas.

Dad shook his head. "Wanda, you tell her. It makes me too sad to talk about it."

Mom sighed. "All but two of them OD'd. So tragic."

"OD'd? What?" I cocked my head to one side. "How can a goat OD?"

"Remember that marijuana crop we had going? God, that was spectacularly lucrative." Mom shook her head. "Well, the goats broke out of their pen one night and demolished half of the crop. We found two goats the next morning, laying on their sides, dead as door nails. The two survivors were sent to rehab and now live on an animal reserve in Sequim."

I rubbed my temples. "Wow. Okay. What did you do with the rest of the marijuana crop?"

"There was still a fairly good portion left. We sold it to pay for the addition to the house."

I felt the beginning of a severe headache coming on. "Why don't you show me how the vegetable garden is shaping up. I'll take some photos of that and the flower garden as well."

When all the exterior shots had been taken, I was ready to see the interior. I stepped inside the door to the addition, my jaw dropping. It was absolutely beautiful. The lobby or common area was flooded with the light streaming in through the windows. The walls were painted a soft, buttery yellow.

"Do you like?" Dad grinned.

"I'm speechless." I walked around the room, inspecting the craftsmanship. "And the weed paid for all of this?"

"Just about." Mom shrugged. "We may need to grow a little more to cover the final touches."

I would never understand my parents' relationship with pot. It smelled bad and took away any kind of motivation to get things done. Then again, my parents had built this addition, and it looked amazing.

"Why can't you just sell some of the azaleas you've got growing in the greenhouse? Even though weed is legal, you have to have the proper license to sell for commercial use. Seems like it would be easier to grow something else."

"People don't stand in line waiting to buy azaleas, honey." Mom patted my arm. "And pot sells for a lot more than a decorative shrub."

"I guess you're right." I held my camera up to my eye and snapped some photos. "Want to show me the guest rooms?"

CHAPTER 5

The office lobby elevator dinged. I stepped inside, my gaze unfocused as the doors slid closed.

When I reached my floor, I stepped out and stood still while other employees whisked past me. The sterile, ultra-modern workplace hummed with activity, even though the air was thick with grief.

I dragged myself into the spacious office I'd shared with Janice and shut the door behind me. I set the laptop in the docking station and turned on the large flat-screen monitor.

I glanced at Janice's empty desk. My heart squeezed painfully in my chest.

A knock on the door startled me. "Coffee cart!"

"Oh, hang on." I got up to open it.

Jared, the coffee guy, pushed the cart into the room. This wasn't the standard mobile coffee cart—this was deluxe in every sense of the word. My boss spared no expense when it came to making his employees comfortable at work. Or maybe he didn't want us to ever leave, not even for a Starbucks—though that didn't stop us from occasionally escaping for a break. Plus, Paul liked the appearance of wealth and prestige in everything he touched.

"What would you like this morning?"

"Triple Americano with cream," I answered almost immediately. This was definitely a triple-shot kind of day. In fact, every day since Janice had been murdered had been a triple-shot kind of day.

"You got it." Jared ran a cord from the espresso machine to the outlet next to the door. He went to work and soon had a piping hot coffee ready. He slipped a cardboard sleeve onto the paper cup and held it out to me.

"Thank you." I took the cup gratefully and settled back down in my chair as the young man unplugged the machine and pushed it out of my office.

Opening my email, I was stunned to see so many unread messages. I furrowed my brow and noted that nearly all the messages were from my boss, Paul.

The first one read, "Clarity, since Janice is no longer able to complete her assigned tasks, all of her emails and assignments will be forwarded to you. As I mentioned in our previous phone conversation, please add these tasks to your list. All deadlines remain the same, and I'm counting on you to complete her work until we can find a suitable replacement. Regards, Paul."

No longer able to do her work? She'd been murdered for Christ's sake. It had only been a couple of days, and Paul was already cracking the whip on me to do both my own job and my friend's. Plus, the blasé tone and nonchalance of the fact that Janice had been killed. What the hell?

The notion that I should give Paul a pass since everyone handled grief differently flew right out the window and was replaced by a sweltering fury.

I glanced out the glass on either side of my office door and caught a glimpse of him striding by, his expensive suit and trendy haircut on full display. Several minions, including the Grand Poobah of brown-nosers, Russell Jones, flanked him and nodded at his every word. "Jerk," I said out loud. Paul paused just outside my door, as if he'd heard me, and glanced in my direction. I quickly flicked my attention back to my screen, pretending to be immersed in my work. His head turned back toward his destination, and he moved on.

I clicked on the next email. Janice had been in the process of ordering a booth for the tech conference in Vegas. I quickly read through the email thread, and went about ordering the booth, made a few phone calls to hire labor for set-up, and then jumped back into my own job of writing press releases and tweeting details of our latest product.

My eyes strayed away from the keyboard, and I allowed myself a peek at Janice's desk. It was still in perfect order—as if Janice would walk through the door at any minute and sit down in her chair. Her Tower of London tea cup she'd bought on our last trip abroad still had a lipstick stain on the rim. The framed picture of the two of us on a road trip to Yellowstone hung on the wall behind her desk.

Tears brimmed in my eyes, threatening to spill out onto my cheeks. I grabbed a tissue and blew my nose. Suddenly, I didn't want to be alone in my office anymore—didn't want the pain of seeing Janice's shrine laid out in front of me. I knew I wasn't the only one affected by Janice's death. I had an urge to be with Janice's other friends and to draw comfort from them.

I got up and left my office. The main room was busy, as usual. Though, judging by my sullen coworkers' red-rimmed eyes, they too were struggling to keep up the usual frenetic pace of the office. Two long tables with open work stations spaced evenly down the line were fully staffed with developers and designers. A tissue box had been placed at either end, and by the looks of it, the nearly empty boxes would soon need to be replaced with new ones.

"Oh, Clarity!" Brandi, my short and curvy friend ran toward me and hugged me tightly. "I can't believe Janice is gone."

My last shred of stoicism dissolved, and tears spilled onto my cheeks.

She handed me a tissue. "Here."

"Thank you, Brandi." I dabbed at my eyes.

Paul and Russell had just come around the corner and were walking toward us. Paul stopped when he reached the first long table and took in the scene, his eyes skating over the boxes of tissues and the tear-stained faces of his employees.

He cleared his throat. "Everyone, I can see you're taking Janice's death hard—we all are. May I remind you that we have a product launch this Friday? And five more on the heels of this launch. Brandi—I was expecting the financials report on my desk early this morning. The delay is causing a problem for me. Please have it to me within the hour."

Brandi sniffled and nodded. "All right."

"Jonah, you were supposed to have the art for the print campaign to the printer an hour ago. Clarity, you're late with the press release. I'm disappointed that you've let your duties slide—especially since I asked you to come in over the weekend."

I gave my boss a stony look. "She was my best friend, Paul."

He attempted a sympathetic expression. "I know. What happened to Janice was tragic. But we've made promises to our suppliers, our stockholders, and our customers. They won't be so understanding if we don't deliver what we've promised."

Paul turned his attention back to the group and clapped his hands. "Now, let's all get back to work! You guys are what makes this company great. Let's show our competitors that we're leaps and bounds ahead of them, okay? Nothing can get in the way of our success."

"Not even the death of one of our own? That's wonderfully compassionate of you." My words were out of my mouth before I could stop them.

Paul narrowed his eyes at me. "It takes determination and fortitude to be successful in this world, Clarity. You might want to evaluate your own situation to see if you have what it takes to come out on top."

I swallowed hard and bit back a sharp retort.

Paul spun on his heels and continued his crusade through the rest of the office.

Brandi let out a big breath of air and her shoulders relaxed. "You know, Clarity, you should be a little more careful of what you say around Paul. He's been known to let people go for less than what you just said to him."

I grimaced. "I know. I couldn't stop myself. It's just that he doesn't seem to care that Janice is gone. He wants us to pretend that everything is normal."

Jonah got up from his workstation and gave me a hug. "I'm glad you said something. I haven't been able to concentrate since I found out. And he should have some compassion. I know he's an ass, but I didn't realize how callous he is. This is making me question working here."

"Thank you, Jonah." I gave him a grateful look. His meticulously groomed facial hair was on trend, as were his black-framed glasses and his millennial, hipster outfit. I'd always had a soft spot for him—especially because he listened to everyone with an empathetic ear. "Don't lose your job over me or Janice. I'm sure things will settle down with time."

Jonah took a step back. "Stress brings out everyone's true colors. Paul's true colors must be bruised black with a side of jade greed."

Brandi gasped. "God. That's good! You have a way with words, Jonah. But like I said to Clarity, be careful what you say to the boss. He'll use it against you."

"I know, I know." I unclenched my hands, which I hadn't realized I'd balled up into fists. "I'm in no mood to deal with a person who has zero empathy."

"I hear ya." Brandi patted my arm. "Watch your back. He's a shark."

✱✱✱

Back in my office, I sat behind my large monitor and rubbed my tired eyes. I took a deep breath and considered everything that had transpired that day. Paul was a horrible person, yes. But he did pay well, and the perks of my job were numerous.

I thought about my beautiful house and the gigantic mortgage payments. If I left this job, would I be able to find work with another company at a comparable salary? I took this position because it paid nearly double the others I had interviewed for.

Having been poor most of my life, I'd been yearning to make something of myself. I'd gotten a decent scholarship and worked three jobs to get myself through college at

Brown. It was blood, sweat, and tears that got me this job and my home.

I shook my head. No. I couldn't quit. Not yet. At a minimum, I would need to pay off my hefty college loans. Even if I found a job that paid three quarters of my current salary, I didn't think I could swing both my mortgage and my college loans.

With a resigned sigh, I methodically worked through each email and task that had been added to my already-full plate.

I would be more careful around Paul. And I would do what I could to grieve for my friend in private.

CHAPTER 6

The week had flown by with the intensity of a hurricane. I was relieved it was Friday, but dreaded Janice's funeral in the afternoon. I couldn't wrap my head around the fact I would be attending the burial of my best friend.

I'd arrived in the office at six in the morning, and it was now nearly two o'clock. The launch meeting would happen in the main conference room in just a few minutes. I grabbed my laptop and rushed to the meeting, nearly bumping into Brandi, who was on her way to the meeting as well.

"I can't believe the launch is actually happening on time. That schedule was ridiculous." Brandi tried catching her breath as she jogged to the conference room.

"Me neither. I've never been so happy for the work day to be over." I found a seat somewhere in the middle of the long table.

Brandi plunked down next to me as more people filled the seats.

Paul entered the room, laptop in hand, and sat down at the head of the long conference table. "All right. Our official launch happens in exactly one hour, so once our briefing is over, you can tie up any loose ends before we hit the send button. Brandi, let's start with you."

Brandi swiped a dark curl behind her ear and cleared her throat. "We came in just under budget with the BFF Bangle, but we haven't added in the cost of the upcoming tech conference, so we might go a little over."

Paul nodded and turned his gaze toward the opposite side of the table. "How about the tweak we had to do to get the color palette right?"

One of the developers, Bernard, cleared his throat. "Done. It was just a matter of aligning the RGB values. One set of parameters had them listed incorrectly and that caused the irregularity. We went in, discovered the issue, and fixed it yesterday. It's working perfectly now."

Paul grunted. "Good, good. Clarity, how are we doing with getting the word out?"

I glanced at my laptop screen. "I've tweeted, written articles and blog posts—which I sent to all the tech magazines and sites—posted Instagram photos, updated our website with the full color shots we got from last week's photoshoot, and with Jonah's help, put together some gorgeous ads for Facebook. Those launched an hour ago, and we're already seeing conversion rates through pre-orders on our site."

"Good. What about the tech conference details that Janice was supposed to have done?" Paul stared at me intently.

I bristled. Supposed to have done? He said it as if Janice had purposely shirked her duties by intentionally being slaughtered. I bit back a bitter retort and carefully worded my response. "She had most of it done, actually. All I had to do was confirm with the venue, and make sure we had a crew to install everything at the booth."

He shrugged. "Okay, then. Brad, go ahead and activate the launch in full—enable the Buy Now buttons on all of the commercial sites where the BFF Bangle will be sold. Double check with retailers at their brick and mortars too."

Brad nodded. "Got it."

Paul continued around the table, grilling each person on their progress, until at last each one had weighed in. He pushed his chair back from the table and stood up. "Well done, team."

I didn't realize how tense I'd been until Paul left the room. I allowed my shoulders to sag and let out a breath of relief. Then I remembered that Janice's funeral would be in less than two hours, and the muscles in my shoulders tightened, bringing on the beginning of a headache.

"What time should we leave for the funeral?" It was like Brandi had read my mind.

"It starts at four o'clock," I said. "I guess we should head out at around three, so we have a chance to find parking."

"Sounds like a plan." Brandi walked into the hall. "I'll tell the others."

I went back to my office and began straightening my desk and checking items off on my task list.

Two men appeared at the open door. I looked up just as one of them cleared his throat.

"Sorry to bother you. We were told that Janice Trudeau shared an office with you?"

I swallowed hard. "Yes. Can I help you?"

"We're Detectives Beacon and Ross. We need to take a few of her belongings for evidence."

"I thought this was Zen Bloom's case."

Beacon responded. "It is. While the trail is still hot, the Seattle PD has assigned more homicide detectives to it."

I bit back tears. The word "homicide" was still a bitter pill to swallow. I motioned toward Janice's desk. "They've already collected her laptop for evidence, so you can take what you need."

I watched as they carefully packed some of her things—mostly notebooks and post-its, into neat boxes. The door shut behind them when they were finished. The only things they left behind were a few pictures, a plant, and an empty tea cup.

✱✱✱

When three o'clock finally arrived, I grabbed my coat, purse, and laptop bag and headed out for the funeral.

Everyone else was doing the same, their normally loud conversations toned down to somber whispers.

We had just reached the elevators when Paul and his minions appeared from the hallway. "Where are you all going?"

"Janice's funeral." Brandi pushed a curl from her face and adjusted the purse strap on her shoulder.

Paul shook his head. "I didn't say any of you could leave early."

"Paul—the BFF Bangle has been launched. And it's Janice's funeral, for God's sake. We need to be there." Brandi frowned.

The boss was clearly irritated. "I'm glad you were all so fond of Janice, but I'm sorry. You need to sew up those final threads on this project and prepare for the next product launch, which," he paused to look at his phone, "has a very short timeline. There's no time to lose."

"This is outrageous!" Bernard said. "She was a friend— and a loyal co-worker. It would be wrong of us to not attend the service."

Paul's eyes narrowed. "Fine. Go ahead and go. But understand this. If I see any of you leaving this office before five o'clock, don't bother coming back."

His words hung in the air. I was struck with both horror and disgust. How could I work for a company that valued its tight deadlines over its people? Over human lives? I got the overwhelming urge to swing the door open and cross the threshold… to leave behind the company and the monster who ran it.

My coworkers hung their heads and slunk back to their workstations. I, alone, stood and met Paul's piercing gaze.

"Well?" Paul crossed his arms.

Several things flashed through my mind. I imagined myself calling Paul a jackass and flipping him the bird. I could almost feel how good it would be to storm out of the office. But the vision of my beautiful home, my car, and my new furniture being hauled off by a repo company kept me from taking the plunge.

I sighed and quietly went back to my office, the image of Paul's smug face haunting me the entire way.

Once in my chair, anger reared its ugly head. How dare he? Preventing Janice's friends from attending her funeral? I would not allow this to happen. Without hesitation, I picked up my cell and called my brother.

He answered on the first ring. "Detective Bloom, Homicide."

"Zen, you've got to help me."

"Clarity? What's wrong?"

I could tell by the edge in his voice that he thought I was in danger. "Oh, sorry. I'm okay. Everything is fine. I mean, everything is not fine! My jerk of a boss is refusing to let any of us go to Janice's funeral." Now that I'd said it out loud, I got even angrier. "He is a molten lump of turd. How dare he? That dirty, rotten scum—"

"Whoa, whoa. Take it easy!" Zen interrupted my rant. "Take a deep breath."

I paused for a moment. "I'm sorry. I'm just so disgusted. He told us if any of us left the office, we'd be fired."

"Do you have some sort of deadline that he wants you to stay for?" Zen kept his voice soothing. He knew when I blew my top, it took a lot of patience to talk me off the ledge.

"No. That's just it." I thumped my fist on the desk. "We've finished the deadline. All the important work is done. What's left is the last-minute paperwork—stuff that can be done within the next week or so."

"Hmmm. Why do you think he doesn't want you to go?"

"Because he's a control freak!" My voice rose higher. "He enjoys turning the screws, watching us squirm. Sure, he gives us great benefits, perks of all kinds. Sadly, that comes with a price. Now, he thinks he owns us. Like we're puppets he can manipulate and make us do whatever he wants."

Zen sighed. "I'm sorry your boss is an ass. Really, I am. How would you like me to help you?"

I leaned back in my chair. "Is there any way you can use the investigation to make it so the employees can go to the funeral? I don't know how. My brain is seriously sleep-deprived, so trying to come up with a creative solution right now is not working."

Zen was quiet for a moment, and then said, "Actually, I think there is a way."

CHAPTER 7

I scrolled through the documents outlining our next high-tech gadget. I had no idea where to begin. My head had been so wrapped up with the current product—and then with the murder, I couldn't even think about work. The anger and disappointment swirled around inside me. Paul had been firm—we couldn't leave before five o'clock. In my state of mind, there was no way I could focus on the next product in the chute.

I chewed on my fingernails. What had Zen meant when he'd said there was a way that we could go to the funeral?

A knock on the door startled me. I sat up straight and smoothed down my skirt. "Come in!"

The door opened, and Paul stood in the entrance. He cleared his throat. "Clarity, I had a change of heart. I'm allowing everyone to leave work early to attend Janice's funeral."

I stared at him. "Why?"

Paul looked slightly pale. "Well, I gave it some thought. You've all worked very hard to launch the BFF Bangle. It's only right that I let you honor and grieve for one of our own."

I forced a smile and got up to retrieve my jacket and purse. "Thank you, Paul. That's very... kind of you."

He took a step backward into the hall. "By the way, per the investigation into Janice's death, the police will be there, and they're expecting everyone who worked with Janice to answer a few questions after the service. Your brother, the detective, is very persuasive." He strode down the hall and continued to spread the word about the change of plans.

I smiled as I buttoned up my blazer. So, that's how Zen had pulled it off. My brother was brilliant. I owed him big time.

* * *

After the memorial service, everyone joined the procession to the graveside. I suspected if they weren't required to talk with police afterward, most of my coworkers would've skipped watching Janice's coffin being lowered into the ground.

I had gone through my entire pack of tissues already and it felt like my face was melting away.

Janice's family was standing near the open grave, clutching each other and hunched over with grief. I caught a glimpse of Janice's sister, Margaret, whispering something into her mother's ear. Even after enduring the pain of saying goodbye to her one and only sibling, Margaret was still so beautiful. Her auburn hair shone against her black dress, her slim figure accentuated by its tailored cut.

My eyes landed on my brother, Zen, standing behind Janice's family. He was handsome in his dark navy suit. He laid a hand on Mrs. Trudeau's shoulder as she dabbed at her eyes with a lace handkerchief.

Next to Zen stood a striking man. He was taller than my brother, with a muscular, lean build. The breeze caught his dark, tousled hair, revealing the most attractive face I had ever seen. A strong jaw, exotic eyes, and full lips. I momentarily stopped breathing. Who was he? And my God, why was I drooling over a stranger at my best friend's funeral? What was wrong with me?

Brandi and Jonah stood at my side, and all three of us joined hands when the minister spoke his somber words of comfort. I heard none of it as my mind raced between memories of Janice, the grief that was threatening to pull me apart, and the questions surrounding her death. My eyes darted back to the man standing next to Zen. Who was he? Were they friends? If so, why hadn't my brother introduced him to me?

I bit my lip in attempt to focus on the minister's words.

"So, do not fear, for I am with you; do not be dismayed, for I am your God. I will strengthen you and help you; I will uphold you with my righteous right hand." He closed his book. "We now say goodbye to our dear sister, daughter, granddaughter, and friend… Janice Trudeau. We know this is just a temporary goodbye, and that we'll see her in heaven when it is our time to be called home."

The machinery engaged, and the casket was lowered into the ground. Janice's mother dropped a single red rose into the hole and wept.

My stomach tightened. I felt like I was about to throw up.

Sensing my distress, Jonah led me to a nearby stone bench. "I know, I know," he crooned. "It's going to be all right. Janice is in a better place now. You will hurt for a while, but with time, the pain will lessen."

I scowled him. "Are you reading that off the back of the funeral home brochure?"

Jonah looked horrified. "No!" Then a pause. "Yeah, okay, maybe I did read the back of that brochure."

I surprised myself by giggling. "Don't you dare make me laugh."

Jonah shrugged. "It's better than drowning in your tears."

Brandi smiled at the two of us. "You guys. I don't know what I'd do without you." She dug in her purse and took out a tissue. She blew her nose. The sound was so jarring, several of the funeral attendees turned around to see what was making the noise.

This sent me into a fit of giggles, and I quickly lowered my head to make it appear as if I were crying.

A familiar voice came from behind the bench. "Sis. We'd like to talk to the people from your firm in a few minutes. We're gathering over there in the outdoor shelter and talking to folks one at a time."

I turned around to look at my brother. The man I'd seen him with earlier was standing at his side.

"Uh. Right. Okay." I couldn't formulate words properly. Zen's handsome friend unnerved me.

"By the way, this is my new partner, Hunter Ito. He just transferred here from the LAPD. Hunter, this is my sister, Clarity."

"Nice to meet you." Hunter's voice was like smoke and velvet. He reached his hand out to shake mine.

I let the tear-soaked tissue fall from my hand and wiped my palm on my skirt before shaking his hand. "Uh…"

His dimpled smile warmed my heart, which proceeded to skip several beats in a row. "Nice." I shook my head dazedly. "I mean, nice to meet you… Hunter."

"Why don't you introduce your coworkers?" Zen nearly rolled his eyes.

"Oh, sorry. These are my friends, Jonah and Brandi." I stood while they exchanged handshakes. I was angry with myself for acting like a middle school girl drooling over a teen idol crush. Especially given the circumstances.

"Zen, I'm going to head over." Hunter tipped his head toward the covered shelter. "Meet you there?"

"Yeah, sure," Zen said.

"Might as well get this part over with." Brandi grabbed Jonah's arm and gave it a tug. "See you in a few minutes, Clarity."

Once we were alone, Zen asked, "How are you holding up?"

I shrugged. "Okay, I guess. Not great, actually."

Zen put his arm around me. "I'm sorry, sis."

"Thanks for arranging for us to go to Janice's funeral." I looked at my brother with a smile tugging at the corners of my lips. "How did you manage it?"

Zen chuckled. "Just applied a little bit of pressure. Your boss is awful. I don't know how you can stand working for him."

"Me neither. I don't know how much longer I can take it."

"Why don't you quit?" Zen asked.

I frowned. "I don't think I can find a job that pays as well. I wouldn't be able to make the payments on my house."

"So—downsize. Move to a smaller house in a less expensive neighborhood." Zen raked his fingers through his short, brown hair.

"I love that house!" I stepped away from him. "It's everything I've ever wanted in a home. It's the only thing that makes me happy these days."

Zen sighed. "Okay, okay. I get it. It's your life. I just don't want you to get locked into this job. It makes me sad to see you treated so poorly by your boss."

I was tired of thinking about Paul and his oppressive management style. I needed to think about something else. "Have you made any progress with those guys from the online dating service?"

Zen nodded. "Yeah. Of the twenty-three men who showed interest in Janice, we've interviewed five. They all had alibis, except one, who said he was home all day watching the Mariners game. He gave us the score and details about the game, but of course, anyone can record a game and watch it after the fact, so we are looking at him closely."

"That still leaves a lot of men you haven't talked to yet."

"The homicide department is understaffed, so it's going more slowly than I'd like." Zen frowned.

"Understaffed?"

"Budget cuts and an increase in homicides," he replied. "A bad combination."

"Is there something I can do? I mean, in terms of helping to find Janice's killer?" I bit my lip.

"What?" He chuckled. "What could you do? We don't need civilian help."

"I'm really good at stalking people on social media. If you gave me the list of men who contacted Janice, I could scour their online activity. Say, for instance, the guy who stayed home to watch the Mariners. Give me his name, and I'll see if he posted about the game on Facebook, Twitter, or any other platform."

Zen paused. "Hmm. You're right. That might come in handy. How about if I send you a list tomorrow? I'll be interested to see what you come up with."

I brightened instantly. I felt so much better knowing I would be doing something, and not just sitting around waiting for news. "Okay, thank you."

Zen took my arm and guided me toward the group of my coworkers. "Trust me," he said. "I've made this case a priority. We'll get Janice's killer."

✳✳✳

Once I was back in the sanctity of my own home, I was finally able to relax and let my guard down. In flannel pajamas, with a glass of wine in hand, I settled onto my couch. I'd been thinking hard about what Zen had said about finding another job or maybe even downsizing. Placing a pillow on my lap, I set my laptop on top and opened a browser window.

First, I scanned the job boards, searching for a similar position to the one I had. I found a few, and quickly realized I was overqualified. Not only that, the jobs paid half the salary Paul paid me.

Just for fun, I did a nationwide search. There were several positions that paid nearly as much, but were in either New York City, Boston, or Los Angeles. The thought of leaving my home state didn't appeal to me. Besides, those places were even more expensive to live in than Seattle. However, I scrutinized the position in Los Angeles further. At least it was only a three-hour flight from home. I could probably stand to live there for a couple of years.

Impulsively, I went through the online application process and attached my resume. I took a deep breath and clicked "Submit."

Pumpkin entered the living room and hopped up on the couch. He stepped onto the pillow and settled down next to my laptop, his paw on the keyboard.

"You little tiger." I gently scratched under his chin and listened to the deep purr emanating from his chest.

I thought of the position in California as a back-up. For now, I would stay in my current job as long as I possibly could, and in the meantime, I would stop spending so much. I'd put as much money into my savings account as I could manage. What was it the financial experts said—you should save at least three to six months of monthly expenses before you quit your job?

Which areas should I focus on to save more money? The first thing that popped into my mind was my car. I opened a new browser window. My beautiful leased BMW was only two years old. The contract was up soon. I sighed. It was a luxury I could probably live without. That would be first on my list of things to cut.

I'd always scoffed at people who drove practical cars, but now I visited a Toyota dealership's website and looked at a Prius. I frowned. A Prius, for God's sake. They did not meet my aesthetic requirements.

I almost closed the tab on my browser. The cursor hovered over the "x." Then again, with a Prius, I could save a lot of gas money. The payments were certainly more affordable than my BMW. Maybe instead of payments, I could use part of my savings to pay for the car in full. Then, if I quit my job, I wouldn't have to worry the car would be repossessed if I couldn't make payments.

Next was my house. The thought of compromising and buying one of lesser quality in a sketchy location made my stomach hurt. This house was my refuge—the place where I felt most comfortable. The Wallingford neighborhood was perfectly suited for my personality and shopping needs. I had to consider my options. I navigated to a real estate site and did a search. I soon discovered the market was on fire, and the only house I could find within my price range was a dump and in a scary part of town.

"Wait a minute," I said out loud. I went to my mortgage company's site and pulled up my account. My interest rate was sky high! Now was the time to refinance that puppy while I still had a job and current interest rates were at a record low.

I sent my mortgage broker a quick email asking to meet about refinancing.

"There." I felt much better having made a few decisions. I gently nudged Pumpkin off the pillow and got up to pour myself a second glass of red wine.

When I returned to my laptop, I noticed that I had an email from Zen. It read, "We've now interviewed ten of the twenty-three men who were interested in Janice on the dating website. Here are the names and occupations of the three who didn't have verifiable alibis. I'm not giving you addresses because you are NOT going to talk to them yourself. See what you can find out about them on social media. Thanks, sis."

I rolled my eyes. God, why did he have to play the protective big brother all the time? I read the names.

Alan Johnson: waiter at The Waterfront. Alibi: home alone watching the Mariners game.

Evron Niva: manager at Puget Bank. Alibi: alone, on a hike on Cougar Mountain.

Jeff Ortiz: software tester at Jetson Software. Alibi: home alone playing video games.

I started with the most generic name—Alan Johnson. I typed his name into the search bar in my Facebook app. There were a bajillion Alan Johnsons living in the Seattle area. I spent an hour clicking through the long list of Alan Johnsons, feeling frustrated after each dead end. I couldn't rely on some of the occupations matching up—because one of the Alan Johnsons was a writer, which meant he might also be a waiter. Writers were like actors. They'd be hard-pressed to make a living as a writer, so they had to work other jobs, like waiting tables.

I discarded the Alan Johnson who was a professor. He obviously wouldn't be waiting tables after class. I plodded on until, finally, I found an Alan Johnson who looked to be about the right age for Janice. This Alan Johnson's occupation was listed as a musician. That would make sense. It was difficult to make a living as a musician without a side job.

I opened his timeline on Facebook and looked at his pictures. The second picture down was a selfie he'd taken with a friend at The Waterfront restaurant. Okay, this was the right guy, I thought. I scrolled down to the date of the murder.

There were no Facebook posts from Alan on the day of the murder. Hmm. I switched to Twitter, located the correct Alan Johnson and checked his feed.

Alan had tweeted all throughout the Mariners game, and they were all about each inning, the players, and the opposing team. Unless he was posting in the middle of murdering my friend, there was no way he could've killed Janice. He'd even actively tweeted the score as the game progressed.

I opened a Word doc and typed out what I'd found. I pasted a link to his Facebook page and his Twitter feed, took screenshots of his posts, and pasted them into the file.

Next, I methodically researched the other men on the list. Evron Niva had indeed hiked on Cougar Mountain. He'd posted photos on Instagram during the hike and the time stamp showed they were taken during the time of the murder.

Jeff Ortiz had been home alone, playing video games. I checked all forms of social media, but he seemed a bit anti-social, so I couldn't find anything online about him. I texted Zen. "Did Jeff Ortiz mention what kind of video games he was playing?"

"Destiny," Zen texted back.

I replied, "If he was playing in a group, you'll be able to verify his alibi. And if he was playing on an Xbox, you can get his usage records through Microsoft."

"Thanks, I hadn't thought of that," Zen texted.

"No problem," I texted. "Let me know when the next batch is ready."

"Okay, will do."

I made sure all the info I'd collected on each person was correct in the document, then attached it to an email to Zen.

I put my phone on the coffee table and leaned back on the couch. It had been a very long day. What would Janice do if the roles were reversed? I was sure that Janice would do anything she could to find the killer of her best friend.

CHAPTER 8

By Saturday evening, I was feeling just a tiny bit better. I'd made a promise to myself that I wouldn't work over the weekend. So, when my friend Sophia called to ask if I'd like to go out for a drink, I surprised myself by saying yes. I couldn't wallow alone in my grief forever.

When I arrived at The Grizzled Wizard, I scanned the very small bar and immediately spotted Sophia sitting with Brandi and Jonah. Perfect. A small, cozy group—and these three were some of my favorite people.

Sophia had gotten to know us when Janice and I had taken a weekend yoga class. Once Sophia had begun chatting with us, it was instant chemistry. It was like we'd been friends for years. Janice and I had introduced her to Brandi and Jonah, and she fit right in with them as well.

"Hey." I sat down at the bar.

The bartender appeared in front of me. "Hey, Clarity. The usual?"

I nodded.

The Grizzled Wizard was a small but cozy dive bar. My friends and I loved it because it wasn't always crowded, the wizard theme was both nerdy and charming, and because the bartender was a kind-hearted soul who made the place feel like home.

He poured me a glass of Cabernet, glanced at my puffy eyes, then poured another inch or two on top. He gave me a sympathetic look. "I heard the news. So sorry about Janice."

"Thank you." I took a long sip.

Sophia put her hand on mine. "I didn't talk to you at the funeral. I'm sorry I didn't come find you. I couldn't even think. Part of me just wanted to get the hell out of there."

I stared down into my wine. "I should've gone to find you too, but I was such a wreck."

"And there was that little distraction from the police." Brandi took a sip of her gin and tonic.

"What was that all about?" Sophie asked. "I saw them with a group of people at the outdoor shelter. Was that you guys?"

Jonah sipped his beer. "Yeah. The police questioned everyone who worked with Janice."

Sophia's eyebrows shot up. "Even you, Clarity? Isn't your brother a homicide detective?"

"Yes, but he has to go by the rules." I finished my wine. "They weren't necessarily questioning us as suspects. They were asking about her general demeanor before she was killed, if we noticed anything weird at the office, and if we knew of anyone who might be angry with her."

Sophia tucked her straight blonde hair behind her ears. "Was there anyone out to get Janice?"

I was quiet. I motioned to the bartender to pour me another glass of wine. "I can't think of a single person who didn't like Janice—at the office or anywhere else, for that matter."

"Maybe it was a random killing." Brandi, who'd been silent the whole evening, swished her drink, the ice cubes clinking in the glass.

"But the way she was killed. It was so brutal—like someone was enraged... someone who knew her and wanted revenge," I said. Saying it out loud made me question who could hate Janice as much as the person who took her life. "Did any of you know if Janice was seeing anybody? Romantically, that is?"

Sophia was aghast. "Seeing anyone? Wouldn't you know if Janice was involved with a man?"

"I thought I'd know. But..."

"But what?" Jonah asked.

"You guys can't say anything because I don't think the public knows this yet." I looked at each of my friends. "Did you guys know that Janice had signed up with an online dating service?"

All three of them nearly fell off their bar stools.

"What?" Brandi's mouth hung open. "That's not something Janice would do!"

"I know," I said. "I can't figure out why she didn't tell me. It makes me think that I didn't know Janice as well as I thought I did."

"You were so close." Jonah's face had paled. "She would've told you. Unless…"

"Unless what?" I searched his face.

"Unless she was ashamed or something," Sophia finished Jonah's sentence.

"Why would she be ashamed to sign up with a dating service?" Brandi asked. "Lots of people do that."

I thought about my friend. Janice was pretty in that girl-next-door kind of way. Though next to her sister, Margaret, Janice had never felt pretty. In fact, she'd confided in me that she thought she was the ugly duckling of the family. "I think she was embarrassed because men throw themselves at Margaret. Her sister practically has to beat them off with a stick. Imagine how that would feel—watching your sibling be incredibly desirable to men. But then none of those men will have anything to do with you."

"That would suck." Jonah's brows furrowed. "Living in someone else's shadow like that."

Sophia finished her drink and accepted another from the bartender, who had just made a pass back to our end of the bar. "So, you're saying she didn't tell anyone because she felt humiliated using a dating app?"

I nodded. "Maybe. I don't know. I'm just trying to put myself in her shoes. Not that anyone ever asks me out on a date. But at least I don't have a sister who looks like a supermodel."

"Girl," Jonah said. "What are you talking about? I've seen plenty of men ask you out on a date."

I rolled my eyes. "Yeah, like that guy Bubba? The one with the wife beater shirt that actually says 'wife beater' on the front? The guys who ask me out are all pretty much like Bubba."

"That hunky detective partner of your brother's seemed into you." Brandi sipped her drink and gave me a sly look.

I felt my cheeks redden. "What? No, he wasn't. I mean, he's my brother's partner."

Jonah winked at her. "Nothing wrong with that."

"But, but…" I sputtered. "Zen wouldn't like that. It would put an awkward spin on their partnership, and on my relationship with Zen."

"Oh, stop," Sophia said with a sly smile. "I didn't see this hot detective. Do tell."

"He's dreamy," Brandi volunteered. "Tall, dark, and handsome. Right, Clarity?"

"Um, yes. He's very nice-looking." I folded my hands neatly in my lap. My heart was pounding just thinking about him.

"Come on!" Jonah slapped Clarity's shoulder. "You were practically drooling on him. Admit it. He's hot."

I shook my head. It wasn't right to be doing anything other than thinking about Janice. "We shouldn't be talking about hot guys at a time like this."

"So, you do think he's hot!" Sophia chuckled. "But you're right. Let's revisit this conversation for the next time we go out for a drink. We're here to honor Janice."

"A toast to Janice!" Jonah held up his beer. His eyes got a little misty. "To our beautiful friend. May she rest in peace."

"To Janice." I clinked my glass with my pals. I swallowed a lump in my throat and wished with all my might that Janice was with us this evening, so she would know how much we all loved her.

CHAPTER 9

On Monday morning, I felt like a semi-truck had rolled over me. My head was pounding, and my body ached with fatigue and sadness. For the second night in a row, I'd tossed and turned, enduring nightmares of axe-wielding killers coming after me.

There was no way I was going in to work—no way I could face the next project with enthusiasm and energy. I called in sick and sank back into my soft bed.

Pumpkin gave me a quizzical look. "Meow?"

I rolled over onto my stomach and put my pillow over my head in an attempt to shut out the insistent yowls from my darling feline. "Ugh, Pumpkin, I want to sleep! I just want to stay in bed a little while longer."

The cat hopped up onto my back, stuck his head under the pillow, and pressed his pink nose to my neck.

I let out a long sigh and pushed the pillow off. I let Pumpkin snuggle into me, but when he began kneading my shoulder, I'd had enough.

"Fine. I will feed you." I groaned, put on my slippers, and trudged to the kitchen.

When Pumpkin was fed and watered, I made myself a pot of coffee. There was no use going back to bed now. I was just awake enough that going back to sleep wasn't an option.

After two cups of coffee and a bowl of oatmeal, I showered and got dressed in my most comfortable outfit— yoga pants, a tank top, and a soft, oversized hoodie. "Ah, that's more like it." I tried not to think about work and what Paul would say when he found out I'd called in sick.

With restless energy, I began sorting through my closets, bagging up old clothes to give away to charity and throwing away shoes whose soles had worn out.

I was still restless. I needed to keep busy. Then I remembered my parents' website. "I can at least get something done for Mom and Dad."

For the next two hours, I found a web template, and uploaded a bunch of the photos I'd taken at their property. I wrote some copy and added a button so guests could book a room online. It was beautiful—I was sure they would be pleased. My stomach rumbled. It was well past one o'clock. I'd forgotten to eat lunch!

I went to the kitchen and fixed myself some made-from-the-jar spaghetti. I considered making a salad to be, you know, healthy, but determined it would be too much work. I shrugged. "Tomato sauce is a vegetable, right, Pumpkin?"

Pumpkin meowed, hopped onto his favorite chair at the dining table, and settled onto the cushion. The sun had just peeked out from a string of muted gray clouds. His favorite chair was in the perfect spot for the rays of sun to stream down on his orange tabby fur, highlighting the soft, white stripes on the underside of his belly.

I shrugged. Apparently, Pumpkin didn't care for vegetables.

I plated the spaghetti and sprinkled a healthy dose of shredded parmesan cheese on top. I was practically salivating as I set the plate down and was about to sit at the table when the doorbell rang.

My brows furrowed. "Now, who could that be?" I looked at my plate longingly, and on the spur of the moment, snatched up my fork and twirled some noodles onto it before shoving a big bite in my mouth. "Mmm."

A glob of spaghetti sauce escaped the fork and dripped onto my hoodie. "Damn." Now I'd have to wash it.

My phone buzzed. The text from Paul read, "Are you really too sick to come into work?"

Jerk.

My fingers fumbled as I texted back, "Migraine. It's the throwing up kind."

"Get better fast. We need you here."

I growled and shoved the phone back in my pocket.

The doorbell rang again. I got up and shuffled to the door. "Be right there!" Expecting to see the postal carrier or some other type of delivery person, I swung the door open to accept whatever package would be dropped into my arms.

Instead, Zen's new partner, Hunter Ito, stood on my porch with a surprised look on his face. "Oh! Did I catch you at a bad time?"

I looked down in horror at my tomato-stained hoodie and my general lack of fashion. The one day I didn't dress up in designer clothes and shoes... Ugh. "Hunter. Um, hi." I searched blindly for what to say. "Come in?"

He smiled tentatively and waited for me to move out of the doorway.

"Oops. Sorry." I fumbled out of the way and shut the door behind him. "Is there something I can help you with?" I could feel my face turning a deep shade of red, which probably matched the stain on my sweatshirt.

Hunter, on the other hand, looked perfectly calm, cool, and composed—not to mention drop-dead gorgeous. He was wearing a light gray suit, a crisp white shirt, and a dark silver tie. He had gotten a haircut since I last saw him—it was cut short on the sides and a little longer on top. The cut accentuated his strong jaw and his defined cheekbones.

My eyes darted around the living room and assessed the damage. One flannel robe, sprawled on the couch, a dirty coffee mug on the coffee table, three bags of clothes to give away lumped in the middle of the floor, and a stack of papers fanned out on the loveseat. Great. This was just getting better and better. The only thing worse would be if I'd left some granny panties hanging on a clothesline overhead. "Why don't you come into the kitchen. Can I get you cup of coffee or tea?"

"Actually," Hunter said, "I just stopped by to pick up something that Zen left here the other day. His notebook?"

"Oh." I noticed his warm, brown eyes and the dark lashes that fringed them. "Are you sure I can't interest you in something to drink while I go look for it?" God. What was I doing? It was embarrassing enough that I currently resembled a crackhead in a hoarder's hut. This was not the time to make small talk. But I couldn't take my eyes off him.

Pumpkin entered the room and spotted Hunter immediately. He wound himself around and between the detective's feet, leaving a healthy amount of cat fur stuck to his suit. Hunter bent over to pet him.

"Nice cat." He plucked a few cat hairs off his pant leg and watched Pumpkin saunter into the living room. "Is that it?" Hunter pointed toward a smallish notebook laying on the coffee table.

I glanced down. "I guess. That's not mine. It must be Zen's." I opened the notebook and flipped through the pages. "Yup. Looks like notes from various interviews."

"That's the one." Hunter took the notebook from me and smiled. "Thanks. I'll just be on my way, then."

For some reason, I felt genuinely disappointed that he was leaving. It was puzzling. I didn't even know this man. I mean, yeah, I was attracted to him, but I didn't know him. "Okay. Thanks for coming by."

Just before I shut the door behind him, he put his hand on my arm. "Clarity. I'm really sorry about your friend."

My arm tingled. I nodded and swallowed hard. "Thank you, Hunter." I watched him walk down the stairs and to his car.

✳✳✳

The next day, after an unproductive attempt at work, I came home and collapsed on my couch. I eyed my laptop sitting on the coffee table. I thought about the application I'd sent out the day before. What if they'd already responded? I was so tempted to log on and find out. Pumpkin had other ideas.

"Meow?" He hopped up onto the couch and looked into my eyes.

I laughed and stroked his tawny cheek. "Hungry?"

His motor revved, and the purring rumbled his entire body.

"All right, tiger." I glanced at my laptop. "I guess my job search can wait."

I headed for the kitchen. Opening a can of food, I plopped the contents into his bowl. Pumpkin dove into it without hesitation.

I ran my fingers along his back. "You really like the tuna, don't you?"

Remembering that I was kind of hungry too, I peeked into the fridge. I had some leftover spaghetti, so I heated that up in the microwave. The bottle of red wine stood on the counter, calling my name.

I'd been drinking a lot since Janice died. Maybe I should lay off the alcohol for a while. But how could I eat spaghetti without red wine? Even though I was of mostly British descent, the quarter Italian heritage in me couldn't resist.

I made a deal with myself. If I had a glass of red wine, I had to have a salad. I hurriedly cut up half a head of romaine lettuce, chopped a tomato, and dashed some olive oil and red wine vinegar on top. "There."

The doorbell rang.

"Are you freakin' kidding me?" I banged my food on the dining table and marched to the door. Then, I stopped dead in my tracks. What if it was Hunter? I looked down at my clothes. No spaghetti stains. Good. Plus, I was wearing a charcoal gray pencil skirt and a fitted, white blouse. Not bad. Except, the skirt was getting a little tight with all the pasta I'd been eating. Oh, well. At least I wasn't wearing my ratty sweatshirt.

I plastered what I hoped was an alluring, but not too sexy, smile on my face and opened the door.

Zen stood on my doorstep.

I tried not to let the disappointment show. "Oh, hey bro." I let him in.

"Don't act so excited to see me," he said with a wry grin.

"Oh, it's not that." I shut the door behind him. "I thought you were someone else, that's all."

Zen raised his eyebrows. "Were you expecting someone? Am I interrupting a date?"

I laughed. "Yeah, right. Since when have I had a date?"

He eyed the table set for one in the dining area and shrugged. "How would I know? I don't monitor your love life."

"Sit." I pointed at a chair next to mine. "Can I get you something to eat?"

"No, no. I'm actually here on official business." He sat down in the chair.

"Really?" I took a bite of my spaghetti.

"Yeah. I showed the Sergeant the information you put together on the list of suspects you sent me. He's interested in hiring you on a contract basis to help with the investigation."

My fork dropped and clattered loudly on my plate. "Seriously?"

Zen grinned. "Yeah. He said we could really use someone like you to do some digging. I mean, we have good data with records, background checks, and what-not, but we don't have anyone who focuses solely on people's activity on social media."

"Wow." I sat back in my chair. "I never even thought that would be a thing the police would pay a contractor for."

"They pay people for all kinds of things," Zen said. "Police work is not limited to the station or the streets. We have to pay experts all the time."

"Huh." I took a sip of my wine. "I will definitely consider that. I've started looking for other jobs, just like you suggested."

"How'd that go?" Zen got up and got himself a glass of water.

"I don't know yet," I said. "I only found one in Los Angeles. I sent them an application and resume, so we'll see."

Zen frowned. "Los Angeles? Are you sure you want to live there?"

"No," I answered abruptly. "I could live there and work for at least a couple of years. Then, I'd have more experience. It would look great on my resume."

"Maybe." He looked doubtful. "But you'd be so far away from family and friends."

I sighed. "If I leave my job here, I need to find a job that pays well, where I could gain more experience. LA is a great place to do that."

"Mom and Dad would be so sad," Zen said. "You'd break their hearts."

A wave of guilt washed over me. "I know. But they'd still have eight other kids to torture."

He laughed. "Yeah, but none of the others are willing to spend much time with them."

Great. More guilt added to the guilt I just piled on myself. I looked down at my plate and stirred my spaghetti with my fork. "You're not making this any easier."

"You'll figure it out." He stood up and pushed in his chair. "Anyway, call the Sergeant tomorrow. He'll get you set up." Zen placed a business card on the table. "Good night, sis."

After he left, I studied the card. "Sergeant Adams. Hmm. What could it hurt?"

I put my dishes in the sink and opened my laptop. I held my breath as I opened my email. There was a response from the company I'd applied to in LA!

It read:

Dear Ms. Bloom,

Thank you for your interest in Conclave. Your credentials are impressive. We're sorry, at this time, we aren't hiring anyone from outside the Greater Los Angeles area. We wish you luck in your job search.

Sincerely,

Ronald Atwater

Director of Human Resources | Conclave

I stared at the email, disappointment hitting my gut like a two-pound cheeseburger. I couldn't even identify why I felt disappointed—I didn't really want to move to California. Something wasn't adding up. My fingers flew over the keyboard. There! Just as I'd thought, the company hired their employees from a variety of geographical areas—and mostly those outside the LA area.

This was worse than I'd thought. Either I had misjudged my level of experience or something else was at play.

I suddenly suspected it had something to do with where I currently worked. I googled "Opulent Industries reputation."

I swallowed hard as I read the first lines of each hit... Words like cut-throat, unethical, and unscrupulous popped up, along with the names of the CEO and his staff. How had I not googled the company's reputation before taking the job? I shook my head. Even if I'd known, would I have turned down the high salary they paid me? Would I have passed up the opportunity and taken a much lower salary somewhere else?

I sighed and closed the laptop. No wonder the corporation in LA didn't want anything to do with me. My company's reputation was likely the reason. And that scared me even more. How was I going to find a job elsewhere if I was tarnished by the reputation of Paul and how his company did business?

Pumpkin hopped up onto the couch and snuggled in close. Within minutes, I was feeling better. His purring engine kicked into gear, soothing my nerves. Petting his soft fur somehow calmed my fears and brought my heart rate back down to normal.

"I should pay you a salary." I kissed his velvety head. "Cats really are the best therapy."

CHAPTER 10

The new project was a disaster.

It was hard to figure out how to sell The Bathroom Buddy. I was sure that any kind of advertising on social media would bring ridicule in the comments. Besides, the product was absurd. A device that could stick on the lid of your toilet which played only classical music and gave you the latest news reports or read you a variety of magazine articles? Weird and gross. Who was the target audience? People who loved to poop to Mozart and Architectural Digest?

I rubbed my temples. I got up from my desk and paced in front of the huge window facing the city.

Instead of emailing the graphic designer about the advertising theme for The Bathroom Buddy, I thought of reasons why someone would've killed Janice. As far as I knew, everyone liked her. Janice was a vivacious, kind-hearted woman who never spoke ill of another. Who could've been angry enough with her to kill her—and in such a brutal way?

I went back to my desk and texted Zen. "Has your team already looked at Janice's computer? Did they find anything that might lead to her killer?"

I watched the dots on my text screen cycle from dot to dot. Finally, Zen's message came back. "They just finished. No red flags or clues that they could find."

I put the phone down on my desk and closed my eyes. Damn. I was so sure they would discover something that would help further the investigation. But they didn't know Janice like I knew her. Would they notice if something was off with her communications? Something that indicated that someone was after her?

My eyes flew open. "Can I take a look at her laptop?" I texted.

"What for?" he texted back. "They didn't find anything."

"I knew her well. I would recognize if something was out of the ordinary."

The dots on the screen cycled again. One, two, three. One, two, three. Finally, Zen responded. "Okay. I'll send someone over to your house tonight with her computer."

I let myself breathe. "Thank you."

A knock on the door startled me. I opened it and stood face to face with Paul's right-hand man, or as I liked to call him, his main minion.

"Russell." I did my best to fake a smile. "What can I do for you?"

Russell stepped past me into the office and milled around, eyeing Janice's side of the room. "Clarity." He said my name with distaste.

I frowned. "Is there something you need?"

He stopped in front of the shelf behind my friend's chair and pushed his glasses back up on the bridge of his nose as he inspected it. His fingers traced a photo of Janice on the beach. She was standing in turquoise water, wearing her pink and white bikini. Her wide grin lit up her face as she struck a pretend supermodel pose.

"Russell?" I was starting to get creeped out.

He turned to look at me. "Paul said I should check out your office. We may need to move you into a smaller, single office down the hall."

I was taken aback. "Why?"

He glanced at Janice's desk. "Obviously, this is a two-person office."

I wrinkled my brow. "And?"

"And," Russell continued, "you obviously are only one person. You don't need a two-person office."

My jaw dropped. "Are you... are you kicking me out of my office?"

Russell turned his bulgy eyes toward me. "I wouldn't say we're kicking you out. Just relocating."

A small ember began burning in my chest and was spreading up toward my neck and face. "When Paul hires a new event coordinator to take Janice's job, you can move her or him into this office."

"Ah, well, perhaps. Here's the thing, Paul just promoted me to VP of Marketing. So, I'll need this office for myself and my new secretary. That is, if I decide I want this one. I'm also looking at the corner office on the north side of the building."

I bit back a sharp retort. It wouldn't be wise to lose my cool now that Russell had been promoted to... Oh, God. He was now my manager! Instead, I carefully worded my response. "That office has a beautiful view of Puget Sound. Congratulations on your promotion. I had no idea Paul was creating a VP of Marketing position."

Russell's face, normally devoid of expression, actually lit up in the tiniest way. "Yes, well, it was a surprise."

"I didn't realize you had a background in marketing." I viewed him with barely concealed suspicion. "For some reason, I thought your background was in computer science."

He shrugged. "It is. However, Paul says I'm a natural at coming up with product ideas and that my marketing strategies are genius."

"Really?" I crossed my arms. "And which ideas are those?"

"My latest one is what you're working on right now. The Bathroom Buddy."

I wanted to scream, but I only managed to squeak out. "I see. Brilliant."

"Glad you think so." Russell walked out the door. "I'll let you know my decision about your office by tomorrow."

I shut the door behind me. That toad! Russell was the vilest person in the company, besides Paul, and now I was to report directly to him. I couldn't believe what a dark turn my career had taken in just the last week. By adding a VP of Marketing, I now had two layers of douche bags to answer to.

I sat down in my chair and glanced at Janice's desk. How had this all happened? My gaze skimmed Janice's remaining belongings, and I frowned. Something was different. I got up and stood where Russell had been standing not two minutes before. The picture. The picture of Janice on the beach—the one Russell had been ogling. It was gone.

✳✳✳

Jonah, Brandi, and I snuck out of the office for a late lunch at our favorite café. The late afternoon sun convinced us that taking a table outside was the only way to go.

"What the hell?" Jonah took a sip of his iced coffee. "Russell took the picture of Janice off her desk?"

"That is beyond creepy." Brandi took a bite of her salad and munched thoughtfully. "You don't think Russell had something to do with Janice's murder, do you?"

I shrugged. "He's disgusting, but he doesn't seem the type to murder someone. I don't think he likes to get his hands dirty. Now that I think about it, it seems pretty clear he had a thing for her."

Jonah made a gagging sound. "Eww. Just the thought of that makes me want to throw up. That guy is a slime ball."

Brandi pointed her fork at me. "What if he asked her out, and when she said no, he became enraged and killed her in a fit of fury?"

Jonah snorted. "He has no muscle tone. Janice could've taken him in a heartbeat."

"But if he was really, really, angry…." Brandi let the thought hang. "You've heard the stories about people having superhuman strength when faced with a traumatic situation, haven't you?"

"I guess murdering someone because they don't like you back is a traumatic experience?" Jonah scowled.

"Russell is a sniveling suck-up. He's gross, I'll give you that." I sipped my sparkling water. "But I've never seen him show emotion of any kind. He's not so much as raised his voice in the office. Do you really think he could get angry enough to kill a woman?"

Brandi shrugged. "You never know. Stranger things have happened."

I sat back in my chair. "Right now, it looks as though one of those men that contacted Janice through the online dating agency was her killer. That's who we should be focusing on."

"Have the police finished looking into those guys yet?" Jonah asked.

I shook my head. "No. It takes a long time to sort through them all. There were twenty-three. Last I heard, they were about halfway through the list."

"Did Zen tell you that?" Brandi set down her glass of iced tea.

"Yeah. I'm actually helping the police, so he's allowed to share some info with me. You guys can't tell a soul about this."

Jonah's mouth fell open. "You're helping with the murder investigation?"

I could feel my cheeks getting warm. "I probably shouldn't be saying anything at all. But yeah, I'm helping with looking into the men's social media activity. You know, what they've posted on Facebook, Instagram, or any other social media outlet during the time of the murder. We've been able to eliminate some of those guys because of what I found online."

"Wow." Brandi gave me an admiring look. "You're like a P.I. or something. That's way cool."

Jonah sat up straighter. "Can we help? I've always wanted to be a P.I."

"Me too!" Brandi perked up. "Business development and finance is not nearly as exciting as finding a killer."

"It's probably a lot safer," I said. "What if we discovered who the killer was? We could be putting ourselves in a heap of danger."

We finished the rest of our meal in silence, each of us lost in thought. My friends seemed as motivated to find Janice's killer as I was. I hoped that the police would solve the crime. If they didn't, I wondered if the three of us could.

CHAPTER 11

"Absolutely not." Zen crossed his arms over his chest. "Your friends are not going to help with the investigation."

"They want to help." I brought him a glass of water and set it on the coffee table in front of him.

"Look, your skills are great, and that's already helped us tremendously. But bringing Jonah, a designer, and Brandi, a finance person, into the mix will not help. It's like you're enlisting Shaggy and Velma to get the bad guy."

I chuckled. "Those pesky kids will ruin everything."

Zen scowled at me. "Clarity, this is no amusement park costumed villain you can unmask and hand over to the police. This is not a cartoon. This is real life. The killer is brutal with a knife and seems to enjoy hacking up his victims. You cannot let your friends get mixed up in this. They would put themselves at great risk, and I could lose my job if anyone found out I was bringing non-authorized people into the investigation."

"Your boss was fine with me helping." I pursed my lips.

"With you, yes." Zen was trying not to lose his patience.

A long pause hung between us.

"What if I only bounced ideas off them?" I sat down on the couch.

Zen sighed and sat stiffly in the overstuffed chair. Pumpkin sauntered into the room and hopped onto his lap. "What exactly do you mean? Like brainstorming with them?"

I nodded. "Yes. Sometimes, I just need to talk things through. Both Jonah and Brandi are good at listening and offering suggestions if I'm stumped."

He stroked Pumpkin's cheek. "We cannot afford any leaks to the media or to the public."

"They wouldn't do that. You have my word," I said.

Zen struggled to keep his voice even. "You aren't likely to be the one—"

The doorbell chimed.

"Who could that be?" I peeked through the spy hole. My heart picked up its pace. Zen's partner stood on my porch. He was even more handsome in his off-duty attire of a soft gray t-shirt, black jeans, and a leather jacket.

"Oh, hey! Hunter. I mean, Detective Ito." I tried to appear nonchalant. It wasn't working. Not with the way my heart was pounding in my chest. "What brings you here this evening?" I laughed nervously and felt my cheeks burn. "You're probably here to see my brother."

He gave me an awkward smile. "I brought you Janice's laptop." He handed it to me. "Plus, Zen told me to meet him here. We're going out for a beer."

"Oh, sure. Why don't you come in?" I opened the door wider and caught the amused look on Zen's face. Was I blushing? Jerk.

Hunter sat down on the couch. I searched for another place to sit, but Zen was sitting in the overstuffed chair, which only left the other end of the couch for me to sit on. I took a deep breath to calm my nerves and sat down next to Hunter.

"I was just explaining to Clarity that she shouldn't ask her friends to help with the murder case," Zen said.

I glared at him. How dare he bring this up in front of his partner! "Well, I didn't think Zen would go for it. I just thought my friends would be helpful."

Hunter seemed to note the tension in the air and cleared his throat. "In what way were you thinking they could help?"

"I don't know." I glanced at his profile. Strong jaw line, straight nose...

"That's just the thing," Zen said. "One of them is a designer and the other one is a money person. I don't think they'd have anything useful to lend to the case."

If Hunter hadn't been sitting next to me, I would've punched Zen. Instead, I took a few deep breaths and tried to remain calm. "My friends are very insightful people. But I understand if you don't want them to help."

"Now you're thinking logically," my brother said.

I resisted an eyeroll. "You said that involving Brandi and Jonah might put them in harm's way. What exactly did you mean by that? And do you think I'm putting myself in harm's way by helping the police?"

"Not really. As long as you stick to digging on the computer, you shouldn't come across the killer's radar."

"So—I'll be safe, but if my friends get involved through me, they won't be?"

"Clarity." Zen's tone had an edge of warning to it.

I thought I'd probably pushed his buttons enough. I took a moment to think about my involvement. What if I stumbled upon the killer, and he somehow found out I was poking around into his background? If he came after me, I would have no means of protecting myself.

"If you're worried about my safety, and I've got to admit, I'm starting to get a teensy bit worried myself, then shouldn't I get a gun?" I wiped my palms on my skirt. I didn't like guns, but if I was going to get into a dangerous situation, I might need one.

"No!" Zen lifted Pumpkin off his lap and scooted forward on his chair. "Absolutely not. You don't have firearm training. You'd be more likely to shoot your eye out than get the bad guy."

"You could teach me." I gave him a sweet smile.

"No." His eyes narrowed. "No gun for you."

"Then, I should at least take a self-defense course, right? If I don't have a gun, I won't be able to protect myself."

"That's not a bad idea," Zen admitted grudgingly. "Actually, I think every woman should take a self-defense course, just for general safety."

I brightened a little. This was progress. "Okay, good. I'll do that."

Zen stood up and pulled a folder out of his jacket. "Here's the next group of guys we'd like you to look into. We couldn't locate the first two, but we've interviewed numbers three, four, and five on that list. They don't have solid alibis. I've included everything we know in the packet. If you have questions, just email or text me."

I took the folder from him. "Thanks."

"Hunter and I are headed out. I'll call you later." Zen went to the door with his partner right behind him.

Wanting Hunter to stay, I blurted out, "Wait a minute. Are you sure you don't want to stick around? You can have a beer here, and I can order pizza."

"Nah, don't worry about it," Zen said. He walked down the stairs to the stone path.

Hunter was still standing next to me. He pressed a card into my hand. "If you're not busy, meet me there at six o'clock tomorrow night." His deep smoke and velvet voice whispered in my ear. "Wear something you can move in."

He was down the stairs and buckling into Zen's car before I had a chance to respond. My hands shook a little as I opened my palm to read the card. It said "Mojo D'Ojo" in a very sophisticated font. The address listed wasn't familiar to me, but looked like it could be in the Phinney Ridge area, a Seattle neighborhood not far from where I lived.

Butterflies danced in my stomach. I couldn't believe Hunter had asked me out! And he'd done it on the sly, without Zen even knowing it. I felt a crazy grin spread across my face. I had a hot date tomorrow.

I almost rushed to my computer to look up the establishment listed on the card. But I didn't want to ruin the surprise for myself. Was it a swanky restaurant? Wait a minute. He said to wear something I could move in. It had to be a trendy new nightclub or a great bar with live music and dancing. This was so exciting!

Pumpkin brushed up against my legs and gave me a hopeful meow.

"Treat time, huh, buddy?" I smiled all the way to the kitchen and took out a box of Kat Krunchies from the cupboard. I shook a couple into my hand. Not even the smell of crusty tuna could ruin this magical evening. I'd finally broken through my dating dry spell. I hadn't felt this giddy in a long, long time.

When I put the box of cat treats back in the cupboard, my eyes landed on the picture stuck to my fridge with a magnet. It was of Janice and me from our last whitewater rafting trip. We were in the midst of shooting promo videos and photos for The ScoutMaster—our company's high-tech, waterproof binoculars. The best part of our job was going to fun locations together. This had been the last trip we would ever take, and it had only been a month ago.

Suddenly, my spirits tumbled from high as a kite to six feet under. Literally.

How could I be happy and excited to go out with a dreamy detective, when the best friend I'd ever had was gone. Dead. Janice was dead.

My eyes filled with tears. I felt another crying spell coming on. I couldn't go out on a date. I should be grieving the loss of my dear friend.

I took the picture off the fridge and stared into Janice's smiling face. She'd always encouraged me to put myself out there. I could almost hear her voice in my head. "Clarity, you need to get out more. How are you going to meet any nice guys if you're at work all the time?"

What I wouldn't give to hear her voice again—to hear her gentle encouragement. I traced the photo with my finger. What would she want for me?

I sighed. I already knew the answer. She'd want me to be happy.

CHAPTER 12

The work day was almost over. With every second that clicked by on the wall clock, my heart beat a little faster. I had just enough time to get from the office to my house, change clothes, and do my hair and makeup before tonight's big date with Hunter. I was so excited, I was practically hyperventilating.

I grabbed my purse and speed-walked through the office to the lobby. Brandi and Jonah were in the middle of a discussion about shoes. They witnessed my determined march to the elevator and rushed to catch up with me.

"What on earth is going on?" Brandi frowned. "Why are you in such a hurry? It's Thursday… not Friday."

I gave her a big toothy grin. "I just want to get home before traffic picks up."

Jonah pushed the elevator button and held the door open while we entered. "Nah—there's something else going on."

My grin never left my face. "Actually, I have a hot date tonight, and I really want to go home and start getting ready."

Brandi squealed. "Hot date? Oooh! Is it with Detective Dreamy?"

I leaned against the back wall of the elevator. "Bingo."

Jonah scrutinized my face. "Spill it. How did he ask you?"

"Oh, my God. You'll never believe it." I pulled the card out of my purse. "He put this card in the palm of my hand and whispered, "Meet me here at six o'clock tomorrow night."

Brandi glanced at the card. "Mojo D'Ojo. Hmmm. Never heard of that. Posh new restaurant maybe?"

I giggled. "I don't know. I'm thinking it might be a nightclub. He told me I should wear something I could move in."

Jonah furrowed his brow. "Something you can move in? Oh, I get it. For dancing."

Brandi took out her phone. "I'm going to Google it."

"No!" I snatched it out of her hand. "Don't tell me. I want to be surprised."

She pooched out her lower lip. "Oh, all right."

I returned her phone and allowed myself a moment to daydream. Visions of Hunter sweeping me off my feet on the dance floor flitted through my mind. He would be an expert dancer, his strong arms bending me back for a dip... The elevator dinged as it reached the lobby level. My daydream disappeared, and I practically launched myself through the doors. "Gotta go, guys. I'll tell you all about it tomorrow!"

***

Back at home, I fed Pumpkin and hurried to my bedroom closet. What would I wear? The day had been a hot one for Seattle—a sweltering eighty-eight degrees. I rummaged through the clothes hanging in the back.

A sun dress? I held it up to give it a once-over. Way too casual. A fancy tank and a Boho skirt? Ugh. No. I needed sophistication.

"This!" I yanked out the one thing every girl had hanging in her closet—a little black dress. This one was sleeveless and had a plunging neckline. Perfect. And if I dressed it up with some jewelry, I'd look even more sophisticated.

An hour later, I took in my reflection in the mirror. I admired the fit of my outfit complemented by the sparkly necklace and earrings. I had watched a YouTube video on how to create the perfect smoky eye, and I recreated the look down to the last detail. The gray eye shadow made my blue eyes look even bluer. For the final touch, I straightened my dark hair, which now hung to my mid-back in a shiny curtain.

I dug in the bottom of the closet for a pair of shoes. I immediately discounted the Jimmy Choo's. Those were not meant for dancing. Instead, I chose a pair of red, three-inch heels I was fairly confident wouldn't kill me to dance in.

Va-va-voom! I was ready to go.

Pumpkin wandered into the closet and proceeded to climb into the shoe box I'd left open and empty on the floor.

"Silly cat, you'll never be able to fit—well, what do you know? You can fit in there!"

Though I noticed he was squishing out and spilling over the sides of the small box. Maybe I should scale back on the Kat Krunchies.

I twirled around. "What do you think, Pumpkin? Is mommy a knockout or what?"

"Meow." His look of nonchalance suggested he didn't give a hoot what I was wearing.

"Men," I grumbled.

I locked up the house and was in my car in a flash. I plugged the address of the nightclub into my phone and squealed out of the driveway. I only had ten minutes to get there!

My hands were sweating a little. Did I forget to put on deodorant? I surreptitiously sniffed my arm pits as I drove. Good thing my car had tinted windows. Wouldn't want any red light cameras catching that on film... not that I was planning on running any red lights, but I was pushing the speed a little.

I found a parking spot a half block down from the address on the card. I got out and hurried to the nightclub with just a minute to spare. I hated being late, so the fact I was cutting it so close was making my heart pound in my chest.

I scanned the buildings, looking for the address.

There, wedged in a strip mall business area, was Mojo D'Ojo. The exterior was black, and the door was a deep red. The gold lettering of the sign suggested the establishment had an Asian-inspired décor.

I took a few deep breaths before I pulled the door open. Would Hunter like the way I looked? What would he think of me in general? God, I was so nervous.

I pulled the door open.

My breath caught in my chest. Confusion clouded my brain. The place was a flurry of motion. Sweaty guys punched black bags hanging from the ceiling. A few men pushed past me out the front door, bowing to a flag in the corner of the room before they left. Women began emerging from the back room, carrying water bottles and throwing their hair up into ponytails or messy buns.

What on earth?

Suddenly, I caught a glimpse of Hunter, who had just appeared from a hall toward the back of the building. He was wearing a black Karate outfit with a black belt tied around his waist.

His eyes went wide and his mouth hung open when he noticed me standing in the entry. He glanced over his shoulder and then made his way over to me. "Clarity." He took in my appearance. "You look... so... wow. Gorgeous. I thought I told you to wear something you could move in?"

My eyes darted to the women wearing yoga pants and tanks. Heat began spreading from my neck to my cheeks. My fight or flight mechanism kicked in, and I turned to flee.

Hunter grabbed my arm. "Wait!"

I couldn't look at him. Instead, I looked down at my ridiculous red heels. Oh, God. What an idiot I was.

"Clarity." He put a gentle hand on my shoulder. His eyes softened. "I thought you knew... this is a self-defense class I teach. You said you wanted..."

Shame filled me from my head to my toes. How could I have been so stupid? When he pressed that card into my hand, he was asking me to go to his self-defense class, not out on a date.

"I have to go." I tried to leave once again.

"No. Wait. Come with me." He led me to the back hall, into a storage room. There were cubbies against the wall. The cubbies were labeled with sizes. He pulled a wrapped package from the one marked "Gi - Women's Small."

"The bathroom is over there." He pointed to a door on the left. "Put these on. Class is going to start soon. I'll meet you out there."

I wiped a tear from my eye and slunk into the bathroom. I looked into the mirror above the sink. How ridiculous I looked walking into a martial arts studio in a little black cocktail dress! I was so, so stupid.

I stared numbly at the package Hunter had given me. It was a white uniform and came with a white belt. I tore the clear plastic off it and proceeded to put it on. Carefully, I folded up my little black dress and tucked it into my purse along with my sparkly jewelry. Taking a deep breath, I opened the door, carrying my purse and high heels out to the open studio.

"You can put your stuff right over there." A young woman pointed to an area off to the side. "Class starts in just a minute."

There were over a dozen women sitting on rolled up foam mats around the perimeter of the room. Unlike me, they were all wearing Lululemon yoga pants and other high-end sportswear.

Super. The only thing I wanted to do at that moment was to melt into the crowd and not be noticed. In my white karate uniform, I stood out like a redneck in a Neiman Marcus.

Hunter stepped into the center of the studio. The women's heads snapped to attention, their eyes locked on his exquisite form.

"Welcome to my self-defense class," he said. "As you know, this is a single three-hour class. If you like the course after this evening, we have an advanced course which you can sign up for online. Or, if you're interested in our regular Karate classes or kickboxing, you can sign up for those as well."

Hunter introduced his one female and two male assistants. "Later in the class, we'll be having you try out some self-defense moves with them, but right now, we're going to learn how not to be a victim. Let's have you pair up into partners to start our first exercise."

Many of the women had come to the class with their friends. And because I came alone, there was an odd number of people in the class—which left me without a partner.

At this point, I was ready to leave. I'd already felt the sting of humiliation, and I now felt like an outcast. While everyone was talking, I sidled over to where I'd put my purse and shoes. I bent over to snatch them up.

"Where are you going?" A deep voice said.

I stood up abruptly. "Hunter! I mean, Detective Ito."

"You're not still thinking of leaving, are you?"

I could feel my face growing hot. "No. I was just… checking to make sure I'd turned off my cell phone."

He studied my face in that way detectives study possible suspects. "We have an odd number of students. I'll be your partner. So, why don't you put your stuff down and come join me for our first lesson."

*** *** ***

About two hours into the class, I finally focused on the lessons.

"Now you're getting the hang of it." Hunter nodded approvingly as I used my elbow to break out of a hold. "I can tell you're getting more confident."

I blushed. "Thanks."

The more I got into the focus of the class, the more I understood how useful this type of instruction was. There were many nights I worked late and walking through the parking lot to my car alone was super creepy.

By the time class ended, I felt more confident in my ability to protect myself.

"Okay, ladies!" Hunter said loudly. "Let's learn one more method of escape. Clarity, would you like to help me demonstrate?"

I felt the eyes of fifteen jealous women boring holes into me.

"Uh, sure," I said meekly.

Hunter moved closer to me. Was it just me who noticed the electricity between us? Or did he feel it too?

"This move is suited for when an attacker grabs you from behind." He wrapped his arms around me and picked me up, squeezing hard.

I gasped and struggled to free myself.

Hunter set me down gently. "Clarity did exactly what a normal person would do in this situation. She struggled to get free."

I took a step back, wondering how I could've done anything different to get out of the hold.

"The goal of the perpetrator is to pick you up to move you to a car or an alley, where they could rape or kill you." He demonstrated again by picking me up and moving me several feet before setting me down. "When the perp picks you up, your hand will be roughly at the same height as his groin. So, grab him by the crotch and squeeze."

I gulped. I hadn't expected him to say that.

Hunter chuckled once he put me down and saw the look on my face. "Your goal is to inflict enough pain to make him release his hold on you. Then you have other options. You can inflict more pain by using your elbows or knees to his head and neck. Or if he's down on the ground in severe pain, you can simply run."

He moved closer to me and said, "I'll demonstrate— Clarity, you can just pretend to grab me, okay?"

I had a moment of panic where I envisioned myself accidentally coming into contact with his family jewels. "Uh, okay."

Hunter picked me up from behind. His scent was intoxicating. Despite having spent the last three hours working up a sweat, he still smelled fresh—that woodsy scent mixed with a little citrus. "Now, reach your hand down…"

I reached and pretended to grab his privates. The ladies in the class gasped. Concern for Hunter's manhood reflected on their faces.

Hunter feigned pain and dropped to his knees. He lifted his head. "Good! That was excellent, Clarity." He stood up. "Now I want all of you to practice with the instructors. We'll give it about five minutes each and then we'll let you go for the evening."

I sighed. Almost done. When I'd first arrived, I thought I was going to die. But now, I didn't really want to leave.

The women turned their attention to the instructors and began working on the exercise.

"Want to try this a couple more times, Clarity?" The hard edge of his face had softened when he addressed me this time. "And, I owe you an apology for the misunderstanding about tonight."

I felt my cheeks warm. "It's my fault."

He brushed a tendril of my hair off my cheek. "No, not at all. The fault lies totally on me. Just to let you know, if you weren't Zen's sister, I would've gotten one of my other instructors to teach for me and taken you out for a night on the town."

I smiled and blushed even more. "Really?"

Hunter nodded, his warm brown eyes full of regret. "Zen has a personal policy that his partners don't date his sisters. I have to agree. It could cause problems in our relationship at work."

My shoulders dropped. "Oh." My disappointment bubbled up inside. Finally, I had found someone I'd felt real chemistry with, only to find out that dating him was not a possibility.

CHAPTER 13

Jonah covered his mouth in horror. "It was a self-defense class? Not a swanky night club?"

I looked down at my hands. "Yeah. That's not the worst of it. He told me we could never date."

"Say what?" Brandi put her hand on her hip.

I pressed the down button for the elevator in our office. "He said he doesn't date his partners' sisters. It's Zen's request, actually, and Hunter agrees." I was caught between being sad and frustrated.

"Why not?" Jonah stepped into the elevator and held the door open for us.

"Because it could get in the way of their work relationship." I fidgeted with my purse strap.

"Seriously?" Brandi asked. "That seems dumb."

I sighed. "I mean, I get where he's coming from, but I just wish he weren't Zen's partner."

"Maybe you can get him to bend his rule." Jonah gave me a mischievous smile.

"What do you mean?" I asked.

"Well," he said, "what if you were so incredibly charming... and hot, that he couldn't resist you?"

I snorted. "The way I looked in my little black dress is as about as hot as it gets for me. And he still turned me down. Honestly, I don't know what else I could do to get his attention."

"Invite him over and wear nothing but your birthday suit?" Brandi wiggled her eyebrows.

I rolled my eyes. "He'd think I was certifiable and have me locked up."

"You mentioned that there was an advanced self-defense course that his studio offered." Jonah stepped out of the elevator and held the door open for us. "You could enroll in that."

"So I could be even more humiliated? No thanks." I opened the lobby door and walked out into the sunshine.

"No," Jonah said. "So that you could wear him down. The more he sees you, the harder it will be for him to resist your feminine wiles."

I laughed. "Well, maybe I *should* take another self-defense course. I felt like I just touched the tip of the iceberg with all that stuff." I paused for a moment. "He probably just thinks of me as Zen's little sister. I don't want to get needy and annoying."

"You don't give yourself enough credit." Brandi shook her head. "You're a beautiful woman. And you're great company as well."

"Did Jonah pay you to say that?" I nudged him with my elbow.

He pretended to take out his wallet. "How much do I owe you, Brandi?"

"Jonah." The warning note in Brandi's voice stopped our bantering. "Clarity, I'm serious. You are one of the nicest and most gorgeous people I know. Hunter, or any other guy worth his salt, would be lucky to go out with you."

I threw my arm around my short pal and squeezed her to me. "Thank you, Brandi. You're a good friend."

"What do you think of my plan?" Jonah caught up to us as we walked to our favorite lunch spot.

"To make myself irresistible to him?" I glanced at my friend. "I'd like to give it a shot."

"Awesome." He gave me a wide grin. "Let's strategize over lunch."

✳✳✳

When we returned from lunch, I found Russell inside my office, running his fingers over Janice's desk. His bug eyes grew larger when I flung open the door.

"What are you doing in here? The door was locked when I left." I narrowed my eyes at him.

"Clarity—you know that I'm considering this office as my own. I've told you that." Russell adjusted his suit coat over his large belly.

I was just about to lay into him when I felt a tap on my shoulder.

"Russell Jones?" My brother, looking very official in his navy-blue suit, stepped forward with his hand out.

Confusion clouded Russell's always dull expression before he shook Zen's hand. "Yes?"

"I'm Detective Bloom, Seattle PD. You're one of the few folks who didn't attend Janice Trudeau's funeral, so we didn't get a chance to interview you."

Russell stared at him blankly.

"My partner and I would like to chat with you in the conference room, if you don't mind."

"I'm sorry. I guess I don't understand..." Russell said. "Am I under suspicion of something?"

Zen gave him a practiced smile. "No, no. Not at all. We'd just like to ask you a few questions about Janice. Maybe there was something you noticed that might be pertinent to the case. It won't take very long. Just a few minutes."

Russell shrugged. "All right, then. I suppose that would be fine."

I stepped away from the door to let the two men exit. Russell hadn't gone to the funeral? And wait a minute, Hunter was here? In the conference room?

"He's still in there," I whispered to Brandi and Jonah in the break room.

"They've been questioning him for over an hour." Jonah took a sparkling water from the refrigerated case. "Seems to me, Russell is looking more and more suspicious every day."

"I know." I poured myself a cup of hot water for my tea. "Zen told him the questioning would only take a few minutes. Makes me wonder if they've got something on him."

Jonah sat down at one of the tables. "Just the fact that he took that picture of Janice off her shelf is creepy in itself. You think he had a thing for her?"

I shuddered. "I'm sure he did. He used to come by our office to see if we wanted to go to lunch with him. We always made excuses. He asked both of us because he didn't want it to look like he was singling her out."

"Ew." Brandi sat down and took a sip of her coffee. "Poor Janice. He's so repulsive."

And suspicious, I thought.

"Jonah, you work closer to Russell's office—at least until he takes mine." I joined them at the table. "Can you keep an eye on him?"

"How do you mean?" Jonah asked.

"Just watch him and see if he does anything... suspicious," I said.

"Suspicious, like hunt down a woman he works with and kill her?" Jonah wasn't kidding around. The look on his face was dead serious.

"Yeah. Like that. And anything else you think looks out of the ordinary."

He gave me a curt nod. "I can do that."

"What can I do?" Brandi asked.

I sipped my tea. "I'll talk to Zen to see if anyone in the office is lacking a solid alibi on the day and time Janice was killed. Then, you can watch whomever he points out. Oh, something else you could do, but it might get you in trouble."

"What?" she asked.

"Check Russell's expense account. Maybe there's some suspicious behavior in his spending?"

"You mean like, buying knives, ropes or axes?" Jonah said.

My stomach churned, thinking about the way Janice died.

"I like this." Brandi rubbed her hands together. "It's like playing a game of Clue."

Jonah's brows furrowed. "Right. But that means that you think someone in our office killed Janice. Someone like Russell."

I shook my head. "Not necessarily. It just means that not all our coworkers have been ruled out. I still think the killer is someone she met through the online dating service."

"Speaking of which, have the police found any possible suspects in that group of people yet?" Jonah asked.

"Not yet. I need to get another batch of names from Zen." I looked at the time on my phone. "I wonder if he's done talking to Russell. I want to ask him what else I can help with."

"Plus," Brandi said, her eyes sparkling, "it's an excuse to go see Hunter too."

My heart did a little dance inside my chest. "Come on, let's go."

We casually walked by the conference room. I was suddenly grateful for the windows in that room. You could see directly inside—if the people meeting left the shades up. And it was easy to see who was seated at the table.

I peeked in. Russell was gone, and Zen and Hunter were flipping through their notes.

"Go in there," Brandi hissed.

A stab of anxiety hit me in the gut. I knew that if I wanted Hunter to like me on any level, he would need to see me more often—even if it was in a professional capacity.

I turned to look at Jonah. He gave me an encouraging nod.

My friends took off down the hall. I breathed deeply and knocked.

Zen and Hunter's heads popped up from their paperwork. Zen motioned for me to enter, while Hunter looked slightly hesitant. My heart sank. He didn't want to deal with me.

I sat down next to my brother. "You guys were talking to Russell for a long time. Is he a suspect?"

Zen shook his head and said quietly, "Not here. Let's talk later."

My interest piqued. So, Russell *was* a suspect. "Are you interviewing anyone else today?"

"Your boss, Paul Walker," Hunter said, his face unreadable.

My eyes widened. "He's under suspicion?"

"No," Zen said. "He's also one of the few who didn't attend Janice's funeral. We haven't had a chance to interview him yet."

I nodded. "Anyone else?"

"Bill in janitorial services, and Howie, who works in the billing department. Do you know either of them?" Zen asked.

"Nope. This company has gotten a lot bigger in the two years I've worked here. We have over a hundred people in this office alone." I tugged on my earring. "Do you guys have another list for me to look at? I can dig into them this evening."

Zen shuffled through his folder. "Yes, we do." He handed me a paper with a list of names. "These are in the next batch from the dating service."

I took the paper, folded it, and put it into my pocket. "Do you need help with anything else?"

"Yeah, actually," Hunter said. "We'd like to re-interview Janice's sister, Margaret. Last time we met with her, she was so upset, we couldn't get any straight answers. You know her, right?"

I swallowed. "Yes. Not all that well. But I've spent enough time with her to consider her a casual friend or acquaintance."

"Good," Zen said. "Maybe you can put her more at ease. Do you mind coming along with us?"

I shrugged. "I don't mind. I guess."

"Can you meet us back here at four o'clock?" Hunter asked.

I glanced at the clock on the wall. It was just after two. "Sure. I can probably sneak out without being noticed."

When the guys left, I settled in to brainstorm social media strategies for The Bathroom Buddy.

CHAPTER 14

The timer on my phone went off at four o'clock. I looked over my progress. Not bad. I had synched up with our marketing team and had scheduled tweets, Instagram posts, and Facebook ads.

I collected my purse and laptop and met Zen and Hunter in the conference room. They were just finishing up as well and had already packed their stuff into their bags.

"Ready?" Zen asked.

"As I'll ever be."

We left the building and went directly to Zen's unmarked vehicle. I automatically climbed into the back seat, knowing that Zen would want his partner beside him, so they could talk.

Rush hour was in full swing. Traffic was awful. I stared out the window as the men spoke in low tones. I lost myself in thoughts of Janice and the good times we'd had together.

When we got to Margaret's house, a lump formed in my throat. It bothered me that I was about to see her raw grief.

Zen rang the doorbell, and we stood in uncomfortable silence for a few minutes while we waited.

I thought for sure she wasn't home, but then I heard footsteps inside. The door opened.

Margaret stood before us, wearing skinny jeans and a scoop-necked tank top, which hugged her toned form. Her red hair was perfectly gathered into a messy bun. She looked better than most women did on their best day.

I glanced at Hunter to see if he noticed how gorgeous she was. His face did not betray any interest. Just cool professionalism. Zen on the other hand, seemed rattled.

"Margaret," he said. "Detective Bloom and Detective Ito, Seattle PD."

She blinked. "Clarity?"

I stepped forward and hugged her. "Margaret." I couldn't say anything more. Somehow, saying the obligatory "sorry for your loss" didn't seem right. There were no words I could say that would make her feel better. Instead, tears welled up in my eyes. I hugged her even tighter.

Finally, Margaret stepped back. "What can I help you with?"

Hunter cleared his throat. "May we come in? We have a few questions we'd like to ask you."

She hesitated for just a fraction of a second. "Uh, sure. Yes, please come in."

Her home in Laurelhurst was impeccably neat and the décor was something lifted straight off a Pinterest post. I'd been here on several occasions. At the time, I hadn't really taken the time to appreciate its beauty.

We followed her into the living room, painted a slate gray with white molding and cabinetry. "Please, have a seat. Can I get you anything? I just made a pot of coffee. It's decaf. Hope that's okay."

"Decaf is fine," Zen said.

"Can I help you in the kitchen?" I asked.

"No, no. I've got it. Cream and sugar?" she asked.

"Sure. Both, please." Zen wiped his hands on his trousers.

"I'll bring it out." She disappeared through the door to the kitchen.

I sat down on the sofa and was surprised when Hunter sat down next to me. He gave me a slight smile. "Nice place."

"Yeah." I smiled back. "Her parents are loaded."

Zen, still looking uncomfortable, sat down on the sofa across from ours. "Janice's home is in Wallingford. And it's a rental. You said, their parents have a lot of money?"

Hunter's eyes were fixed on the door to the kitchen. I wondered if he was ensuring that Margaret didn't overhear our conversation. Or was he just so caught up in her beauty that he couldn't wait for her to come back?

I cleared my throat. "Her mom worked for Microsoft in the early years and did really well off her stock package. She retired early and just at the right time—before the dot-com crash." I thought for a moment. "And her dad comes from money. So, yeah, they live a comfortable life."

"Why would Janice live in a rental home, and Margaret live in a place like this? And in this neighborhood?" Zen furrowed his brows.

"Because their parents set up trust funds for each of them, and a chunk of it is paid out when the girls turn thirty. Margaret is two years older—so she used part of that chunk to buy this house." My eyes misted over. "Janice's thirtieth birthday is next week. She was so looking forward to buying her own home. She wanted one in this neighborhood, so she and Margaret could live close by."

Margaret swung the door open, carrying a tray with mugs of steaming coffee, a pitcher of cream, and a bowl of sugar cubes.

"It might be a little warm today for hot coffee, but I was in the mood for comfort." She set the tray on the coffee table and sat down next to Zen.

We each took a mug of coffee and doctored it up with cream and sugar. Hunter took his black.

Zen stirred his coffee. "Thank you, Margaret." He took a sip. "This really hits the spot."

She nodded and sipped her coffee. "You said you had questions for me?"

"We just want to run through the day... the day Janice passed. Can you walk us through all the interactions you had with her on that day? And maybe the days leading up to it?" Hunter leaned forward.

Margaret cringed. "I'll do my best. I'm trying hard to move on with my life."

"Move on?" I blurted out. "She's only been gone for two weeks."

Zen shot me a warning look. "I think what Clarity means is that everyone needs time to process the death of a loved one."

I bit my lip. I'd overstepped my bounds. How could she expect to move on so quickly after her sister's death?

"I understand." Margaret looked stricken. "But every time I think about the reality of what's happened, my brain just shuts down. I want to grieve, but I'm too scared."

"Scared?" Zen put his cup down.

Margaret's shoulders slumped. "Scared that if I grieve, it means that Janice is truly gone. That I'll never get her back." Tears slid down her cheeks.

Zen put his hand on her shoulder. "I'm sorry."

I immediately felt bad for what I'd said about moving on so soon. But the clock was ticking, and I knew that every minute we put off getting answers was a minute the killer would use to slip further away. "Margaret, I know this is hard. Believe me, talking about this is the last thing I want to do. But I think we all want to get to the bottom of this. There's a killer out there. We need to get the guy who murdered Janice. What if he kills again?"

Margaret blinked, as though the thought had never occurred to her. "Do you think he will?"

I shrugged. "I don't know. But I do know that if he does, and we haven't done everything we can to find him, I will never forgive myself. Please—we need your help. Maybe something you remember will help Zen and Hunter track down the man who did this to your sister... to my best friend."

Margaret broke. Her sobs wracked her body, and the coffee spilled over the rim of her cup onto her lap.

Oh, man. What had I done?

Zen gave me a frosty glare and reached for a napkin to mop up the spill.

I jumped up and grabbed more napkins. I got on my knees where Margaret sat and helped to clean as well. "I'm so sorry. I didn't mean to make you even more upset."

"No, no." She watched helplessly as Zen wadded up the wet napkins and put them on the tray. "You're absolutely right. I can't stick my head in the sand—especially if the killer is planning on murdering someone else."

I gave her a quick hug and then sat back down on the couch.

Hunter eyed me curiously. He seemed to be more of an observer rather than a participant in this strange unfolding of events.

I took a deep breath and let it out slowly to steady my nerves. "What can you tell us about that day?"

Zen settled back into his spot on the couch and took out his notebook. "Start at the beginning. Right after you woke up that morning."

Margaret wiped a few tears from her face. "I don't know. It was normal, I guess. I got up at five-thirty and made a pot of coffee. And I made toast and soft-boiled eggs."

"You got up at five-thirty on a Saturday?" My eyes were wide with disbelief. Why would anyone in their right mind get up so early on a weekend?

Margaret gave me a slight smile. "I'm an early riser. And a creature of habit. Because I get up early all week for work, my body can't sleep past my normal wake-up time."

I marveled at her discipline. The only reason I got up early on a weekend was to feed Pumpkin. But then I went straight back to bed after he was fed.

Zen nodded and jotted something down in his notebook.

"I went for a run at around six o'clock."

"What was your route?" Hunter asked.

"That morning?" Margaret frowned, trying to remember. "I'm pretty sure I ran down 41st and past the Beach Club. I turned around there and ran back the same way I came. It was a shorter run than usual because Mom and Dad wanted me to help them pick out new furniture for their beach house. It's due for a cosmetic update."

"So, you went to your mom and dad's place after your run?" Hunter asked.

"I showered first." Margaret allowed herself a small smile which didn't seem to reach her eyes. "Then I met them at their house. We drove to that little coffee shop off 39th—Charlie's Café? I really needed another cup of coffee since I'd been out late the night before."

Zen looked around her living room and took in the high ceilings, the art on the walls, and the way the fireplace had just the right combination of rustic and elegant pieces set upon the thick wood mantelpiece. "You certainly have a knack for decorating."

Who was this guy? Certainly not my brother—the one whose only decor was a large glass display case filled with a boyhood baseball card collection.

"Margaret's an interior decorator, Zen." I almost rolled my eyes. "Of course she has a knack for it."

Zen's face flushed. Was he embarrassed? Honestly, what was going on with him?

He cleared his throat. "Did you hear from Janice that same day?"

"I did. Yes." She paused for a moment. "Janice called me at around noon on Saturday. She asked for my help with her house hunting—she wanted my opinion."

"Did you meet her in person?" Hunter asked.

"Yes. She came here, and we talked about locations, neighborhoods, and the style of home she was interested in."

"Did she tell you about her date?" Zen had his pen poised over his notebook. "Who she was meeting from the online dating agency?"

Margaret let out a mirthless laugh. "See, that's the thing! The thing that keeps niggling at the back of my mind. The online dating thing is not something I would've expected from Janice."

I pointed at her. "Yes! That's what I keep saying! No way would Janice sign up for a dating service... especially without telling you or me first."

Margaret nodded. "Exactly. Janice was a busy woman. She was so focused on her career. I think if the right guy had come along, she might've considered dating. But actually making the effort and signing up with a dating service? That's not her."

Zen glanced at me, and I nodded vigorously. "Right."

"So," Hunter said slowly, "why do you think she did?"

She shook her head. "I have no idea."

"Anything else you can tell us about that day?

She thought for a moment. "Right before she left here, she said she had to run by her office to check on something. Then she went home to get ready for her date."

Hunter's eyebrows rose. "She stopped by her office?"

Margaret nodded. "That's not unusual. She often stopped by work on the weekends."

"That's true. We both do." I frowned. "Did."

"Did she talk about anything specific that she planned to do at the office that day?" Zen asked.

"No. She did seem a little anxious, though. I attributed her nerves to be about the date, not the office." Margaret set her cup down on the coffee table.

"I must have just missed her. I was at the office all morning, but then left to go grocery shopping in the afternoon." I scooted to the edge of the couch. "Did she say what the guy looked like? The guy she was going out on the date with?"

She shook her head. "No. In fact, she didn't say anything else about the man. Just that she had an afternoon date through the online service."

Zen closed his notebook. "Okay, I think that's it for now. Thank you, Margaret, for answering our questions."

We got up and went to the door. I turned and hugged Margaret briefly. "I'll call in a few days to check on you. Do you need anything?"

"No, but thanks for offering." Margaret gave me a half smile. She opened the door and watched us walk out. "Please call if you find out anything."

"Of course," Zen answered. "I'll keep you informed."

She gave him a more sincere smile than she'd given me. "Thank you, Detective."

"Zen. Call me Zen." He stumbled on one of the stairs, but quickly recovered his balance.

"Zen," Margaret repeated.

***

"What the hell was all that about?" I demanded as we went back to the car. "Zen. Call me Zen," I said in a mocking tone. "You were interviewing the victim's sister. Do you tell all the people you interview to call you Zen?" I rolled my eyes at him. "You better not have a thing for her."

Zen glared at me. "I don't have a thing for her. I was just... being compassionate, that's all. I wanted Margaret to feel more comfortable around me."

Hunter had stepped back to avoid coming between us. He raised an eyebrow at Zen's latest defensive comment and gave me a little shrug.

We got to the car and Zen opened his side and unlocked the doors. To my surprise, Hunter moved ahead of me, opened the front passenger door, and motioned for me to get in.

I stood there for a second, dumbfounded, wondering what to do.

"Please." He motioned again.

"Uh, thank you." I got in, and he shut the door once I'd buckled my seat belt.

Hunter got in the back. Zen gave him a bewildered look in the rearview mirror.

I bit my lip to keep from smiling. Maybe Hunter was into me after all.

CHAPTER 15

Zen dropped me off at work, and he and Hunter drove back to the station.

I ran up to my office to retrieve my stuff and snuck back out without anyone noticing I'd left.

I should've talked to Brandi and Jonah about what I'd learned from Margaret, but I knew they would grill me on Hunter too. For now, I just wanted to keep him to myself and think about those subtle cues he'd given me.

Still unsure about what would happen with my job now that Paul seemed annoyed with me, I drove to the Toyota dealership and asked to test drive a Prius. The lease on my BMW was up soon, and I needed to make a fiscally responsible choice for my next vehicle. If I could purchase a car for around twenty-five thousand dollars, I'd be able to pay for it in cash.

Two hours later, I'd made a deal at just under the amount I'd wanted to pay. I would pick up the new Prius later, after I took my BMW back when the lease was up.

With a self-congratulatory smile, I drove back home.

Pumpkin was at the door to greet me, giving me an anxious look.

"Hungry again?" I picked him up and cuddled him. I looked at the wall clock. "My sweet baby. Sorry I'm late. I'll get you some dinner right away, okay?"

I set him down in the kitchen and got out a can of chicken vittles. I set the bowl down and without a single thank you, he dove in.

While he was eating, I changed into a pair of jeans and a t-shirt. I walked back into the living room and noticed Janice's work laptop sitting on the coffee table. I'd been so caught up with my faux date with Hunter that I'd completely forgotten about it.

Opening it up, I was glad to see that one of the police techs had left a post-it stuck between the keyboard and monitor. It was the login and password to get into the machine.

I turned it on, logged in, and opened the documents folder. Most of the files were labeled with the subject and date within the file name. Everything looked in order.

"Nothing suspicious here," I mumbled.

Pumpkin finished eating and wandered into the room. He hopped onto my lap and stretched across the keyboard.

I sighed. "You seem very determined to keep me from getting things done."

Eyeing the toy mouse on the couch, I picked it up, and dangled it in front of his face. "Ooh, look, Pumpkin. A mouse!" I threw it across the room. He purred and rolled onto his side, now covering the entire keyboard with his body.

"This won't do." I gently pushed him off the computer and got up. "Want some outside time?"

Next to the French door that led to my deck, I'd installed his cat door. It led to a completely separate portion of the deck, where there was a sandbox, a scratching post, and two benches he could sit on. I called it his "catio." He loved to watch the birds in the backyard. What made it extra special was the metal fencing over the decorative wooden arches that were attached on either side of the railing. There was no way Pumpkin could get out—and no way that raccoons, coyotes, or other predators could get to him.

If the weather was nice, I kept the cat door unlatched, so he could enjoy the sights and smells of the outdoors.

I went into the kitchen and shook a handful of Kat Krunchies into my hand. Letting him smell them, I went to the cat door and threw the treats through the flap in the door and watched him shoot through it like a circus tiger jumping through a ring of fire. I chuckled. "There. Now I can focus."

I went back to Janice's computer, and opened up her work email app. Like me, Janice saved everything, so she could refer back to the emails if there was a problem with an event she'd booked.

"God, there are hundreds." My stomach dropped as I stared at the screen. It made me sad to realize she would never read these emails.

I decided to start a week before Janice died. Maybe if the man who had killed her was the one she'd had a date with, he might've emailed her a week in advance? It was as good a place to start as any.

Most of the emails had to do with the conference our company would be attending next week. There were emails from vendors who set up booths and emails from the hotel we'd booked lodging with. There was nothing out of the ordinary—they all seemed to be work-related.

Suddenly, my eye caught the "From" column and the name Russell Jones. I held my breath and opened it.

It read:

"Janice, I have an extra ticket to the Seattle Symphony on Saturday. Would you like to go? We can meet at five o'clock for dinner. The concert starts at seven. Let me know."

"Gross." Russell had asked her out on a date. "Oh, my God! Saturday was the day Janice was murdered!"

Why hadn't she told me about this? I opened her "Sent" folder and looked for the correct date and recipient. "There it is." I held my breath and opened the response from Janice to Russell.

"Russell, that's so sweet of you to think of me! Thank you. Unfortunately, I won't be able to join you for the concert, though it sounds lovely. I already have plans. I hope you find someone to enjoy the concert with!"

God, she was nice. Too nice. She let him down so gently. He probably didn't even realize she was rejecting him. What were the "plans" she'd spoken of? Or was that just an excuse she'd just made up to avoid going on a date?

I sat back and let my mind wander. What if Russell had gotten mad that she'd rejected him? Maybe he was so disappointed she'd said no that he went to her house and confronted her. And maybe they argued, and he got rough and killed her. Was it possible? Could Russell be a deranged killer?

* * *

I found nothing, aside from Russell's email, in Janice's inbox. But this was Janice's work laptop. Where was her home computer?

I texted Zen. "I forwarded some emails from Russell that I found on Janice's computer. Your team has probably already checked this out, but maybe they've overlooked Russell's email? Better to be safe than sorry. I couldn't find anything else on Janice's work laptop. Do the police have her personal computer?"

A few moments later came the reply. "I was about to take it to her sister's house. Do you want to take a look first?"

"Yes!" I replied. "When can you bring it over?"

"Tonight. Around seven?"

"I'll be here."

I put my phone down and stared at her laptop. Where else would she have kept information on the guys she'd dated?

I dug through her file structure, hoping to find anything out of the ordinary. Nothing. It was all strictly work-related.

My stomach rumbled. Pumpkin wasn't the only one who was hungry. The refrigerator was an empty wasteland. I sighed. I really needed to do some grocery shopping. I looked at the time. It was just after six o'clock. Not enough time to shop before Zen came by with Janice's other computer.

I called my favorite Thai food restaurant and ordered delivery of three different entrees with rice, figuring the leftovers would last me the rest of the week.

Remembering the latest list of online daters, I pulled it out of my purse and hunkered down in front of my own computer. There were six names on the list.

I got through three of them when the doorbell rang.

My food had arrived! I opened the door and handed a tip to the delivery guy in exchange for the bag of deliciousness.

I'd just sat down at the table with a plate when the doorbell rang again. That would have to be Zen. I yanked the door open, anxious to get back to my dinner.

My breath left me. Both Zen and Hunter stood on my doorstep.

"Hey, sis." My brother stepped past me into the house. "What smells so good?"

I stole a glance at Hunter, who was looking fine in a dark gray suit.

"Uh, Thai food." I closed the door behind them.

Hunter gave me a crooked smile. "I love Thai food."

My mind raced. He loves Thai food. What was the thing I was supposed to say in response? My thought process stalled. There was an awkward moment of silence and then it came to me. "Sit down, you guys! I'll get some plates."

Zen grinned. "God, that would be great. We haven't had a chance to grab dinner yet."

I fled to the kitchen. Did I look all right? I scrutinized my reflection in my kitchen window. I still had my work clothes on, and they were a bit rumpled, but I was presentable. "Okay, okay. I've got this. It's fine," I whispered to myself.

I took out two more plates, some utensils, and paper napkins. I rushed them out to the dining table and then went back for water.

Zen looked slightly disappointed when I set a glass of water in front of him. "Do you have any beer?"

"No, I'm sorry. You drank it all the last time you were here."

"That's too bad. How about if I run to the corner store and pick up a six-pack?" He stood up.

"If you really want to," I said. "Sorry I didn't buy more. I haven't been shopping in a week."

"That's okay. Be back in a few." He left and closed the door softly behind him.

Suddenly, I was aware that Hunter and I were alone.

He smiled at me. "Hi."

I blushed. "Hi."

The wall clock ticked, ticked, ticked.

"Shall I plate it for you?" I dipped a large spoon into the box of rice.

"Oh. No, that's okay. I've got it."

Was he blushing? This was good. He was nervous around me. Nervous meant...

He stood up and took off his suit jacket. "I don't want to spill anything on this."

His biceps stretched the fabric on the arms of his white shirt so that it was taut when he bent his arms.

A trickle of sweat rolled down my back and pooled at the waistband of my skirt. "Is it hot in here? I think it's hot. I'm going to turn up the air conditioning."

I got up awkwardly from my chair and pushed the buttons on the thermostat. "There," I said, as I came back into the room.

"So, how's it going with the dating stuff?" He took a bite of his food and closed his eyes as he chewed. "This is delicious."

I flushed. "Dating stuff? Oh, I'm not dating anyone at the moment."

His eyes opened, and a look of amusement crossed his face. "No. I mean, how are you coming with sifting through the profiles of the online daters who'd contacted Janice?"

I was sure my face turned a lovely shade of Shoot Me Now Red. "Oh, ha ha! Of course. I knew that. I was just kidding. You know—after that thing at the karate studio." I was making it worse. Much worse.

The corner of his lip drew up in a slight smile. "Look, Clarity, I wanted to talk to you about that. I think—"

The door opened. "I'm back!" Zen announced cheerfully. "Did you miss me?" He saw the looks on our faces. "Is everything okay?" He set the beer down on the table.

"Yeah, yeah, of course." I got up to get the bottle opener and brought it back to the table.

"We were just talking about the work Clarity has done with the social media profiles." Hunter snatched the bottle opener, cracked his beer open, and took a long swig.

Zen furrowed his brow. "Yeah? Did you find anything?"

I hesitated. "No, not yet. Of the six you gave me today, I combed through three. They were all clear. I'll look at the other three after dinner."

My brother frowned. "I was hoping you'd find something sooner. Our leads are drying up."

Guilt washed over me. "I should be dedicating more time to this. Maybe I'll take the day off tomorrow."

Zen seemed surprised. "I didn't mean to give you the wrong impression. You're doing fine. We're just getting pressure to solve this quickly." His cell rang, and he pulled it out of his pocket. "Detective Bloom."

He listened for a moment. "When?"

Hunter set down his fork.

"Where?" Zen listened.

The wall clock ticked.

"We'll be right there." Zen met Hunter's gaze. "There's been another murder."

CHAPTER 16

My mouth hung open. "Another murder?"

Zen nodded, his lips set in a grim line.

"What happened?" I shuddered at the thought of how the killer had dismembered my best friend. "Did the victim die the same way as Janice?"

"Not exactly. This one was similar, but she wasn't killed with the same kind of wrath as Janice was."

I blinked. "I don't get it."

Zen sighed. "I don't have a lot of time to explain, but basically, the victim was a young woman around Janice's age. She wasn't married and didn't have children. Her body was found in a dumpster."

My eyes widened. "In the same dumpster Janice was found?"

He shook his head. "In the alley behind the victim's office building in downtown Seattle. Which might explain why the body wasn't hacked up like Janice's. The killer was probably operating on limited time."

"What? How could someone get away with a murder in such a public place? I bet there were at least three homeless people sleeping in that alley—you know how downtown is. Someone must have witnessed the murder."

He shrugged. "That's all I know for now. Hunter and I need to get down there right away."

"Can I come?" I blurted out before I even realized it was coming out of my mouth.

Zen frowned. "Absolutely not. Your job is to be behind the scenes, digging through the social media profiles of our suspects." He gestured toward Hunter. "Let's go."

They went to the door and stepped onto the porch.

"Call me if you turn up anything on the latest list of men. And, if you could send me a document with all their online activity like you did last time, that would be great."

I watched them get into their unmarked car and drive away. Were all older brothers such jerks? I went inside and slammed the door.

Zen and Hunter's beers sat, half full, on the table. I narrowed my eyes at the bottles. Why couldn't Zen take me seriously? I picked up the bottles and stomped into the kitchen to pour the contents down the drain.

Wait a minute. Why was I about to waste perfectly good beer? I mean, I wasn't really a beer drinker, but...

Zen's bottle had the least amount left in it. I drank it down in one swig. Next was Hunter's beer. This one I would savor.

I carried it back to the living room. I opened my laptop and resumed my work.

The next guy on the list, Max Vanderlin, was hot. Tall, broad-shouldered, square chin... Janice would've been attracted to this one. He was her type. I pulled up his LinkedIn page. He owned a financial planning company near the Green Lake area.

I dug through his Facebook profile, Twitter and Instagram feeds, but didn't find anything he'd posted during the time of Janice's murder. I poked around some other lesser known social media sites and again, came up blank. How was I going to find out if this guy had anything to do with Janice's death?

My eye caught the laptop case Hunter had set on the coffee table. Janice's personal laptop. I bit my lip. What if?

I took out the computer and booted it up. Once again, the police tech had left a sticky note with login and password information. I keyed it in and held my breath as her desktop background image loaded. It was a selfie of Janice and me, wearing sunglasses and clinking our umbrella'd daiquiri glasses.

My eyes watered. "For you, girl. I'm doing this for you." I brushed away a tear and loaded her internet browser.

What was the name of that dating site again? I did a quick search for match-making companies in Seattle. The second one on the list was highlighted in purple rather than blue, indicating that it had been clicked on before. It was called "Pursuit." I made a face. Ugh. Very forced and creepy—like some aggressive safari hunt, instead of a dating company.

I clicked.

The home page came up. I didn't know what I was expecting, but it wasn't this. The site looked more like a high-end financial corporation than a dating site.

It was minimalistic. Stark white. Clean lines. "Hmm." I clicked on "Login" in the top ribbon. The user name and password were pre-filled. Jackpot! Janice had saved her login information, so the browser had retained it.

Interesting. The name on her account was listed as Jan Magnuson, not Trudeau. Magnuson was her mother's maiden name. I shrugged. A lot of women did that when they didn't want to be stalked. And I could see why, especially on a dating website. You couldn't be too careful these days.

I clicked on the "My Profile" button on the home page. The screen changed to a headshot of Janice, looking very corporate. The shot was taken of her profile, rather than straight on. It didn't even look like her. A small photo gallery with scrolling arrows showed three more photos. One was a full-body shot of Janice wearing a light gray suit and a crisp white blouse. The second one was of her standing in front of her parents' luxury car. The third photo showed her in profile, raising a glass of white wine to her lips as she sat in a ritzy-looking bar. None of the pictures showed her entire face. What in the world?

I'd never seen her so corporate-looking. She always looked professional at work—but Janice had an air of casualness about her that put people at ease. This didn't look like the same person.

I scratched my head. What would've prompted her to set up a dating profile on a site like this? I clicked on the "My Account" button, which showed the details of her payment info. My eyes went straight to the field that said, "Member since July 18, 2018."

My fingers flew to my mouth. That was two days before her murder! In my gut, I knew with one hundred percent certainty that Janice joining this site had something to do with her murder. But how? And why didn't she tell me what was going on?

Another thought struck me. If Janice had been murdered by a guy she'd met on this dating site, then the only way I could find out who the killer was...

Setting Janice's laptop on the coffee table, I grabbed my personal computer and navigated to the Pursuit page. I stared at the "Join Now" button. This could be a big mistake. I was playing with fire, and I knew it.

Hunter's bottle of beer was still sitting next to the laptop. It was now empty. I went into the kitchen to grab another one. "Zen would throttle me if he knew that I was thinking about baiting a killer."

He'd been so adamant about me not coming to the latest crime scene. My cheeks flushed. How dare he dictate what I could and couldn't do? Just because he was my older brother didn't mean he could treat me like a kid.

Staring at the beer, I frowned. Beer was not my choice of drink. Who did he think he was, coming in here, forcing his opinions and his cheap beer on me? I made a raspberry noise with my lips and put the beer back in the fridge. I stomped over to the counter, where a nice bottle of merlot sat, just waiting for me to pop the cork.

I nodded. Yes, red wine was more my style. I was a strong, independent woman. My friend needed me to solve her murder. I poured myself a big glass of the burgundy-colored liquid and marched back into the living room.

Pumpkin meowed and followed me, his tail swishing in time to my march. "At least you have my back, buddy. You never tell me what to do." I gently scratched his soft cheek. "Except when it's feeding time."

I took a fortifying sip of my merlot and put the two computers side by side. I would copy all the parameters that Janice had put into her bio. So, if that psychopath was attracted to Janice's profile, he would also be attracted to mine.

Once I had everything complete, I stared at my screen. No. This wasn't right. It was too easy for this guy to research me online.

I looked down at Pumpkin. "What if he comes after me? You're not exactly a guard dog."

Pumpkin meowed and hopped up to the back of the couch. He wedged himself behind my neck and nestled into my shoulder.

I needed to make up a different name—one that he couldn't trace back to me. And, I needed to use someone else's photos. I didn't want him to recognize me out in public and follow me home.

My heart pounded. God! What was I doing?

Janice's screensaver came on and began rotating through photos. Janice and me riding horses in Snoqualmie. Janice and Margaret as little girls, their toothless grins and freckles lighting up the screen. Janice and me laughing hysterically as we sang karaoke at one of our favorite bars. Dang, she was tone deaf. I did a half sniffle and laugh that came out as a snort. I took another sip of wine.

I loved that girl. She was the best of the best.

Having strengthened my resolve, I squared my shoulders, trying not to jostle Pumpkin. Now was the time for finding the monster who'd killed her.

I backspaced over the name field and entered the most generic name I could think of, aside from Jane Doe. Ashley Brown. I mean, who didn't know an Ashley? They were everywhere.

Next, I had to figure out what to do about the pictures. If I uploaded current photos of myself, then the man who killed my friend would know what I looked like. If I used stock photos, any fool could upload them into Google's image search and know something wasn't right.

I took a couple more sips of wine and rubbed Pumpkin behind the ears. His motor kicked in and his rumbling chest soothed my jangled nerves.

A thought crossed my mind. Several years ago, I had made the unfortunate mistake of dyeing my hair red. I got tired of it and ended up going back to my natural dark color. If the killer was attracted to Janice because of the way she looked, maybe he would also be attracted to me as a redhead.

I searched through my pictures folder.

Fifteen minutes and an empty wine glass later, I shouted "Eureka!" Pumpkin gave me a dirty look and left his perch, jumping down off my shoulders.

"Sorry," I muttered.

In an old folder, I found three photos of me where I somewhat resembled my friend. Fear was starting to gnaw at me. Was it stupid to bait a killer?

I chewed on my lip. My gut was telling me that I was walking on thin ice. Zen would not approve. After a few nail-biting moments, I made my decision.

"Whoever did this to Janice has to be caught."

I knew I had to create a different email address. The risk of using my own was too great. "That's okay," I said to myself and the cat. "I can do that."

Pumpkin sauntered back over and began washing his paws.

I created a new, non-descript email account, and once it was confirmed, I made it forward to my home email address.

I paid the exorbitant monthly fee to the dating site and collapsed back into the couch. I gulped the rest of my wine and set the glass down on the table. "Now—I wait."

CHAPTER 17

"You did what?" Brandi grabbed my arm, nearly knocking the bite of salad off my fork.

We were seated at a new lunch place a few blocks from our building in downtown Seattle. The low hum of people talking and the clinking of silverware created a pleasant atmosphere.

I took a sip of my water. "I'm baiting the killer."

"Dang, girl. You're catfishing him." Jonah leaned back in his chair and put his hands behind his head. "I'm not sure if that's stupid or just plain crazy."

"Does Zen know?" Brandi's eyes were as wide as saucers.

"Uh, no." I shuddered. "If Zen knew, he'd handcuff himself to me."

"What happens if you go out with the guy and he kills you?" Brandi whispered.

"That won't happen." I sounded a lot more confident than I felt.

"How do you know?" Brandi leaned forward, her elbows on the table. "He did kill Janice…"

I put my hand up to stop further discussion. "I created a fake profile, I didn't use my real email address, and if I get any dates through this service, I will only do a coffee or lunch place in a really crowded area. What could go wrong?"

Jonah snorted. "Said every victim in a horror movie before they got offed."

Brandi pushed her half-eaten salad away, crumpled her napkin and tossed it on the table. "This is a bad idea. It's beyond your expertise. You're not a cop."

Inside, I knew she was right. I couldn't let her see how nervous I was about what I'd done, and I was having serious second thoughts. "I'll be fine."

Jonah came out of his relaxed position and leaned forward in his chair. "I think this is way too dangerous. But here's the deal. We cannot let you do this alone. If you set up dates with these guys, you will tell us, and we'll be there watching. Got it?"

I'd never seen Jonah speak so forcefully. I instantly felt better. "Okay. Sure."

"And we should have Zen on speed dial in case something weird happens." Brandi took out her phone. "What's his phone number?"

Feeling a flicker of annoyance, I pulled out my phone anyway and sent both Brandi and Jonah his contact info. "There."

"Okay, then." Brandi relaxed her shoulders.

"Right." Jonah sighed. "Excuse me," he said to the server who'd just passed our table. "I'd like a double scotch, no ice."

✱✱✱

When I arrived home after work, I anxiously approached my laptop. Had anyone chosen me for a date? I bit my lip. What if no one had?

I laughed, startling Pumpkin, whose emerald eyes narrowed in annoyance. "I mean, that's stupid. It won't be me who's rejected. It'll be the fake me."

I turned on the computer and waited for it to load. My fingers brushed nervously through Pumpkin's fur. Maybe I should do something while it loaded. Mom always says, "A watched pot never boils." I went into the kitchen to scrounge up a meal. Then I remembered I still hadn't gone grocery shopping. I would have to settle for boxed macaroni and cheese. I opened the fridge and took out the milk carton. I opened it and gave it a sniff. "Pee-yew!" There went the macaroni and cheese idea.

Rummaging through my pantry, I found a package of Top Ramen. "This works." I put a pot of water on to boil and then opened a can of cat food and emptied it into Pumpkin's bowl.

He came running, his tail in the air, ready to dig in.

While the water was boiling, I hesitantly went back to my laptop. I clicked on my browser and loaded the Pursuit page.

There were three messages.

My fingers shook as I opened each one. I first scanned through a photo of the men, then read their messages.

"Pursuit Member: Pierce Padgett

Message: Hello, Ashley. I saw your profile on Pursuit and would love to connect. I am free for lunch or coffee on Thursday at 11:00 a.m. Are you available to meet? I work in downtown Seattle. There's a coffee shop in Pioneer Square which I enjoy very much—Zeitgeist Kunst & Kaffee. Please let me know if you are available. Sincerely, Pierce."

Well, he certainly was polite. And non-threatening too. Strangely enough, that coffee shop was only two blocks away from work. I pulled up the list of men Zen had given me who had messaged Janice through Pursuit. My finger slid down the list until it landed upon Pierce Padgett. I was half pleased with myself for constructing my profile to mirror Janice's and half terrified that it had worked.

What did Zen's notes say about Pierce? I opened the document. My finger traced the information on the screen. "Subject said he was home reading a book," it said. I frowned. That was something I couldn't verify on social media. Unless he was reading the book on an e-reader. Would the e-reader company have a way of tracking reading progress and the date and time it was being read? I wondered if the police had gotten a warrant to get that information if he'd been reading electronically.

Before I agreed to anything, I had to check this guy out. First, I searched for him on Facebook. There he was! But he had locked down his privacy settings tightly. Even his friends list was hidden from me.

Next, I read his LinkedIn page. He had a master's degree in finance and was a certified CPA. I opened a new browser window and went to the company website. His picture and bio appeared in the About Us section. He'd worked at his accounting firm since he'd graduated from college. Pretty boring. That was good. Boring might mean that he wasn't a killer.

I scanned Instagram and couldn't find him. Likewise with Twitter. Guess he wasn't the most social person ever.

There was just enough mystery there that I needed to meet him in person. Scrutinizing the photo he'd posted, I couldn't detect any serial killer vibes. He was handsome, with refined features, light brown hair, and glasses. He looked like the clean-cut guy next door. I read his message again and then typed a reply that matched the tone of his.

"Pursuit Member: Ashley Brown

Message: Hello, Pierce. I would be happy to meet with you at Zeitgeist on Thursday at 11:00 a.m. Coffee would be great. See you then. Sincerely, Ashley."

Now, what was I going to do about my hair? It wasn't red anymore, and I liked my natural dark hair. A wig? Or maybe I should tell him that I just got it colored?

While I worried about my hair, I opened the next message and checked out the man's profile picture. His dark hair was greased back and his fake tan was a little obvious.

"Pursuit member: John Finn

Message: Hey, Ashley! Saw your profile and you are smokin' hot. Would love to hook up with you. I can probably squeeze you in for a lunchtime quickie on Wednesday at noon. Just so you know, this is a one-time deal. No attachments allowed. You game?"

I groaned. There was no way Janice would date him.

Searching through the notes Zen had sent me, I discovered that John Finn was not on his list. Good. I could eliminate this guy from the line-up of suspects. I typed my reply.

"Pursuit member: Ashley Brown

Message: John, I don't think so. Bye."

I opened the next message with one eye open, cringing at the thought of encountering another dirt bag.

"Pursuit member: Max Vanderlin

Message: I would like to meet with you. Friday, 7:00 p.m. at The Graywater. See you then."

This guy was on Zen's list! And he seemed to be a presumptuous creep. He didn't even ask me if I was interested. He just assumed I'd meet him when and where he told me to meet him. Yeah, that's the kind of boyfriend every girl needed. What if he was the killer?

The message seemed cold enough to come from a person who would nonchalantly murder women...

I went back to the file Zen had sent. In his statement to the police, Max Vanderlin said he'd been hiking on Mt. Si on the day of Janice's murder. He claimed he'd gone by himself, so no one was there to back up his story.

Pumpkin hopped down from the couch and rubbed his cheek on my leg. I reached down to stroke his back.

I needed to focus. Checking Google, I discovered that the place he wanted to meet, The Graywater, was an out-of-the-way restaurant in Ballard. There was no chance I would meet a guy I didn't know in a place I was unfamiliar with. Especially at night.

Goosebumps prickled my flesh as I thought about replying to this guy. He could be the one. I took a deep breath and typed my response.

"Pursuit member: Ashley Brown

Message: Hello, Max. I would prefer to meet for coffee or lunch somewhere closer to downtown Seattle. How about coffee on Friday at 10:00 a.m. at the Starbucks on Occidental?"

I reread my message several times before I clicked send.

Maybe he wouldn't agree to my terms, but I was not going to meet him unless he did. Even I knew it was far too dangerous.

CHAPTER 18

"I have a big announcement to make." Paul adjusted his tie.

We'd been summoned to the main open work area in the center of the office, and each of us stood fidgeting. Was the company being bought out and swallowed up by a bigger fish?

"This afternoon, I'm giving everyone half a day off." He smiled broadly and held his arms out, as if expecting to receive a bouquet of flowers and a showering of praise.

I was stunned. This kind of thing never happened at Opulent.

The employees suddenly wore surprised expressions, and the low buzz of whispers spread through the small crowd.

Paul held up his hands. "Okay, I know—you're shocked." He gave a practiced devilish grin. "I just wanted to reward you for a job well done. Mondays aren't usually my favorite day of the week, but today is different. The BFF Bangle is topping the sales charts. It's currently the number one bestselling high-tech wearable in the history of our company. Well done."

He and his minions clapped and the rest of us hesitantly joined in. I was sure my coworkers were thinking the same thing I was. What was the catch? Double the workload when we returned the next day?

"And," Paul said as he made a shushing motion, "it's been brought to my attention that I was a little hard on you about attending Janice's funeral. I owe you an apology."

I glanced at Jonah and he raised an eyebrow.

Paul continued. "So, this afternoon, I invite all of you to come over to my house for a backyard barbecue."

Paul's minions smiled and patted him on the back. Russell, who stood on Paul's right, nodded his head and grunted his appreciation.

I glanced at Jonah and Brandi, who were both frowning—likely because we'd all been led to believe we were going to get a half-day off, only to find out we were required to go to Paul's house.

Paul checked his Opulent Smart Watch and pushed a button on the tiny screen. Cell phone chimes went off from various pockets and desks, one after the other, like some kind of disjointed Jingle Bells tune.

I took the phone out of my jacket pocket and glanced at the screen. Before I could read the text, Paul said, "I've just sent you all directions to my house in Medina. It's early enough in the day that traffic shouldn't be too bad going over the bridge. See you all in about a half hour."

When everyone disbursed, I fell into step with Jonah and Brandi. "That was weird."

"Yeah, he's never given us time off before. Even if there is a catch." Brandi looked down at her stilettos. "I wish I'd known we'd be going to a barbecue, though. I would've worn more sensible shoes."

"The weird part is being invited over to his house." Jonah grabbed his messenger bag off his ergonomic chair.

"It's weird that he lives in a house." I frowned. "Seems like he never leaves this place—he's always hovering and looking over everyone's shoulders."

Brandi laughed. "I know, right? Wish he would lighten up and at least try to be human once in a while."

Jonah shrugged. "Well, maybe now is our chance to see if he truly is human. If he resides in a normal house instead of a robot charging station, we'll know he's for real."

***

"Holy Park Avenue, Batman!" Brandi stared, open-mouthed, at the estate spread out before us.

A man with a safety vest waving an orange baton directed us toward a parking space on the side lawn.

"Good Lord. It has to be at least ten thousand square feet." I got out of Jonah's car and took in the sight of the expansive home. It was built in the Italian villa style, with a cream exterior and landscaping to die for.

A tent had been set up on the front lawn. Caterers were busy arranging trays of food on the buffet tables while bartenders poured glasses of champagne, martinis, and microbrews for guests to enjoy.

"I thought he said this was a barbecue." I took off my sunglasses and stared at the decadence on display. "This is amazing."

Soon the lawn was filled with the rest of Paul's employees, looking dazed.

"Come on." Jonah took my hand. "Let's go get some food before it's all gone."

We got our drinks and then stood in the buffet line until it was our turn to load our plates.

I caught a glimpse of Paul with his arm around a beautiful blond woman. She was wearing a classic Jackie Kennedy-style Chanel dress. Her golden hair was twisted into a classic chignon.

Paul and the woman approached us. "Clarity, Jonah, and Brandi, I'd like you to meet my wife, Audrey."

"Nice to meet you!" She stuck out her hand, and I shook it.

She was even more beautiful up close. With porcelain skin and cornflower blue eyes, she was impossibly perfect.

Peals of laughter floated in the summer air as two small children came running toward us at full speed.

The woman smiled and swung the little boy onto her hip, while Paul hoisted the little girl onto his shoulders.

"This is Mason," Audrey said, tipping her chin toward her son. "Can you tell them how old you are, Mason?"

He tried in vain to hold up three little fingers but had to use his other hand to push his other two down.

I gave him a big grin. "Three! You're so grown up."

He smiled shyly at me.

"And this is Victoria." Paul held onto her legs as she sat perched up high.

"I'm five." She grinned, revealing a missing front tooth. "I don't need to show you how many fingers. That's for babies."

Her brother frowned. "I'm not a baby."

"It was a pleasure meeting you," Audrey said to us. She set her little boy down on the grass. "Run and play now. I'll get you some food in just a bit."

Mason ran off, and Victoria nearly leap-frogged off Paul's shoulders to run after him.

"Nice meeting you too," I said.

We watched them move onto the next group of people.

"Have you ever heard him talk about his wife and kids?" I asked. "I didn't even know he was married."

"He has pictures of them in his office." Jonah scooped a mound of mushroom risotto onto his plate.

"Really?" I frowned. "I guess I don't go into his office very often."

"There's really no reason to go in there," Brandi said. "He's always roaming the halls checking on people anyway."

"He sure has good taste in women." I carried my plate to a nearby table. "Audrey is lovely."

"And his kids are adorable." Brandi took a bite of the shrimp pasta. "Mmm. This is delicious."

"He's a self-made man." Jonah took a sip of his beer. "I heard that he started out with nothing. Look how much he's accomplished! And he's only thirty-seven."

My opinion of Paul was beginning to change for the better. It took a tremendous amount of courage and smarts to do what he'd done. He'd built the company from the ground up. I suddenly felt a lot better about working for him. Perhaps I didn't need to look for another job after all.

Russell walked by our table, heading back for seconds at the buffet line. He stopped short when he caught sight of Audrey. He stood there for a long moment before his attention went back to the heaping plates of food at the serving tables.

"What a creeper," I whispered in Brandi's ear.

"Totally." Her gaze followed Russell as well. "What's up with guys pining after women they can't have?"

I shrugged.

After we finished eating, I got up and looked around. "Any idea where the restrooms are?"

"Restrooms?" said a voice behind me.

I turned around to see Audrey standing behind me, a smile on her face.

"Oh! I didn't see you there." I laughed.

"Come on." She took my arm. "I was just heading to the house. I'll show you."

Inside the palatial home, my mouth hung open. I stood on the marble floor and stared at the double staircases curving upward to the second floor. To the left was an expansive living room. A massive fireplace with a heavy mantel displayed family pictures. To the right was a huge kitchen with marble countertops and stainless-steel appliances.

"Wow." I felt a tiny twinge of jealousy. My home was charming and cozy, but this place belonged to a lifestyle I'd never be able to afford.

"You like it?" Audrey glanced at me.

"I do." I studied the ornate wrought-iron railing on the twin staircases. "You have a beautiful home."

Audrey smiled. "It's nice. It took me a while to get used to it. I grew up in the country and a much simpler life. Sometimes I miss it."

"Oh?" I peeled my eyes away from the splendor of my surroundings and looked at her. "Where did you live?"

"Up in the Skagit Valley. I sure miss the tulips… and the lavender fields."

"My parents live up there!" I said. "They just built an addition onto their house and made it a bed and breakfast."

Audrey's expression turned wistful. "A bed and breakfast? That sounds lovely. Do you get a chance to visit often?"

"I was just up there taking photos of it for their website. But I must admit, I don't see my parents enough." Feelings of guilt spiraled through my chest. "I should visit my folks more."

"I'd love to get Paul away from work. He's been traveling so much lately. It would be nice for us to have some down time."

Traveling? I wasn't aware of Paul taking many business trips. Then again, I was trying to avoid the man most of the time. He could've easily gone on a trip or two without my noticing it.

"My parents moved to New York City right after I graduated from high school," Audrey continued. "So, I haven't been to the valley since then."

"Well, let me know if you ever want to go back up for a weekend. My folks' place isn't anything fancy, but it's nice if you want to get away from it all." The growing urgency to find the bathroom made me antsy. I shifted from one foot to the other.

Audrey must have noticed my discomfort. "I don't want to keep you from your mission." She pointed to the hall to the left of the staircase. "The bathroom is the first door on the right."

"Thanks!" My heels clicked on the marble as I trotted to the open door.

When I emerged from the bathroom, Audrey was nowhere to be found. I let myself out of the house and rejoined my friends at our table.

"Looks like the party is winding down a bit." Jonah finished his iced tea. "Do you want to get out of here?"

I checked the time on my phone. "Maybe we should. Traffic will be in full swing in another half hour."

But then the caterers came out with trays of delicious-looking desserts.

"Uh, after I get some of that cheesecake. Traffic already sucks—we might as well be high on sugar to get us through the afternoon grind." I made a beeline for the table before the line got too long.

Brandi and Jonah swiftly joined me, and soon our plates were loaded with more than we could—or should—eat.

As we sat back down at our table, Paul slid into the chair next to me. "Audrey said your folks have a bed and breakfast in Skagit Valley."

"Yes, they just opened their doors for business." I raised my eyebrows. "Why do you ask?"

Paul leaned in conspiratorially. "Our anniversary is coming up soon, and I'd really like to surprise her with a getaway."

I thought of the lavishness of his home and the standard of which he was accustomed.

"Honestly, Paul, I'm afraid you might not be happy with their place." I motioned toward his palace. "It's nothing fancy like this. Maybe you'd be happier booking a nice resort? Maybe something in La Conner?"

Paul shook his head. "No, you don't understand. Audrey misses the simpler life. You should've seen the look on her face when she mentioned your parents' bed and breakfast."

His blue eyes pleaded with me. "Please?"

I smiled. "Of course. But you can't hold it against me if you hate it."

Paul held his hand up in the boy scout promise. "I won't."

I took out my phone and called my parents.

When I hung up, I nodded to Paul. "Okay, it's all set up. They're thrilled to have you and Audrey." I watched Paul's children playing tag in the distance. "Oh! I forgot to ask if you wanted to bring your kids?"

"Uh—no kids." Paul chuckled. "We can get a nanny to stay with them for the weekend."

I grinned. "Great idea. I'm glad it all worked out."

Paul put his hand on my arm and squeezed. "Thank you. I owe you one."

"Well," Brandi said after he left. "That was quite the love fest. Looks like you've forgiven the Grand Poobah after his insensitivity surrounding Janice's death."

"Maybe a little. It's a good reminder for me that I should consider giving people a second chance. Nobody is all bad, you know?"

Jonah finished his last bite of chocolate cake. "Come on, let's hit the road."

CHAPTER 19

It was Thursday—the day of my first date with a potential serial killer. I arrived at the office earlier than usual, carrying a shopping bag containing a red wig and some other supplies for pinning my hair up underneath it.

My hands shook as I set the bag under my desk. Could I really pull this off without getting myself killed?

I shook off my doubts and dug into my work. There was a lot I had to get done before my coffee date with Pierce Padgett.

My laptop hummed to life, and I settled in to check off all of my to-dos.

Before I knew it, it was time to get ready for my first attempt at sleuthing.

There was a knock on my door. It swung open and Brandi peeked her head in. "Ready?"

I swallowed. "Ready." I gathered up the bag and my purse and followed Brandi to the women's restroom.

She checked under the stalls. "All clear."

Brandi was so business-like and serious, I almost giggled. She'd probably watched too many James Bond flicks as a child.

"Let's do this." She dug out a comb and bobby pins from my shopping bag.

I nodded solemnly, echoing her serious demeanor.

After about fifteen minutes, we had my hair done up in pin curls. Brandi put the wig cap over the top and then positioned the wig into place.

"Damn, Jessica Rabbit." She stood back and appraised me. "You don't look half bad as a redhead."

"Thanks. I think." I wondered who Jessica Rabbit was as I stared at myself in the mirror. The auburn-hued locks did look pretty nice with my skin tone. The wig looked better than my real hair had when I'd dyed it years ago.

If I was meeting the serial killer today, would a wig be enough to keep him from recognizing me if I bumped into him later?

"I have one other thing I need to add." I rummaged in my bag and pulled out a contact lens case. I carefully put the contacts in and blinked.

Brandi gasped. "A redhead with emerald green eyes. You don't even look like yourself anymore."

I smiled. "That's the point."

On the way out of the office, my coworkers gave me uncertain smiles. Maybe they thought I was a new employee.

We grabbed Jonah and made our way to the coffee shop, just a couple of blocks away from our office.

Pioneer Square was the old part of downtown Seattle, and in recent years, it had gone through a surge of revitalization. There were coffee shops around every corner, little bistros, and artsy shops carrying blown glass and specialties of every kind.

I loved that they'd retained the historical look of the place, with the brick town square filled with pigeons, and overflowing flower baskets hanging from the black lamp posts.

My nerves got the better of me as we approached the coffee shop. I took a deep breath and opened the door.

The place was filled with the aroma of brewing java. I salivated in anticipation of a Grande Americano with cream. I bought my coffee, my eyes darting around the shop looking for my date.

"Is that him?" Brandi hissed.

I followed her gaze to the only single man sitting at a table for two in the far corner.

His light brown hair, refined features, and glasses matched the photo I'd seen on the dating site. "That's him."

Jonah gave me a nod and whisked Brandi away to an unoccupied table where they could keep an eye on me.

I straightened my blouse, took a deep breath, and approached the man. "Pierce?"

He stood up, tall and lean, and stuck out his hand. "You must be Ashley."

I shook it, noting the firm grip and coolness of his fingers.

"Can I get you anything?" He motioned toward the order counter.

"No, thanks. I already got my Americano."

"All right. Be back in a minute."

I turned to look at Brandi and Jonah, both of whom gave me a worried look. I gave them a thumbs-up and attempted a confident smile.

Pierce came back with a steaming mug of coffee. The aroma somehow put me at ease, and I settled into my chair.

"Thank you for meeting me." His voice was steady and measured.

He didn't offer anything further, and the silence hung over us like the morning fog on Lake Washington. I couldn't handle the quiet, so I said. "Tell me about yourself."

He cleared his throat. "I believe I've covered everything in my online profile."

I laughed and then realized he wasn't joking. My laugh tapered off into a thin sigh. I straightened up in the chair and folded my hands on the table near my coffee cup. "You wrote the basics, if I remember correctly."

He blinked. "What I wrote is pretty much it."

I took a sip of my coffee, spilling a little on the table top.

He frowned and immediately grabbed a napkin from the dispenser and mopped up the spill.

I noted the precise and efficient manner in which he cleaned up the mess. "You're an accountant and you've worked for the same firm since you graduated with a master's degree in accounting."

Pierce nodded. "That's correct."

"Do you—have any hobbies or things you like to do outside of work?" I leaned in and batted my eyelashes to see if I could get a reaction from him. Nothing.

"I like to read," he said.

"Oh, okay!" I said a little too enthusiastically. "Do you read e-books, by chance?"

The look of disdain on his face gave me the answer.

"I only read paperbacks. E-books are ruining the reading experience for this generation and generations to come."

"I see." I took a gulp of my coffee but was careful not to spill this time. "What kinds of books do you like to read?"

"Classics and historical fiction mostly. Occasionally, I enjoy a wild romp through science fiction, if I'm feeling daring."

Wow. What a bad boy.

More silence. Obviously, he wasn't interested in finding out about me. In this case, that was a good thing.

"Do you like to participate in any sports or outdoor activities?"

His expression stayed the same. "No, I do not."

He was a tough nut to crack. Did he even have a personality?

"What do you do for fun, then?" I was getting tired of talking to a wall.

"I already told you." He narrowed his eyes. "I like to read."

"Mmmhmm." I desperately wanted to roll my eyes. This guy was the most boring person I'd ever met. In fact, if I dated him for real, I'd probably offer to kill myself just to get out of the relationship. "Family. How about family?"

"What do you mean?" He took a sip of his coffee.

"Are you close with your family? Do you have brothers or sisters?"

"I live with my mother, and we are close. I do not have brothers or sisters, and my father passed away ten years ago." The monotone of his voice began grating on my nerves.

"I'm very sorry to hear that," I said.

"Sorry to hear what?" His eyebrows rose a fraction of a centimeter.

"About your dad." I gritted my teeth. And speaking of teeth, it was like pulling them to have a conversation with this guy.

"That's quite all right. He wasn't the nicest man. Mother and I were relieved when he died."

I swallowed. Maybe he'd killed his father too? "Oh. Do you go out much, Pierce?"

"No. That's why I signed up with this dating service. Frankly, I was hoping to find an engaging partner that I could have meaningful conversations with. I see that assumption was wrong." He glanced at his phone. "It's time for me to get back to work."

Wow. This man was colder than an iceberg. I shrugged. "Okay. Thanks for meeting with me."

He stood and pushed his chair in. "Goodbye, Ashley."

"Bye, Pierce. Have a nice day."

He walked stiffly to the door and was gone.

I breathed a sigh of relief and got up to ask the person behind the counter for a bag. Giving Brandi and Jonah the thumbs up, I took the bag into the bathroom, ripped off my wig, and stuffed it inside. Then I carefully removed my contacts and returned them to their case.

Even though I didn't get any murderous vibes from Pierce, I was pretty creeped out by him. I wanted to erase all vestiges of my disguise so he wouldn't recognize me out on the street somewhere.

✳✳✳

"He sounds like a real peach," Brandi said after I recounted my experience with Pierce.

"Do you think he could be the killer?" Jonah swiped at a fly as we walked back to the office.

I shrugged. "My first instinct is to say no—because he's literally the most boring person I've ever met. I can't see him killing anybody because that would mean he'd actually have to get up and do something. Murder seems way too exciting for this guy."

Brandi scowled. "That sounds really wrong."

"Yeah, sorry." The crosswalk light was blinking, and we hurried across the street. "I don't know. Maybe his cold and calculated personality does smack of a serial killer."

I almost wished I'd gone to school for criminal justice. If I only had the skills necessary to identify the traits of a killer, I could either eliminate Pierce as a suspect or finger him as the perpetrator.

"What are you going to tell Zen about him?" Jonah held the door to the building open for us.

"The truth. I'm going to say that I did a thorough scrub of all social media outlets but couldn't find much about him. His book-reading alibi is all the police have. They'll keep him on the list of suspects and maybe question him further."

"You're not going to tell Zen you met with Pierce, then?" Brandi pushed the elevator button.

"No way. There's no need to get Zen all riled up. If he knew I met with a potential serial killer, he'd tell the captain, and I'd be summarily removed from the investigation."

Brandi frowned. "True, but I think you should either stop trying to bait serial killers or at least let your brother know what you're doing. Maybe the police will go along with your idea and back you up."

"Absolutely not!" I narrowed my eyes. "At least not yet. I need to do this now before too much time has passed. The trail is getting colder the longer we wait. And if the police get involved, all the red tape will make this take longer. We have to strike while the iron's hot."

We got on the elevator and Jonah pushed the button for the twelfth floor. "I swear to God, Clarity, if we see any sign of a wacko trying to get you, we will call Zen in a heartbeat."

I groaned. "I know, I know." Geez. They were as bad as my brother.

CHAPTER 20

After work, my mind wandered back and forth between Hunter and the serial killer. Not that the two were intertwined. The more I thought about possibly baiting a dangerous criminal, the more I thought about my own safety. And the more I thought about my own safety, the more I thought about Hunter and the class he taught.

I went online and checked out Mojo D'Ojo's website and read up on the advanced self-defense course. It wasn't just a workshop—it was a three-day course which met evenings at six o'clock. And it began tonight. I bit my lip.

What were the pros and cons of signing up? Con: I would be drooling over a man I couldn't have. Pro: I would be drooling over a man I could possibly have if he got to know me better. Another pro: I would learn how to protect myself if I was attacked by a serial killer.

That last pro alone should've been enough to convince me. But why Hunter's class and not some other self-defense class somewhere?

What was it about Hunter that made me so attracted to him? Was it because there was an air of the forbidden about him? That certainly made him more exciting. But it was more than that. Aside from his physical attributes, which were obvious, he had a quiet strength that I really liked. And I was drawn to him in a way I just couldn't explain.

This was my chance to gauge if Hunter was into me as much as I was into him. I filled out the online form and clicked submit. Seconds later, I received an email confirmation that my registration and payment had been received.

All right, then. I quelled my nerves and went about my early evening chores. I fed Pumpkin, made a grocery list, unloaded the dishwasher and then got dressed for class.

Luckily, I'd gone to Lululemon before my worries about money had hit. I paired my new yoga pants with a pretty exercise top in a robin's egg blue, which made my eyes sparkle. I grabbed my gym bag and headed out the door.

✳✳✳

Hunter seemed surprised to see me walk through the doors of Mojo D'Ojo. "I didn't think I 'd ever see you here again."

I attempted a casual laugh, but it came out more like a croak. "Well, I've got to learn how to defend myself somehow." Why did I act so awkward around this guy? "Since Zen is unwilling to teach me how to use a gun, I figured this is the next best thing."

Hunter grinned. The dimples in his cheeks appeared. "Tell you what. If you do well in this class, I might just teach you how to shoot."

My heart skipped a beat. "Seriously?"

He put his finger to his lips. "Do not tell your brother."

I crossed my heart. "I promise."

"Come on." He pointed at the clock on the wall. "Class is about to start."

In the first half, we learned about being aware of our surroundings, not to wear headphones if we were walking alone, to make eye contact with the men we encountered, and most importantly, to make it known that we were watching them.

In the second half of the class, as Hunter talked, I suddenly became aware that every woman in the room was hanging on his every word. Well, maybe not every woman, but the majority were. I frowned. There was a lot of competition in this class.

"I know we've already covered most of this material in the beginning of class," Hunter said, "but for the second half, we're actually going to put this into practice by walking to our cars in the parking lot. Some of our instructors are hiding behind vehicles and other objects to try and catch you by surprise. After each person has a turn, the instructors will hide in different locations so you won't know where they're coming from."

The women whispered nervously to one another.

Hunter continued. "It's getting pretty dark out there now, so this will be a good test of what you've learned so far."

Our group filed outside to the sidewalk. It was a warm evening. The air carried the scent of fast food and beer.

We watched as the first woman attempted to walk to her car.

An instructor hiding behind a large SUV emerged just as she took her car key out of her purse. The woman turned to face her attacker and kicked him in the groin. Luckily, the man was wearing padded protection.

"Rachel, great job!" Hunter called to her. "In a real-life situation though, you'll want to shout for help or say 'fire.' I'm glad you didn't here, since we don't want the police and fire department to show up."

A few women snickered. The tall blonde next to me said, "Why would you yell fire?"

"People seem to react more when the word 'fire' is yelled than they would react to the word 'rape.'" He frowned. "It says a lot about our society, doesn't it?"

When it was my turn, I kept my radar tuned to my surroundings. I was confident I would hear or see someone before they could attack me. I'd taken my ponytail holder out of my long dark hair. I knew attackers often used ponytails to grab and render their victims helpless as they pulled them into an alley or behind a bush.

My classmates watched me intently from the entrance of Mojo D'Ojo.

I spotted my car across the parking lot and made my way to it while glancing from side to side. My ears were tuned to the sounds of traffic from the distant freeway. I focused on hearing approaching footsteps or the rustle of fabric.

Aside from traffic noise, it seemed quiet. I walked with my head up, alert and ready to take on anyone who approached me.

A glint of white caught my attention. What was that? On the side of a dumpster to my right—a shoelace? That's where my so-called assailant waited. I took a deep breath and readied myself. Knees bent, arms out front, hands ready to gouge, pull, or scratch.

The fake perpetrator stepped out from behind the dumpster.

In a flash of adrenaline, I went full-on fight mode, kicking the instructor in the padded groin and delivering a well-aimed, but not too forceful blow to the back of his neck.

The man grunted and went down.

"Clarity!" The alarm in Hunter's voice behind me snapped me out of my single-minded task.

I froze.

The rush of power I'd felt as I fought the attacker turned to confusion. Why was there a homeless man laying at my feet in a fetal position?

The man held his hands over his crotch and groaned.

I stared at the shoelace dangling from his ill-fitting shoe. "Oh, God." I looked back and forth between Hunter and the man on the ground. I stepped back in abject horror. "What have I done?"

Hunter gently nudged me out of the way and knelt beside the man. "Sir, are you all right?"

The man whimpered.

My hands trembled. I bent over and touched his shoulder. "I'm so, so sorry! I thought you were an instructor. Did I hurt you?" As soon as the words were out of my mouth, I realized how ridiculous they sounded. "Here, let me help you." I pulled at his oversized coat until he was sitting up.

He stared at me with bloodshot, frightened eyes and shielded his face with his hands as though the moonlight was blinding him. "Please don't hit me!"

Like Alice in Wonderland, I felt myself shrinking. Smaller and smaller. I wished I could become so tiny that I'd disappear under a rock or some other pint-sized object. How could I have attacked a homeless man? Heat warmed my cheeks.

"Do you need an ambulance, sir?" Hunter asked. He glanced at me, his lips quirking up at the corners.

Was he laughing at me? I glared at him.

He laid his hand on the old guy's shoulder.

The man shook off Hunter's hand and scrambled to his feet. "No. No ambulance. No police."

Hunter stood and turned toward the martial arts studio. "Wait here."

The homeless man looked like he wanted to make a run for it—but I didn't think he'd make it very far.

I swallowed hard. "I apologize. We're taking a self-defense class, and we were practicing going to our car in the dark. I thought…"

He held up his hand. "Save it. I'm fine. Now, let me get back to my spot before someone else takes it." He motioned toward the dumpster.

The door of Mojo D'Ojo swung open and Hunter jogged back to us. He pressed a wad of money into the man's hand. "Here. Get yourself some dinner and a hotel room for the night, okay?"

The homeless man looked bewildered by his sudden stroke of luck. "Thanks." He sprung up, much more nimbly than I expected after the abuse I'd delivered and made his way to the dive bar across the street.

One by one, the heads of the instructors popped up from behind cars and bushes, reminding me of the curious prairie dogs I'd seen on a drive to Eastern Washington.

I felt the eyes of the women in my class boring into me. Scared to look at them, I kept my chin down and walked back to the entrance of the martial arts studio.

Whispers and nervous laughter greeted me on the sidewalk. My stomach twisted. I'd assaulted a homeless man.

Hunter cleared his throat. "Though, that was an unfortunate chain of events, Clarity did all the right things if indeed her attacker had been... an attacker."

I kept my chin down and avoided eye contact with my classmates.

"Let's continue with our exercise," Hunter said. "Who wants to go next?"

✳✳✳

At home, I tried to dwell on the positives. I'd learned some handy techniques on how to disable an attacker. That was a good thing. And, I got to spend time with Hunter— although, not in the way I'd hoped.

The more I was around him, the more I liked him. It was frustrating to know that even if he liked me back, we could never be a couple. I loved my big brother, but dang, he was getting in the way of my love life.

I sighed. "Right. Back to work, then."

Pumpkin appeared through the cat door and meowed. He pranced over to me and dropped something at my feet.

Revulsion hit me hard. "Ew!"

The dead mouse was nearly decapitated. Blood soaked its light brown fur and puddled on the floor.

Fighting the urge to vomit, I carefully sidestepped the unfortunate rodent. In the kitchen, I grabbed an arm's length of paper towels. Sometimes, I wished I had a man by my side... one who would take care of things like squishing spiders, fixing leaks, and disposing of small dead creatures that my cat brought me as a gift. But I was an independent woman who could take care of myself. I could do this.

I stooped over, paper towels billowing out from my shaking hand, scooped the mouse up, and gagged. "Oh, God. Disgusting!"

Pumpkin gave me an incredulous look. Like, he couldn't believe how rude I was for not thanking him for his little memento.

"I love you, but this is completely gross." I swooped the dead thing into the waste basket and tied up the plastic garbage bag. After dumping it into the outside garbage bin, I went back in the house and stared at my killer cat. "Now, where did that mouse come from, anyway?"

I eyed the cat door. "Let's go see."

The sliding door leading to Pumpkin's personal deck was locked, as usual. I clicked it open and walked outside. Pumpkin followed me via his cat door.

A slight breeze carried the scent of honeysuckle in the warm night air. I breathed it in and looked up at the stars— the ones that were visible through the light pollution, anyway.

The deck wasn't a huge space, but it gave Pumpkin enough room to sit outside and admire the trees, birds, and insects flying by.

I figured the mesh enclosure over the top would protect him from predators like raccoons and coyotes, as well as keep little animals like rodents and birds safe from my feline hunter.

"How did you get in here, little mouse?" I examined the mesh, looking for holes.

Pumpkin wandered around and stopped to sniff at a spot where the floor of the deck joined one of the posts.

"Well, look at that." I knelt down beside him. The mesh had come loose from the post, and there was an opening of a few inches… just large enough for a mouse to get through. I stood back up. "I'll have to fix that later—before you bring me another present."

Pumpkin blinked lazily at me and went about inspecting the opening again. At least it wasn't big enough for a cat to get through.

Back inside, I opened my laptop, ready to comb through date requests with potential serial killers.

There were a few requests for meet-ups, but none of the men matched the names from Zen's list. I wrote polite rejections to those men and was about to power off my laptop.

Ping. A message had just come in on the dating website. It was from Max Vanderlin, the man who had requested a dinner date on Friday. I'd been uncomfortable with dinner and had suggested a daytime coffee date instead.

"Pursuit member: Max Vanderlin

Message: Hello, Ashley. I think I can make a 10:00 a.m. coffee at the Starbucks on Occidental. I'll be wearing a blue Boglioli sport coat. I'm six-foot two with an athletic build. See you there."

"Oh, ho, ho!" I laughed out loud. "This guy thinks highly of himself."

Pumpkin jetted off the couch and ran into the bedroom.

"Sorry, kitty," I yelled. I opened a tab on my browser and looked up Boglioli sport coats. Just as I expected... very pricey.

I popped back onto the dating website and looked at his profile pic. "Handsome, in an entitled sort of way." Blond hair, blue eyes, chiseled features. He looked like the kind of guy you'd expect to see in the Preppy Handbook... and named Biff or some other sort of pretentious name. But was he a serial killer?

Maybe I would find out tomorrow.

CHAPTER 21

When I got to my office early the next morning, my key didn't fit in the lock. I frowned and tried again. The key just wouldn't go in.

I turned around and stared down the empty hallway. The office was quiet. I wasn't sure if anyone else had come in yet.

After walking around and peeking through the narrow glass panels beside each office door, I determined that I was indeed the only person there. "Oh, well. I could use a cup of coffee anyway."

The mobile coffee cart guy was just getting set up down the hall. He looked up when I approached the cart. "Good morning!"

"Good morning." I smiled. "Are you ready for your first customer?"

Jared the latte boy grinned back. "I am. Grande Americano with cream?"

I giggled. "You know me too well."

Once I took the first sip, the elevator doors opened, and a few people trickled into the office.

Jonah was among them. He nodded in my direction and joined me at the coffee cart. "Venti latte, no sugar, please."

While we waited for Jonah's coffee, I told him in hushed tones about today's date with the next person on the list.

"I hope I can get free at 10:00. I have a ton of work to do on our website graphics." His brows furrowed.

"No worries," I said. "If you can't be there, I'm sure Brandi can back me up."

More people began making their entrance into the office. The elevator ran steadily for the next few minutes.

I noticed the office manager walk into the main area. She slid off her light jacket and made her way to her own office at the end of the hall.

"Barbara!" I hurried after her. "My key isn't working in my office door and I can't get in."

The slightly-built woman cocked her head to her side. "Your old office, you mean? I haven't given you a key to your new office yet."

I blinked. "My new office?"

Barbara frowned. "Don't you remember? You were assigned a new one. Russell and his new assistant are in your old office."

My heart stopped. I blinked a few more times, buying time while I tried to comprehend what she was telling me.

Her mouth formed the shape of an O. "Paul didn't tell you, did he?"

I shook my head and looked down at my feet.

Barbara opened her office door and rummaged around in her desk drawer. "This is the one." She pulled a key out and laid it in my palm. "It's number 1212. Next to the copy room."

I nearly choked. Next to the copy room! I wiped away the angry tear that had spilled over onto my cheek. "Okay, thanks."

Her look of pity nearly broke me. I turned and hurried back to the open work space and down the other hall which led to my new office, trying not to be seen by my coworkers. The tears had probably streaked my makeup and would be noticeable.

My hands shook as I inserted the key. The door swung open.

Inside the bare, windowless office, a lone desk was pushed against the far wall. All of my things had been boxed and sat atop the desk in a heap. My philodendron plant was perched on top of the largest box of books. Great. No windows. No light for the plant.

I hitched in a sob. How could Paul do this to me? What had I done to deserve this? He'd been nice to me at his house. I'd arranged a getaway at my parents' B&B for him and his wife. I knew that Russell had been interested in my office, but to give it to him without telling me ahead of time? With no opportunity to pack up my own things or have some say in the matter?

I set down my purse, my laptop, and the bag containing my wig and disguise for my coffee date with a serial killer.

"Clarity?" Jonah somehow appeared behind me and put his hand on my shoulder. "What are you doing in the old storage room?"

I sniffled and turned to face him. "Apparently, it's my new office."

The look of shock on his face brought a fresh wave of sadness, and more tears filled my eyes.

"I don't understand." Jonah hugged me and patted my back. "Why did you give up your old one?"

I pulled away and wiped my face with the back of my hand. "I didn't give it up. I was kicked out. Did I tell you that Russell is my new boss?"

Jonah frowned. "I'd heard about that. Wait... did he take your office?"

"He and his new assistant." I sniffed. "God, Jonah, this is demoralizing! What should I do?"

He crossed his arms. "If I were you, I'd quit. Between Paul being an ass when Janice died and Russell taking your office, it's pretty evident that neither of them are human."

"I can't quit. Not now. I have a mortgage, a car, and credit card debt. There's no way another company would pay me as much as what I get here." I leaned against my desk. One of the legs came loose and the whole thing slumped down, sending boxes crashing to the floor.

I crumpled to the floor in a puddle of tears.

Jonah knelt down beside me. "Hon, you've got to pull yourself together. You can't let the idiots win. Come on." He pulled me up. "Put your game face on. Don't let them get to you.."

Sniffling, I pulled something out of the box next to me. "At least I found my Kleenex." I tugged one out and blew my nose.

Jonah laughed. "Good. You haven't lost your sense of humor. Let's get your office put together."

A half hour later, Jonah left to work on his deadline. I'd fixed the leg of my desk and positioned it in the corner furthest away from the copy room wall. I sniffed the air. I could still smell the copy machine toner, but it wasn't as bad from where my desk was standing. Now all I needed was a small bookshelf to display my books and pictures.

As I appraised my new office, a seed of anger began to grow in my heart. The defiance I'd buried after being admonished by Paul several times since Janice's murder had resurfaced.

But Jonah was right. I couldn't let anger get the better of me.

"Shake it off, Clarity," I told myself.

I picked up my plant. "Well, Phil. It's time to meet your new owner."

I marched down the hall with a purpose and knocked on the door of my old office.

"Come in." The weasel was in there already.

I opened the door and gasped. My office, my beautiful office was completely redecorated. How had he had the time to do this? There was a new, abstract carpet laid underneath the desk area. The colors matched the signed Seahawks photos from one of the years we'd gone to the Super Bowl— framed in blue and green. Tacky.

My eyes nearly bugged out when I spied the picture of Janice he'd snatched from her shelf shortly after her death.

I turned to gape at the desk where my friend had once sat. A young woman stood up from her chair. "Is there something I can help you with?"

"You..." My throat became dry as I took in her appearance. "You look just like my best friend."

Her hair was a strawberry blond, just like Janice. She was roughly the same height, too. Her pale skin and blue eyes were so similar, I almost ran to give her a hug.

Russell cleared his throat and stood up. I hadn't noticed that he was sitting at my old desk. "Clarity, I'd like you to meet my new assistant, Naomi."

I looked back and forth between Russell and Naomi.

"Nice to meet you, Clarity." Naomi stepped out from her desk and shook my free hand. "What have you got there?"

I glanced down at my plant. "Uh, it's a gift. My new office doesn't have any windows." I glared at Russell. "So, it needs a new home. Would you like it?"

Naomi smiled. "Why, thank you! That's so sweet of you." She took the plant from me and found a place where the light hit it just right. In the same spot I'd had it when I occupied this office.

"His name is Phil," I said with a sad smile. "Take good care of him."

"I will." Naomi squeezed my arm. "It was nice meeting you. You can come visit Phil anytime you like."

Russell's bulgy eyes stared at me, his expression neutral.

I backed out of the office and fled to my storage room.

＊

I couldn't believe I'd forgotten to tell Zen that Russell had swiped the picture of Janice. Surely, that was important. I texted him and waited until he sent back a message.

His response was, "Glad you told me. I made a note of it and will follow up."

Good. Maybe I should notify HR while I was at it. But if Russell was the killer, I didn't want him to know I'd gotten him in trouble.

An hour later, I was still stewing over the injustice of losing my office and my best friend. But I needed to get ready for my date with the potential serial killer. Then, I realized I'd forgotten to ask Brandi if she could watch over me.

I texted her. "Are you free at 10:00? I have a coffee date with one of the Pursuit members."

Brandi texted back immediately. "OMG. I have a meeting with Paul to go over financials. Can Jonah go?"

My shoulders slumped. Could this day get any worse?

"No. He's got a deadline."

"Oh no!" Brandi texted. "I'm adding you to my Find Friends network on my phone. That way I can track you if anything happens. You just have to accept my request on your mobile."

"Thanks for the vote of confidence. Ha ha. Okay, I'll accept the request."

A few seconds later, I got her message and clicked the accept button. Done. Now, if the guy I was going on a coffee date with tried to kill me, at least Brandi could tell the police where to find my body.

Next, I set an alarm on my phone, so that I had an excuse to leave during the coffee date, especially if things were getting scary.

I grabbed the bag with my disguise in it and took the elevator down to the lobby. No one ever used the bathroom down there, so I could get ready without anyone seeing me.

Once I was done putting on the wig, a low-cut blouse, and tight skirt, I stashed the bag with my regular clothes in the back of the cleaning closet next to the restroom. I tried to prepare myself by taking deep breaths as I left the building.

Would this be the guy? The man who killed Janice? Was I foolishly putting myself in the path of a psycho?

Ten minutes later, I arrived at Starbucks. Alone.

CHAPTER 22

"Are you Ashley?" A blond-haired man stuck out his hand for me to shake. He was tall and wearing an expensive blue jacket… the Boglioli sport coat he'd said he would wear. And he wasn't boasting when he said that he was athletically built. Hot-cha-cha! Maybe this date wasn't such a bad idea after all.

"That's me." I smiled and shook his hand.

His movie star smile lit up his handsome face. "Max Vanderlin. Nice to meet you. Can I buy you a coffee?"

"That would be great. Thank you. I'd love a tall Americano with cream."

"You've got it, gorgeous. Why don't you grab a table?" He winked and stood in line to order.

Interesting. He was certainly more charming than the last one. Maybe he was a little too slick. Was he like Ted Bundy, the charismatic and attractive serial killer who'd murdered at least thirty women? A chill ran down my spine.

"Here you go, sweetheart." He set the coffee in front of me.

"Thank you." I took a sip. It tasted great. I hoped he hadn't added a date-rape drug to it. I started to sweat, thinking it had been really stupid to come here alone.

But here I was. I needed to figure out a way to ask what he'd been doing on the day Janice died. I couldn't be obvious or he'd be on to me. "So, Max, I'd love to know more about your interests. What do you like to do when you're not working?"

He grinned. "I love fast cars, golfing, and mountain climbing." He leaned in and whispered, "And I love fiery redheads with long, lean legs." His eyes journeyed down my body, gliding over my legs.

Ew. I had the sudden urge to take a bath in bleach. But I had to play the part, or I'd get no information out of him.

"Mountain climbing, huh?" I batted my eyelashes. "I love the outdoors. Are you an avid hiker, too?"

"Sure. Hiking is good. I mean, hiking has got to be hardcore or it's not worth it, you know? For me, it's all about the extreme."

I played into his game. "I love extreme—and I love men who like to sweat."

His eyes sparkled. "If you'd like, I can take you sometime. I'll start you off with something easy, like a romantic stroll around Green Lake. We can work our way up to the more sweaty forms of exercise later."

I pretended to not get his innuendo. "Green Lake's not much of a hike, but I'd still like that." My mind raced. How could I steer the hiking conversation to the day that Janice had died? If I could get him to talk about what he did that Saturday, maybe there would be evidence that he was where he said he was. Or not. Perhaps there were traffic cameras on the way that could've captured photos of him in his car.

"Do you go out hiking or climbing every weekend?"

He took a sip of his coffee. "If the weather is good, I never miss it."

"Do you stay out all day?"

"Sure—all day." He flashed me a white smile.

Zen's report said he'd been alone on the day that Janice had died. In fact, he'd said he'd been hiking on Mt. Si. That had to be my angle. "You know, I've always wanted to climb Mt. Si. Have you ever done that?" I leaned forward, giving him a better view of my cleavage.

His eyes went straight there and lingered on my chest. I resisted the urge to shudder and pull my shirt up to my chin. As gross as this was, I had to do it for Janice.

"Have I ever climbed Mt. Si?" he scooted closer to me. "As a matter of fact, I was just there not long ago." He puffed out his chest. "I was training for my next Mt. Rainier climb."

I gave him a coy smile. "I want to hear all about it."

He frowned. "You want to hear about my hike up the Mount Si trail?"

"Mmhmm. Mountain climbing is so hot." Gag.

He frowned and ran his hand over his hair, patting it in place. "Well, I got up real early."

I gazed into his eyes. "Uh huh. Did you stop for coffee on the way? Coffee is the only thing that will motivate me to exercise in the morning."

"Of course, yes. At the Starbucks at Eastgate."

"Right on the way," I said. "Smart. What were you wearing?"

One of his eyebrows raised and he gave me cat-like grin. "I was wearing my North Face mountain shorts and a tight, moisture-wicking shirt. It was a little uncomfortable on me—since I've bulked up since I bought it, but it still worked fine."

"Tight, huh? Was it blue? Blue would match your eyes." I stared intently into his baby blues and tried to convey I was interested.

He chuckled and patted his hair. "How did you know? Yes, it was blue."

Why did he keep patting his hair? I looked more closely at his head and noticed that his scalp was a little red. I could see little dots on the skin.

"How long did it take you to go up the mountain and come back down? I bet you were pretty fast compared to the other climbers because you're in such great shape." I was buttering him like a Thanksgiving dinner roll.

He puffed up a little more and scooted his chair even closer to me.

"I was up the mountain in about two and a half hours or so. Back down in half that time." He took off his sport coat and hung it on the back of his chair.

"Oh, my. I had no idea Mt. Si could be conquered in such a short time." I scooted back just a tiny bit, to make a little space between us.

Max reached for his coffee, making sure I saw the muscles rippling in his arm as he bent it. "Like I said. Extreme is what I do best. Hardcore."

My eyes wanted to roll, but I commanded them to stop. I pushed my chair back and pretended to fan myself. "Incredible. I bet you went home and crashed for the rest of the day."

He put his arm on the back of my chair. "No. I went home and took a shower." He licked his lips. "And then I went to the putting green and worked on my golf swing."

"Wow. You are an amazing man." My phone timer went off. Thank God. I wouldn't have to stay and stroke his ego any longer. "Oh, gosh, I have to get back to work. It was so nice meeting you, Max."

He seemed bewildered. "Wait—you're leaving?"

"Yeah, so sorry. I have a meeting with my boss in ten minutes."

His face fell. Geez. Now I felt really bad. My gut instinct told me he wasn't a serial killer. Just a pompous ass who wanted to impress women. Still, I needed to follow up on the information he'd given me. If there was proof he'd gone hiking and then to the golf course, he was in the clear.

"Tell you what. Contact me again through Pursuit. Maybe we can go for that walk around Green Lake?" Where there were lots of people milling about at all times.

"How about this Saturday?" He stood up and stepped closer to me.

"I'll check my calendar. Thank you for the coffee." I stood up on my tiptoes and kissed him on the cheek. It was a pleasure meeting you, Max."

His face flushed. "The pleasure was all mine."

I whisked out of the coffee shop and headed back to the office. Wait a minute. Why was I going back to Opulent? I didn't really have a meeting with my boss. And my new office was freaking depressing. I turned around.

A metro bus heading to Westlake Center stopped a few feet from me. I ran to it and hopped on. I needed some shopping therapy. If I bought a pretty rug to cover the ugly gray tiles—and maybe some art for the wall, it would brighten the place up.

I took a seat and thought about my office, the revenge I wanted to wreak on Russell… and Paul, and how humiliating it would be when everyone found out that they stuck me in the old storage room.

By the time I made it to Westlake Center, my mind had wandered back to Max Vanderlin. Could he really have killed her? I guessed anything was possible, but he sure didn't seem like the type who would kill someone. A player, yes. But a killer?

I stepped off the bus and took a breath of somewhat fresh air. Why did buses always smell like pee and sour sweat?

The light scent of salt air tickled my nostrils, and I instantly felt cleaner.

I located the downtown Nordstrom not far from Westlake and dashed inside. This would only take about twenty minutes, I thought. At the most.

I finally emerged from Nordstrom loaded down with a rolled rug and a big bag containing a picture and a fake plant. I needed to make one more stop into Westlake to find a fun wall hanging. As I approached the entrance to the downtown mall, the sound of sirens filled the air. An unmarked police car came screeching around the corner and nearly took out a couple of pedestrians as it came to a hard stop on the pedestrian walkway.

I stared in horror as my brother flung the driver's door open and ran toward me, Hunter on his heels.

Brandi climbed out of the back seat, looking shaky, worry lines etching her face.

My heart stopped. The bag of stuff I was holding dropped to the sidewalk.

"Clarity, where is he?" Zen boomed.

"Where's who?" My mind was spinning. What was happening?

"Where's the man you were meeting for coffee? Did he get away?" My brother's face was stony, and his blue eyes searched the crowd for a criminal.

Hunter, too, was scanning the people walking around us.

"God." I turned my attention to Brandi. "You told Zen?"

She wrung her hands and bit her lip nervously. "I had to. Neither Jonah nor I could back you up today. So, when you didn't show up after a while, I was sure you'd met with the actual killer—and that he got you!" Tears rolled down her cheeks.

"Oh, Brandi. I'm so sorry. I'm perfectly all right, see? Why didn't you text me?"

"I did." Brandi sniffed. "Check your phone."

I fumbled in my purse and pulled it out. There was a long list of missed calls and frantic text messages. I'd really messed up big time. "Oh, my God. I'm really sorry. I must've turned my ringer off before the coffee date. Will you ever forgive me?"

Brandi ran to me and threw her arms around my neck. "I'm just so glad you're all right. I thought you'd ended up like Janice."

Guilt washed over me. I gave Hunter a pleading look as Brandi squeezed the life out of me. His face betrayed no emotion. He must've thought I was the world's dumbest person.

Zen grabbed my arm. "Get in the car, Ginger. We need to talk."

I adjusted my red wig and let him pull me to the vehicle. Once I was seated in the back with Brandi, he put my bags in the trunk and slammed it hard.

I gritted my teeth in preparation of the verbal onslaught I knew was coming.

He got in, started the car, and pulled into traffic. Instead of unleashing his fury, an icy silence hung in the air. That was almost worse.

We drove two more blocks, then Zen pulled into a loading zone and put on his hazard lights.

I held my breath.

Zen turned in his seat to glare at me. "What in the world were you thinking? You could've gotten yourself killed."

My hands squeezed together on my lap. "I know. I'm so sorry."

"You're sorry?" Zen's jaw tightened.

"Hey, hey." Hunter put his hand on Zen's arm. "I think Clarity realizes her mistake now." He turned to look at me and gave me a sympathetic smile. "While what she did was completely reckless, and frankly, really stupid, she knows not to do it again. Right, Clarity?"

Humiliation plus a little bit of anger dripped through my veins. I couldn't decide whether I should tuck my tail between my legs or flip them both off.

"Right, Clarity?" Hunter said between clenched teeth.

I sighed. "Right."

"However," Hunter continued, "I would love to know what she found out about Max Vanderlin."

A few moments of silence went by before I spoke. "He said he was climbing Mt. Si, just like it said in the report. He told me he stopped at the Eastgate Starbucks in the morning before he drove up the pass. I got the distinct feeling he wasn't quite telling the truth. If you could check the video footage at Starbucks for that day, maybe that will help."

"Why don't you think he was telling the truth?" Brandi asked.

"Because he seemed like he was trying to impress me with his athletic ability. Like, too much." Another thought popped into my head.. "And something else. Max kept patting his hair while he talked. It made me look at his scalp. I don't know if this means anything or not, but there were little red dots that I could see through his hair."

Brandi frowned. "Dots?"

"Yeah." I shifted in my seat. "Like he may have had some kind of medical procedure. It wasn't totally red though. So, maybe a week or two ago. Other than that, he seemed fine. Very full of himself."

Zen snorted. "He was a pompous airbag when we interviewed him too. I wouldn't be surprised if he's a trust fund baby. He seems to be very enamored with material things."

"Not everybody who likes nice things is materialistic," I huffed.

"He drives a Maserati." Hunter raised his eyebrows. "Someone who drives a Maserati is either a serious car collector or he's really materialistic and likes to show off his wealth."

I shrugged. "Look, I'm not defending the guy. Check into traffic cams or video footage from the Starbucks he said he went to on the day Janice died. If there's nothing there, go back and press him for answers."

"That's actually some good stuff you uncovered." Brandi patted my leg. Then she whispered, "I'm really sorry I got you in trouble with your brother."

I gave her a half smile. "It's all right."

Zen's eyes narrowed. "No more sleuthing on your own. I see the value in you interviewing the guys from the dating website in disguise." He glanced at my wig. "Work with the police so you can be wired—and safe."

Hunter nodded. "I agree with Zen. What you did was way too risky. You could've been hurt. We have female detectives who can do this, and I won't hesitate to ask if one of them can do this instead of you."

My shoulders tensed. "Message received. But I knew Janice better than anyone. I will work harder than any cop on the force to get the answers we need." I stared out the window as we drove back to Pioneer Square. This day couldn't get much worse.

CHAPTER 23

Brandi and I retrieved my clothes from the cleaning closet on the ground floor of our office building. I took off my wig and changed back into the outfit I'd worn to work.

By the time we got upstairs, it was noon.

Jonah was pacing in front of my new office. "Where the hell have you two been? I've been worried sick!"

Brandi squeezed his arm. "I'm sorry. You were in that meeting with George, and I didn't want to barge in. All hell broke loose—and I'm afraid I got Clarity in trouble with her brother."

I unlocked the door and pushed them both inside. "Shh! I don't want anyone to overhear." I shut the door behind us. "Basically, I met with that guy, Max Vanderlin, from the dating website. He's pretty narcissistic, but I didn't get a sense that he was a serial killer or anything."

"Said every woman who got picked up by Ted Bundy," Jonah said under his breath.

Ignoring his comment, I opened the bag of stuff for my office and pointed to the rolled-up rug I'd dropped on the ugly gray tiles. "After I met with him, I needed some shopping therapy—because number one, I lost my office to that bloated boil, Russell. And two, I didn't get any solid evidence that Max killed or didn't kill Janice."

Brandi looked down at her hands. "When I couldn't get a hold of Clarity, I panicked and called Zen. He was, shall we say, upset that Clarity met with a suspect without telling him."

Jonah crossed his arms. "Can you blame him? I told you this was a bad idea."

"If there's a next time, I'm going to work with the police, and they'll put a wire on me." I handed him the rug. "Make yourself useful and help me center this on the floor."

Soon the carpet was arranged, and the picture and fake plant were in their new homes. Brandi and Jonah went back to work, looking as harried as I felt. What a crappy day.

I rearranged my desk and set my laptop into its workstation, fired it up, and caught up on the dozens of emails I'd missed.

My desk phone lit up. A woman's smooth voice said, "Hello, Clarity, this is Russell's assistant, Naomi."

"Hi, Naomi." I cradled the receiver between my shoulder and head while I typed. "What can I help you with?"

"Russell would like to see you in his office in five minutes." Her voice was cool and professional. Clearly, she hadn't spent enough time with Russell to become annoyed yet.

"All right. I think I can do that." I checked my calendar. "Looks like I don't have any conflicts. I'll be there in five."

God. What kind of fresh hell was this? If it was about The Bathroom Buddy, I was going to flush myself down the toilet.

I opened my desk drawer and took out a hand mirror. Wanting to make sure I'd gotten rid of any evidence of my disguise, I took a quick peek. Good thing I did. I'd accidentally left the green contact lenses in. With shaking fingers, I took them out and put them in their case. Russell would definitely have noticed that. He noticed things about the women in the office.

Next, I unplugged my laptop and tucked it under my arm, locked the door behind me, and made my way to my old office. My awesome, luxurious, window-walled office with the stellar view of Puget Sound.

The door was open. I knocked on the glass next to the door.

Russell's bulgy eyes appeared over his large-screen monitor. "Come in, Clarity."

I nodded to Naomi and approached his desk. "Hello, Russell."

He grunted and said, "Pull up a chair."

I set my laptop up and scooted a plush office chair toward the end of his desk and sat down. I looked at him expectantly.

He cleared his throat. "I just wanted to let you know that we're starting on a new product now that The Bathroom Buddy has been launched."

"Okay." I opened a template where I kept product information for each item the company manufactured. "What is it?"

Russell sniffed self-importantly. "It's my best idea yet."

I tried hard to keep the sarcasm out of my voice. "Even better than The Bathroom Buddy?"

His fleshy face broke out into a rare smile. Well, not quite a smile, more of a weird smirk. Like a smile from someone who is rarely happy but is testing it out to see if he could be. "It's called The Womanizer." He emphasized the title, as if that made it all the more special.

My jaw dropped to the floor. "The Womanizer? You're joking, right?"

He looked perplexed. "Why would I joke about this?"

I cocked my head to the side. "Russell, have you looked up the definition of that word?"

He grunted. "I know what it means, Clarity. It's a play on words."

"Okay. What exactly is it, then?" My fingers hovered over my keyboard.

"It's an electronic organizer for women. Get it? The Womanizer?"

I rubbed my hand over my face. "Russell, that's called a smart phone—and pretty much every woman, and every man, in America has one. Why would we have to make a separate device? And by the way, no self-respecting woman would buy a product called The Womanizer. Have you run this by the research and development team?"

"Clarity, don't you watch the shopping network? It's filled with useless devices and people are snapping them up by the thousands every single day. And the name is clever. It'll sell like hotcakes." He scowled at me. "Just write down the specs I give you and do your thing with social media and marketing, all right?"

I gritted my teeth. "Whatever you say, boss."

"By the way, Paul approved and fast-tracked The Womanizer, so there's no need to get R&D involved. We're recycling the technology from our old digital organizer. It's straightforward. We're just updating the software and changing the outside from black to pink. Women will buy anything if it's pink."

***

When I finally left Russell's office, I was drained. Any joy I'd ever experienced in my career at Opulent had been sucked out of my body and replaced with sadness, fear, and regret.

How had I gone from being an upwardly mobile career woman to glorified flunky willing to stoop to all-time lows to get a paycheck?

I sat in my storage room office and robotically carried out the duties of promoting Russell's stupid product—which in my opinion, wouldn't sell in the most misogynistic society.

After I'd come to a stopping point, I leaned back in my office chair. This was the first time I'd seriously contemplated quitting. I mean, I'd briefly entertained the thought right after Janice was killed. But it was more of a knee-jerk reaction to how Paul handled the aftermath of her death... and the fact that he was being a slime ball.

My mind sluggishly processed all the reasons why quitting wasn't a possibility. Beginning with my mortgage and ending with my student loans.

I refused to become a hippie like my parents. I cringed, and thought about their carefree lifestyle... with goats, weed farms, and all the other ridiculous things they did for money—just to get by.

I blew out a breath. Nope. I wasn't going there.

When four o'clock rolled around, I was ready to get out of my prison and go home. Everyone was still busy working. I snuck out the front doors and pushed the button for the elevator. Somehow, I managed to escape undetected.

Once on the road, I stopped at the store and stocked up on all the essentials plus snacks and beer for Zen and Hunter, in case they dropped by. And a couple of bottles of red wine for me, in case I needed to drown my sorrows. Again.

Halfway home, my phone rang. I pushed the Bluetooth answer button on my steering wheel. "Hello?"

A deep voice said. "I'm looking for Clarity Bloom."

"That's me." I turned left onto North 40th Street and stopped at the next stop light.

"This is Mike at Seattle BMW. I talked to you last week—I just called to remind you that your lease is up today. Will you be coming in to renew it or can I interest you in an upgrade?"

"Oh, shoot. Thank you for the reminder." How could I have forgotten this? My stomach twisted. "I've actually purchased another vehicle. It won't be ready until tomorrow though. Is it possible to let me have the BMW just one more day, until I can pick up my other car?"

"No, I'm sorry." His irritation was apparent in the tone of his voice. "We'd have to renew the lease in order to let you keep the car another day, since you didn't purchase your new vehicle from us. When will you be bringing it in?"

I clenched my jaw. Now I was the one who was irritated. "Well, I guess this evening then. How late are you open?" I wanted to go home and unpack my groceries and clean out anything I'd left in my trunk and glove compartment.

"Our leasing office closes at six o'clock."

It was five-thirty. Not enough time to go home and unload. "I'll come by right now." I ended the call and stroked the steering wheel. "Goodbye, awesome car. I love you."

On the way to the dealership, I consoled myself with the thought of having no lease payments each month. I'd taken money out of my savings account to pay for my new Prius in full. Even if I kept my job at Opulent, it was the responsible thing to do. Most Americans were just one paycheck away from being homeless. A crazy thought flitted through my mind. What if I ended up homeless? Would the Prius be big enough to live in?

I sighed. Maybe I should've paid off my student loan debt before I'd purchased the Prius. No. I had to quit second-guessing myself. "One negative thing at a time, Clarity," I muttered as I pulled into the dealership parking lot.

Thirty minutes later, I was loading my groceries and a bag of stuff from my former car into the Uber I'd summoned to take me home.

My emotions squeezed my chest tight, and I quickly turned my head to stare out the window before the driver noticed I was about to cry.

We pulled into my empty driveway a few moments later. "Thanks for the ride." I hauled my stuff up the short flight of stairs to my front door.

Pumpkin was waiting for me, meowing for his dinner.

"Hey, tiger." I bent down and picked him up. He let me snuggle him for about ten seconds, leaped to the floor, and headed for the kitchen.

As I fed him and unpacked my groceries, I had a flashback of doing this same exact thing the day I'd found out Janice had been murdered. The tears broke free, and I found myself sitting on the floor, wracked with gut-wrenching sobs.

The doorbell rang.

"Dear God in heaven. Why are you doing this to me?" I got up off the floor and reached for the tissue box. I blew my nose and dabbed at my face, trying not to smear my makeup.

Feeling a bit guarded after Zen's reaction to my going it alone with a potential serial killer, I peeked through the peephole in the front door. To my dismay, Hunter stood on the porch, looking devastatingly handsome in a fitted dark suit, white shirt, and designer tie.

I sighed. I seriously could not catch a break. I opened the door. "Hi, Hunter."

He took one look at my face and stepped in beside me. "What's wrong? Has anything happened?"

I shut the door behind him. "Nothing is wrong." I paused. "And everything is wrong."

He raised his eyebrows. "You're not making sense. Are you still upset about what Zen said?"

My feet hurt, standing on my fashionable but cruel heels. "That's only half of it." I motioned toward the couch. "I'm going to change into something more comfortable. Want a beer?"

"Sure. I'll get it. You go ahead and change."

"Okay. Be right back." When I got to my bedroom, I rummaged in my dresser for my yoga pants and tank top. I was too depressed to even care what Hunter thought of my outfit, let alone my blotchy red face.

I padded back out to the kitchen, poured myself a glass of red wine, and joined Hunter in the living room. I sat down on the couch across from him. "Thanks for waiting. As you can see, I'm a hot mess today."

His smile seemed tinged with pity. "I'm sorry you're feeling bad. Want to talk about it?"

I shrugged. "I don't know." A few moments of silence went by. "I guess it's everything. Ever since Janice was killed, I feel like I slipped off the side of a mountain and I'm just tumbling my way down. You know?"

"I can imagine." He set his beer on the coffee table between us.

"Not only is Zen mad, but my new boss took the office that Janice and I shared. He moved me into the old storage room." I bit my lip. "Now he's making me work on his latest product, The Womanizer."

Hunter barked out a laugh. "Very funny." He paused at my blank expression. "You're not kidding?"

It was the only thing that'd made me laugh all day. "No." I started to giggle, and then found that I couldn't stop. It was infectious, and Hunter soon joined in.

A strange feeling overtook me. I hadn't really laughed a good belly laugh since before Janice died. It felt so good, and at the same time, I felt guilty for laughing. Guilty for being alive when Janice was laying six feet under in her grave. My laughter turned to tears.

Hunter came over and sat next to me. He pulled a tissue out of the box sitting on the coffee table. "Here."

"Thank you." I choked back a sob and blew my nose. "I'm sorry."

"No need to be sorry." He scooted a little closer to me. "With all you've been through lately, it's no wonder you're out of sorts. You're human."

I let my shoulders relax. He was right. Here I was, pretending that I was just fine while my world was crumbling around me.

"Thank you," I said. "I'm glad you're here." I tilted my head to the side. "Why are you here again?"

He laughed. "I came to see if you were coming to the self-defense class tonight. And I wanted to check on you. Zen was a little harsh with you earlier. And while I agree that you put yourself in danger, I didn't want you to think that I'm as angry with you as your brother is."

"Thanks." I gave him a curious glance. "So, you think it was okay to make a date with a potential serial killer without the protection of the police… or my friends?"

"No. I don't." His face was stern. "Don't ever do that again. But I think your observation skills are impressive. We actually got a lot of information from your little meeting with Max."

"Like?" I took a sip of my wine.

"We checked with that Starbucks he said he'd been to on the morning of his Mt. Si climb, and there was no footage of him at all. And, none of the traffic cams picked up video evidence of him driving through North Bend or on any sections of I-90."

"Really?" My heart pounded. "Does that mean?"

"No, it doesn't mean he killed Janice, if that's what you were going to ask. However, your observation of the red dots on his scalp were key. On the day he said he'd been climbing Mt. Si, the day Janice was killed, Max Vanderlin was getting a hair transplant in Seattle."

I was floored. "Why didn't he just tell you that the first time you interviewed him?"

Hunter smiled, his dimples creasing his cheeks. "Because the guy is vain as hell. There was no way he wanted to admit his good looks were anything other than natural."

I threw my head back and laughed. "Oh, my God. What an idiot."

"Yup." He took a sip of his beer. "You have a nice laugh, you know that? You should do that more often."

Was he flirting with me? "Well, you'll have to come by more often to make me laugh then," I said.

His dark eyes met mine. "I think that can be arranged."

Well, this conversation sure took a turn. My stomach did a little flip. What was going on with me? First I was happy, then sad, then happy, and now... "Detective, I believe you're sending me mixed signals."

"I'm not sure what you mean." His gaze held mine.

I took a gulp of my wine. "For example, you told me you didn't date your partner's sister. Then, you come by here to check on me."

"Because I'm getting to know you a little more, and I'm concerned about you." He looked down at his hands.

I furrowed my brows. "And just now, you seemed kind of... flirty."

One corner of his mouth turned up, and he looked up to meet my gaze. "Flirty?"

I sat back and scrutinized him. "So, are you?"

"Am I what?" He leaned toward me.

I caught the scent of sandalwood and bergamot. And maybe hint of something smoky, but I couldn't quite put my finger on it. I was in deep trouble. There was nothing sexier than a man who smelled good.

"Flirting with me." I scooted closer to get a better whiff.

Hunter's phone buzzed. He sat up straight and glanced at the screen. "Damn. It's time to leave for our class. Are you coming?"

Disappointment at the interruption pulled me out of my reverie. I stood up and set my wine glass down on the coffee table. "Uh, yeah. Hang on. Let me get my stuff."

Hunter dug into his pocket and pulled out his car keys. "I'll drive."

CHAPTER 24

Saturday morning, I got up early and fixed myself an extra strong cup of coffee. I had to work on Russell's latest harebrained product, The Womanizer. Did Russell seriously think that anyone would buy a useless product with a name like that? However, I was willing to give it a try. It was my job, and I had to do the best I could with what I was given.

I chugged my coffee and tried to figure out where such a product would sell the best. Or sell at all. I decided to try the usual social media tactics first. I emailed Jonah and asked if he could design some ads for Facebook, Twitter, Instagram, and LinkedIn. I asked him to work with the copywriters to come up with some text that worked with the images.

Russell had fast-tracked the product using a previously manufactured product, so the prototypes were already out and had been photographed by the advertising team.

I set up a placeholder Facebook page for the product, as well as a special Twitter account just for The Womanizer, so the company itself wouldn't get all the hateful tweets I expected. It was sure to get hammered by angry women, and by keeping the product on a separate Twitter account, I would hopefully avoid having Opulent become the primary target for their ire. If they wanted to bash the product, let them.

The YouTube video would have to wait until the ad team had finished filming short commercials. Good luck to those guys. I couldn't imagine what kind of video they could put together that would actually make the product seem appealing.

Next, I scouted publications in different parts of the country where I could buy ad space—both in print and in digital markets. That took the better part of the day. I'd chosen magazines and sites that were on the extreme end of the political spectrum—like the ones who offered conspiracy theories for every news headline—in hopes their audience would be more accepting of the product than the mainstream public.

By the time five o'clock came along, I was drained. I sat back and took a deep breath, letting my shoulders relax. Going out with Brandi and Jonah tonight was going to be that much sweeter now that my work for the day was done.

A knock on my door startled me. I got up and cracked it open a smidge.

Jonah stood there with an amused look on his face.

I let him in.

"Just wanted to let you know that it's not April 1st." His lopsided grin was full of good humor.

"Huh?"

"Those emails you sent me about creating images for ads for The Womanizer? Come on, Clarity, I know that was a joke. You normally don't mess with the creative team like that, so—what gives?"

I gave him a blank look. "It's not a joke."

He crossed his arms and narrowed his eyes but remained silent.

"I'm not kidding." I was exasperated and tired. I really didn't feel like revisiting my irritation with Russell. Jonah deserved an answer, though. "Look, ever since Russell got the marketing director job, Paul has been letting him come up with some product ideas. First, he came up with The Bathroom Buddy, which I thought was the dumbest idea ever. But this one takes the cake. I told him no one would buy a product like The Womanizer—for so many different reasons. He shot me down and told me to do my job. So, that's what I'm doing."

Jonah uncrossed his arms. "You are serious, aren't you? Holy crap. Paul usually has a good handle on what will sell and what won't. Why is he letting Russell tarnish our product line?"

I rubbed my hands together. "I don't know. There has to be a reason, but I have no idea what it is."

He shrugged. "Let's not worry about that for now. You're still up for drinks with me and Brandi, right? You obviously need to loosen up and have some fun. How about karaoke, too?"

I laughed. "Sure. Why not?"

***

When I finally got home after my night out, I fixed a Chop Chop salad with the works and congratulated myself on eating healthy. The nachos and fried food I'd eaten at the bar were sitting like bricks in my stomach. I ate while I sifted through the emails I'd received from the men on the dating site. None of the guys who'd emailed me were on Zen's list.

I sent my brother a message, giving him a status update. Even though he was still mad at me, I knew he'd want whatever information I'd gathered so far.

"If you have any more people you need me to research, let me know." Before I clicked send, I chewed on my lip. Then wrote, "I'm sorry I put myself in danger and didn't tell you what I was up to. It was a stupid thing to do. I hope you can forgive me."

I sent the mail. Pumpkin wound himself around my legs. I picked him up and snuggled with him on the couch. "You're the best furry person I could ever have. Want to watch Outlander with me?" I ran my fingers through the fluff on his cheeks. "You're the perfect man, Pumpkin. Always there when I need you."

He purred loudly to the sound of bagpipes and drums in the opening scenes of the show. This was the first time in months that I'd been able to relax and watch television. I would do more work for Opulent tomorrow. Tonight, I was spending quality time with my ginger.

CHAPTER 25

"I hate Mondays." Brandi accepted the fragrant vanilla latte from our office coffee cart vendor. She took a sip and closed her eyes. "Thank God for caffeine."

"The usual, please," I told our personal hero standing behind the counter.

I tried to wait patiently while he concocted my triple Americano with cream. "I worked most of the weekend, so it doesn't even feel like I got a break."

The elevator doors opened, and Paul whisked in, looking tanned and relaxed. He spied me and made his way over to us. "Clarity, I have to tell you—Audrey and I had the best time at your parents' B&B this weekend! Thank you for arranging it."

I'd forgotten all about that. I had meant to call my parents to ask how things went, but I'd completely forgotten.

"I'm so glad you had a good weekend!" I smiled and took a sip of my coffee.

He nodded at the coffee guy. "Coconut milk macchiato. Make that a grande."

"So, it wasn't too rustic for you there?" I wondered if there was still a stoned goat or two wandering the property.

Paul laughed. "No, no, it was great. I mean, I prefer going to Europe or somewhere tropical. But Audrey really loves the country life. She even went with your mom to pick up a couple of goats and some chicks. I got a kick out of your dad showing me his new chicken coop."

"More goats, huh?" I shook my head, thinking about the emergency phone calls I'd probably be getting from them soon.

As long as they didn't plant another crop of marijuana, I think the goats would be relatively safe.

"Those little critters were cute." Paul grinned. "I had a hard time convincing Audrey to not take one home."

My heart lifted. Paul was happy with me. Maybe he'd cut me some slack and find a nicer office for me.

The barista handed Paul his drink. "Here you go."

"Thanks. Back to work!" He whistled as he disappeared down the hall leading to his office.

"Brownie points for you." Brandi gave me a sly look. "Be ready to accept the perks coming your way."

She was right. Paul had a habit of handing out little bonuses and perks when he was pleased with his employees. He wasn't all bad.

My savior, Jared, handed me my Americano. "Here's your drink."

"Thank you. You're the best."

I high-fived Brandi and went to the storage room to get some work done.

***

Later in the afternoon, I was startled by a soft knock at my door. "Come in."

The door opened, and Hunter stepped in. "Hey. Thought I should let you know, we're here to do another round of interviews."

"I didn't realize you weren't finished." I motioned toward the chair against the wall. "Are you going to tell me who you're talking to? And why?"

He shook his head. "Zen is waiting in the conference room. I don't want to say too much here." He glanced down the hallway. "I'll fill you in later—over dinner, maybe?"

My cheeks flushed. "Are you asking me out on a date?"

His smile faded. "If Zen asks you, then no, it's not a date. We're discussing reasons for why you should never try dating a potential suspect again."

"Got it." I grinned. I couldn't help myself. Hunter really did like me.

"Pick you up at seven?"

"Seven works." I shuffled a stack of papers on my desk. Suddenly, I didn't know what to do with my hands. Or, what to do at all.

He seemed to notice my awkwardness. His eyes twinkled. "See ya."

The door shut behind him.

My mind raced. He liked me. He asked me out on a real date. A real sort-of date. Oh, God, if anyone walked into my office right now, they'd see the goofy grin plastered on my face.

Then I remembered why Hunter was here in the first place...Who were he and Zen interviewing?

I texted Brandi and Jonah. "Need some intel. Who's in the conference room with Zen and Hunter?"

Several seconds later, Jonah replied. "Can't tell. The blinds are shut on the windows."

"Can you keep an eye out to see who comes out?"

"Will do," Jonah texted.

I tried to focus my energy back to the big monitor on my desk. Did Zen and Hunter really suspect someone here at the office? Or were they just being extra thorough with their interviews?

My desk phone rang. "Clarity Bloom."

"It's Paul. Can you please join me in my office?"

"Sure. Be right there." I hung up. Why would Paul want to talk to me? He was probably going to thank me for his relaxing weekend getaway. Maybe he would even give me a bonus or extra time off.

I made my way down the hall to Paul's door and knocked.

"Come in."

I opened it and stood, waiting for him to acknowledge me.

He looked up from his screen and motioned to one of the chairs across from him. "Have a seat."

"Hi, Paul." I sat down and folded my hands in my lap.

He made direct eye contact with me. "How's it going? Have you been able to keep up your social media work plus Janice's duties?"

"I'm doing okay, I guess. It's been a bit stressful, but I'm surviving." I waited for him to go on—sure that he would offer me something for my extra efforts.

He inspected his manicured fingernails. "You know that ad you placed for Janice's position?"

"Yes?" I'd placed it per Paul's instruction, not long after Janice had been killed. I wondered why the position hadn't yet been filled. "Did you hire someone?"

"Not exactly. I had HR take the ad down." He drummed his fingers on his desk.

I frowned. "What? Is Opulent not doing conferences or events anymore?"

He shook his head. "It's not that. I've decided to merge Janice's job with yours. I figured you've been doing just fine taking over her tasks. Why hire another person to do something that you're already doing?"

Shock reverberated through me. "I took on Janice's responsibilities for only a short time. I'm not going to lie, it hasn't been easy doing both her work and mine. Coordinating events is a fulltime job—just like social media is. Not to mention, now that I've been reporting directly to Russell, I've been doing most of the marketing as well."

"Good for you. I'm glad that's settled then. You've proved that you can juggle multiple tasks." He stood up. "If you'll excuse me, I'm running late for a meeting."

"Wait!" I stood up. My head was spinning. I came in here thinking he would give me a bonus. Instead, I got double the work. "Since you're essentially assigning me two fulltime jobs, I'm assuming you'll be increasing my salary to reflect the extra workload?" There had to be an upside to this somehow.

One side of his mouth quirked up, giving him a roguish appearance. "Of course not. Your salary is already more than generous. Count yourself lucky that it was this high before you took on these additional responsibilities."

Paul ushered me out of the room. "Opulent is going to be doing a demo of our new products at GadgetCon in Vegas at the end of next month. You'll need to start making arrangements today. In fact, you're kind of behind the power curve on that."

I glared at him. "No one told me about this."

He waved his hand at me. "Check in with me tomorrow morning. I want to make sure the contracts for the exhibit have been signed and submitted."

How could he put all of this on my already overflowing plate? "But Paul..."

He hadn't heard me—he was already ten strides ahead, on his way to the next meeting.

***

I worked non-stop until after six o'clock. My chest was tight from tension, and my butt was sore from sitting too long.

My phone buzzed.

It was a text from Hunter. "What kind of food are you in the mood for?"

Oh my God! I'd forgotten all about our date. My heart began beating so fast, I thought I'd pass out. How was I going to get home and ready for my date in time?

Calm down, Clarity, I thought to myself. I took several deep breaths. Finally, I texted back, "Something casual? I'm still at work. Need to get home to change."

"I know a great informal place," he replied.

Grabbing the contracts Paul had asked for, I threw my laptop in its case and slung my purse over my shoulder. I ran through the office and knocked on Paul's door. The lights were out. Apparently, he got to go home whenever he wanted. I shoved the contracts under his door and went to catch the elevator.

***

I'd just pulled on a pair of skinny jeans and a cute blouse when the doorbell rang. "Just a minute!"

My hair hadn't been combed since this morning. "Damn!" I quickly ran a brush through it and swiped on some lipstick.

I ran to open the door. "Hunter! Come in." He stepped inside, looking absolutely delicious in his jeans and army jacket. "You look really nice."

"So do you." His dimples creased his cheeks. "Are you ready to go?"

Pumpkin trudged into view. His angry meowing started the minute he laid eyes on me.

"Almost. I have to feed my cat." I whisked into the kitchen and put his favorite food in his dish. "I'm sorry, Pumpkin." I got out some smoked salmon from the fridge and added it to his bowl.

The annoyed meows turned into purring. I ran my fingers through his soft fur. "I'll be back in a little while, tiger."

Hunter reached down to give Pumpkin some love, too. Pumpkin purred and rubbed his cheek on Hunter's pant leg.

"He's a good cat." Hunter gave him one more scratch under his chin. "Let's go."

Pumpkin promptly sauntered back to his bowl and ignored us.

I locked up the house and we got into Hunter's car.

The sun was out but it was occasionally blocked by clouds as the wind rushed them across the sky. Hunter turned on the heat. "It's a little chilly tonight. Tomorrow is supposed to be overcast."

"I don't think I'll be able to go outside tomorrow anyway. My boss told me that he's not going to hire someone for Janice's job. He's going to make me do it."

"You're not going to do social media anymore?" He turned left at the light.

"No. I'm still doing that, but I also have to take on all of Janice's responsibilities—for the same pay."

"What? Why?" Hunter glanced at me, concern etching his face. "That's like taking on two fulltime jobs, isn't it?"

"Exactly," I said.

"That's crazy. You won't have a life." He shook his head in disbelief.

I wondered if this would be my first and last date with Hunter. "I know. I'm not happy about it."

"Can you quit?" He watched a SUV make an illegal U-turn and mumbled under his breath, "If I weren't off duty right now..."

I cleared my throat. "So, where are you taking me?"

His attention focused back on me. "I told you. Somewhere casual."

He was being very mysterious. I studied his profile. His dark eyes were fixed on the road ahead, watching for anything out of the ordinary. As a cop, his observation skills were probably much more acute than most people's. I realized at that moment that I felt safe with him. Safe from the threat of serial killers, dangerous daters, and any other real or perceived threats.

We turned onto 65th, heading toward Ravenna. We drove under the freeway overpass and past all the informal places to eat. Where was he taking me?

When we ended up on a residential street away from the restaurants, I had to ask. "What's going on?"

He grinned as we pulled into the driveway of a cute gray house with white trim. "I'm taking you to the most casual diner I know—Chez Hunter."

"This is your place?" Wasn't this a little too forward for a first date?

"It's actually my folks' place." He got out of the car and came around to the other side to open my door.

"You live with your parents?" Now I was regretting every decision I'd made to get myself into this situation.

He snorted. "No. Do you really think I'm that pathetic? They're living in California now. They rent it to me. Someday, I'd like to buy it from them."

Relief washed over me. "You had me worried there for a second." I got out of the car and appraised the outside of the house. The yard was enclosed by a picket fence—an actual white picket fence. "And also, I was wondering how a cop could afford a place in Ravenna."

He laughed. "Let's go through the front door. I'll give you a tour." Hunter unlatched the gate and led us through the front yard.

The landscaping was fairly sparse, but there was a nice low deck that wrapped around the front and one side of the structure. Inside, I was pleasantly surprised by the wood floors and elegant, but comfortable furniture. The house was clean, but not sterile. It looked lived in and cozy.

Hunter gave me a quick tour. "Don't look in here too long. This is the guest room. Translation—this is where I throw stuff when I don't know what to do with it."

I peered inside the room. There was a bed and a dresser, plus several cardboard boxes filled with paperwork and other things. A baseball glove peeked out of the top of one box, and an old trophy peeked out of another.

"I'm actually relieved to see that you're human." I grinned at him.

"You had your doubts?" He led me to the kitchen.

"This is beautiful." I took in the granite countertops and wood cabinetry. Everything looked new and shiny.

"Thanks. I just used up a big chunk of my savings to have the remodel done."

"You said your parents own the house? They didn't chip in to help with the cost?"

He shook his head. "No, I didn't want them to. This was my project."

I picked up a photo perched on a little shelf in the corner. "Is this your family?"

"Yep. That was taken last year."

Hunter's dad was slender and wiry. "You have his dimples," I pointed to the photo. "And your mom is gorgeous." I stared at the stately woman with the caramel-colored hair and gray eyes. Her skin was half a shade lighter than Hunter's. "She looks like a movie star."

"Thanks! She was actually an actress in Sweden for many years."

"Sweden—I wouldn't have guessed that by looking at her picture." Then I realized I was probably being presumptuous. I felt my cheeks get warm.

He caught my expression and laughed. "It's okay. Her mother is Swedish, but her dad immigrated there from India. Don't ask—it's a long story."

I smiled. "And how did your mom and dad meet?"

"In a café in Paris. It was crowded, and the waiter told them he could seat them both, but they had to share a table. They had each just graduated from college and were looking for adventure."

"And they found love." I practically swooned. "That's so romantic."

"They're still crazy about each other. It's kind of gross." He made a face.

I swatted his arm and looked at the picture again. "And these are your sisters? They're beautiful."

The two young women were gorgeous. One of them looked a lot like their mom, and the other favored their dad.

"That's Britt," he said, pointing to the picture. "She just got her law degree from Columbia. And that's Anja—she's a senior at UCLA."

"Impressive. Are you all close?" I put the picture back on its shelf.

"Very," he answered without hesitation. "Family is everything."

A stab of guilt hit me in the gut. Family. My mom and dad were constantly reaching out to us kids. I had so many brothers and sisters, but not one of us did a good job of keeping in touch with them.

Hunter grabbed my hand and led me out the French doors to the back patio.

My face lit up. "A barbecue?"

"How's that for casual?" He grinned. "I cut up some veggies, lettuce, tomatoes, and other stuff. And of course, I've made up some burgers, too. Help me pull the food out of the fridge. We'll set it up on the outdoor dining table."

My stomach grumbled. Burgers!

Hunter and I worked as a team, and soon, the burgers were sizzling on the grill. "How do you like your buns?"

I stopped what I was doing. "Excuse me?"

"Your hamburger buns? Toasted or not? Firm or soft?" The quirk of his mouth told me he was playing with me.

"Lightly toasted," I replied. "I like them firm but still a little soft, so they melt in your mouth."

"Whoa! A little too much information." Hunter laughed.

I had intended it to be funny, but after that sentence came out of my mouth, I regretted it instantly. It sounded a lot more naughty than funny.

"I'll go get a plate to put the cooked burgers on." I disappeared into the kitchen, wishing I could disappear altogether. God. Why was I so awkward? I'd been out of the dating loop too long. This was hard work.

I found the plate cupboard and took one out. When I joined Hunter by the barbecue, I set it on the side.

"Perfect timing." He scraped the burgers off the grill and put them on the plate. They smelled heavenly. "Would you like a beer?"

"Sure," I said. "Unless you have some red wine?"

"I have red wine. Cabernet or merlot?"

"Merlot sounds good."

"Be right back," he said. "Why don't you fix up your burger and have a seat while I get you a glass?"

Once he left for the kitchen, I pinched myself. Was this for real? A handsome single man, who knew how to cook and take down bad guys? This was too good to be true.

Hunter came back out with a beer for himself and a glass of wine for me. "Here you go."

"Thanks!"

While he fixed his own burger, my eyes wandered to the back yard. It was sparsely landscaped as well. Just a lawn and a few fruit trees toward the back. Douglas fir and cedar trees provided privacy between his lot and the next one over.

"I've been thinking of putting in a koi pond." He took a sip of his beer.

"That's awesome. I've always loved koi. I don't dare get them for my own backyard. Pumpkin would want to go fishing every day."

He laughed. "Don't you have that wire netting enclosing the deck? That should keep him from koi fishing."

"You noticed that? Theoretically, it should keep him enclosed. I'm afraid he would pull a Houdini if there was the temptation of fish nearby."

The sun was sitting low, and the sky was painted with pink and orange clouds. A few birds fluttered off to the evergreen trees, ready to roost for the night.

We finished our dinner and Hunter went inside to turn on the lights. I helped him carry our plates to the kitchen.

"Would you like another glass of wine?" He tipped the bottle toward me.

A warm buzz was already curling its way through my body. What could it hurt? "Maybe just a little." I held my glass out.

He splashed some into my glass. "How about some music?"

"Sounds nice." I took a little sip of the wine, letting it linger on my tongue.

Within minutes, the silky sound of John Legend's voice filled the silence.

"God, I love this song." I swayed to the gentle lilt of the music.

Hunter smiled. "So do I." He put down his beer and moved closer to me. "Dance?"

My heart skipped several beats. "I'm not so good at dancing."

"I'll teach you." He took one of my hands in his, and his other wrapped around my waist. "See, it's easy. Just move with the rhythm."

He pulled me closer. I looked up into his eyes and felt his heart beating against mine. He bent to kiss me.

The banging on the door made me jump.

Hunter froze. "Damn." He walked reluctantly to the door and flung it open.

"Zen! What are you doing here?" Hunter tried to close the door behind him, but apparently, it wasn't fast enough to hinder my brother's view of me.

My heart sank.

Zen pushed the door open wider and stared at me. His eyes lingered on the wine glass on the kitchen counter. "What's going on here?"

The soft music playing in the background now seemed to scream, "Your little sister and your betraying partner are about to hook up!" I cringed at the thought.

Hunter cleared his throat. "Clarity and I were just discussing her conduct regarding the baiting of criminals without police protection. I was explaining that—"

Zen stepped inside. "Are you two seeing each other?" His voice had a hard edge to it.

"No!" we both said simultaneously.

I laughed nervously. "Of course not. It's just as Hunter said. He was reprimanding me for my impulsiveness. I'm now completely aware that I need to run everything by you before I interact with suspects."

Zen glared at me and then at Hunter. "Is that right? You were rebuking Clarity—with wine and soft music? Well, that ought to put the fear of God in her."

I didn't know what to say. What could I say? There was no fooling an experienced detective. I tried anyway. "He was softening the blow. He felt bad about being so angry with me."

"Why didn't you answer your phone? I called you several times in the past half hour." Zen's eyebrows were cinched, creasing his forehead. He reminded me of a grumpy old man who was about to scold a kid who'd dared venture onto his lawn.

Hunter paled and patted his jean's pocket. He took out the phone and pushed the home button. "I guess I had the ringer off."

"I'll bet you did." Zen's face was turning red.

"I was just leaving anyway," I interrupted. "I have a ton of work to do." I snatched my purse off Hunter's couch and headed for the door. Then, I remembered that Hunter had driven me here. I couldn't just leave. I swallowed hard. "Can you guys give me a ride to my house?"

Zen growled. "There's no time. Hunter and I need to get going. There's been another murder."

"Oh, no." My stomach twisted. "I can take an Uber then."

"Forget that. Come on." He pulled me out the door. "You're coming with us. I want you to see what you're getting involved in."

CHAPTER 26

We drove west until we reached the Ballard Locks. We passed a beautiful botanical park and the famous fish ladder built for salmon to swim up. I watched a few white boats traveling through the open locks between Lake Union and Puget Sound.

The atmosphere in the car was chilly—and it wasn't because of the air conditioning. The tension was thick between Zen and Hunter. My brother's stiff shoulders and clenched jaw told me exactly how angry he was. Hunter, on the other hand, was exuding nervous energy. He opened the glove box, pretended to look for something, then closed it. His eyes flitted back and forth between the road ahead and Zen's profile.

I needed to break the tension with some conversation. But discussing what'd happened at Hunter's house was not a good idea right now. Somehow, I needed to distract Zen and get the two of them talking about anything but Hunter and me.

"Why would someone dump a body in a place where there are so many tourists?" I asked from the back seat. I'd intentionally chosen to sit behind Zen, so he couldn't glare at me.

When Hunter remained silent, Zen spoke. "The office believes it was dumped in the middle of the night. And it isn't a body. It's a body part."

"A part?" I made a face. As if finding part of a dead body was any less horrific than finding a full dead body.

"A hand, to be exact," Zen said. "It was in a dumpster behind a restaurant. It fell out of the dumpster when it was mechanically picked up by the truck."

"The garbage man found it, then?" My stomach dropped.

"Yes. The hand was in a plastic bag. The bag ripped open when it fell. Otherwise, the garbage man wouldn't have noticed it when he jumped out of the truck to pick up the bag."

"Where's the rest of the body?" I stared out the window as we pulled up to the flashing lights and police activity. Dusk was losing its battle with night, and the blue and red lights of the police cars reflected off the side of the buildings and onto the darkening road.

Hunter cleared his throat. "Probably dispersed in separate trash bins in different locations. There will be teams all over, scouring dumpsters nearby."

"Gross." I was thankful I didn't have that job. Scouring trash bins for body parts? No thank you.

Zen pulled over behind a Seattle PD vehicle. "Stay here." He and Hunter got out of the car and approached a group of cops.

I tried to pick out what they were saying, but I couldn't hear through the noise of the sirens and engines in the surrounding area.

Craning my neck, I looked out the window to see what was happening. A woman wearing a jacket that said "Medical Examiner" bent over something on the ground. A ripped plastic bag was lying to the left of the object she was examining.

A photographer was there, his digital camera clicking rapidly as he took pictures from different angles.

Zen and Hunter walked past the car. Hunter made eye contact with me and attempted a smile. I waved and started to get out of the vehicle.

My brother thrust his palm out at me. "Stay put."

I sighed and leaned back against the seat. Zen was really mad. I couldn't tell who he was angrier with—me or Hunter. Somehow, I had to make amends and patch things up with him.

That would have to wait until later. Because now, I was really curious about the remains they'd found in the dumpster. Unfortunately, though, I didn't think Zen would be forthcoming with details. He was too disgruntled to share anything with me at the moment.

After a few minutes, I looked out the other window and spotted Hunter and Zen following a couple of police officers toward another dumpster away from the building.

Quietly slipping out of Zen's car, I walked stealthily toward the man with the camera. I needed to get close enough to see what they were looking at, but not close enough to arouse suspicion or draw attention to myself. Carefully peeking around the camera man, I spied a chalky white hand in the dirt. It was cut off at the wrist. The appendage had clearly belonged to a woman. The long, delicate fingers were elegant. The fingertips were blackened. Had the killer burned off his victim's fingerprints to keep her from being identified?

I heard men's voices coming around the corner of the building. My heart pounded. I snuck back into Zen's vehicle without a minute to spare.

Still not being able to hear much, I opened my door a crack to let their words filter in.

"Pat, you need to widen your circle to include the more industrial areas a few miles away," my brother said.

Pat, an older officer with graying hair, nodded. "I'm way ahead of you. I've got men branching out at least three miles from this location. But it's going to take a while. There are a lot of dumpsters out there."

"I'll notify waste management to postpone garbage service until you finish the search." Hunter stepped away to make the call.

Zen's phone rang and interrupted their conversation. "Detective Bloom," Zen said. "Where?" He paused and listened to the person on the other end. "Okay. Barricade the street and tape off the area. We'll be right there."

***

We pulled up to the next site where more remains had been found in a dumpster just a mile down the road.

This time it was a leg.

Zen got out of the car and gave me a semi-empathetic glance. "You can come out too, but don't get in the way."

I nearly hurled myself out of the back seat. By now, it was pitch black, save for the streetlights. The night air held a chill that foreshadowed the upcoming autumn.

Hunter watched me shiver and opened the trunk. He took out a Seattle PD jacket and handed it to me. "Here. Put this on."

"Thank you." I put the large jacket over my shoulders and wrapped myself up in it. It smelled like him. I pulled it tighter around me.

Zen scowled at Hunter and me. I knew what he was thinking. He was feeling betrayed by the two of us, and he was not happy that I was within touching distance of his partner.

My attention drifted from the circle of officers to the leg that was laying on the ground a few yards away. The medical examiner and photographer hadn't yet arrived.

While Zen and Hunter spoke with the others, I scooted closer to the gruesome appendage. I wanted to get a good look before anyone noticed.

Like the hand from the other dumpster, it was chalky white. The leg had been cut at the top of the thigh. The cut was jagged—as if someone had taken a chainsaw to it. My eyes glided down the rest of the leg. Her calf muscles were shapely and toned. A runner? Or at least someone who exercised on a regular basis. The toenails were painted a shell pink. This woman wasn't a poor homeless person. She took care of herself. Her appearance was important to her.

The entire time I was gawking at the dismembered appendage, I expected my stomach to rebel. Something so horrible would make most people hurl. I was surprised that I felt more curious than repulsed. I wasn't sure if that was a good thing or a bad thing. Was I somehow flawed because I wanted to take a closer look? I needed to understand what had happened to the poor young woman.

Zen was suddenly by my side. "Are you okay? If you're feeling nauseous, you can go sit in the car."

This was unexpected. "I'm actually fine." I looked up at him. He seemed uncomfortable. "Are you still mad at me?"

He groaned. "Maybe."

I winced.

"I guess I'm more upset with Hunter." He paused for a moment. "He betrayed my trust. Partners should not date one another's sister."

His phone buzzed.

I glanced at the screen before he answered. The call was from Janice's sister, Margaret.

"Hang on. I need to get this." Zen walked a few steps away and turned his back to me. But I could still hear him. "Hey. Sure. Tomorrow at the Canlis? Okay, I'll pick you up at seven."

The Canlis? That was one of the most expensive restaurants in Seattle.

He came back to join me next to the severed leg.

"So," I said. "If I remember correctly, you also have a rule about not dating the victims' family members. At least until the investigation is over."

Zen froze. "That's different."

I grinned. "How so?" I was so tempted to do a victory dance.

"She's not Hunter's sister." He blinked.

"Nice try. I get it. Double standards, bro." I turned to go back to the car.

He put his hand on my arm. "Clarity. Wait. I don't want you to date Hunter because I don't want you getting hurt."

"I can get hurt dating anyone. Are you going to ban me from dating altogether?" I snorted. As if he could.

"No, but if you and Hunter break up, it could get super awkward for me. What if it's a bad breakup and he has a lot of animosity toward you? Would he have my back in a situation where my life was in danger?"

My mouth hung open. "You have that little faith in him?" I thought for a moment. "Or are you afraid if he hurts me, you'll be the one who won't have his back?"

"No, that's not it," he blurted out.

"What is it, then?" I put my hands on my hips.

He groaned. "Can't you just respect my wishes? Personal stuff shouldn't get mixed up with professional stuff."

I sighed. Hunter was the only guy I'd liked—really liked—since my last relationship. And that was two years ago. I finally said, "If it means that much to you that he and I don't see each other, then fine."

He gave me a curt nod. "Thank you."

All the air in my lungs rushed out. He truly expected me to sever my budding relationship with Hunter. The thought made me physically ill. How could my brother do this to me?

"Look, we're going to be here for a long while. I'm going to call that Uber so you can get back home." Zen took out his phone.

Hunter had overheard Zen's last words about calling an Uber. "Don't bother calling a car for her. I'll run her back home."

Zen gave him a hard glare. "It's fine. I'll call her a car, and we can get back to the investigation."

Hunter raised his eyebrows. "It won't take long to drive her. It's later in the evening. Traffic is much lighter now."

"Hey, Zen!" one of the officers called from across the alley. "Come take a look at this."

Zen ran his fingers through his short hair. "This is totally against my better judgement. Go ahead and take her home. But hurry back. We need all hands on deck."

"Got it." Hunter pointed to the car. "Let's go."

Once we were on our way, I turned to look at Hunter's profile as he drove. "Hunter, I think—"

"You don't have to say it," he interrupted. "I know." He gave me a mournful look. "I really, really like you, Clarity. But I've got to respect Zen's wishes. He's my partner."

My heart sank. "I understand. It would make things awkward if we became a couple. Zen is the one sibling I'm really close with. I don't want to damage our relationship."

He sighed. "Trust me, if things were different, you wouldn't be able to get rid of me."

I laughed, even though I felt like crying. "I just wish that Zen weren't so hard-nosed about this. He has all these rules, you know? He's allowed to break them when it's convenient, but we're not allowed to break them at any cost."

"He's breaking his own rules?" He glanced at me.

"Yeah. He's dating Janice's sister, Margaret."

"The redhead?" He turned at the light.

"Yup."

"She's gorgeous." The corner of his mouth quirked up.

I rolled my eyes. "Great. Maybe you can both date her. Unless that's breaking Zen's rules, of course."

Hunter chuckled and put his hand on my arm. "I'm hoping that Zen comes around. Especially when he realizes that what he's doing is just as wrong in his book as me dating his sister."

"I already pointed that out to him. He didn't see the irony." I sighed.

We pulled up in front of my house.

Hunter gave me a sad look. "We should hold off for a while. If you need anything or you feel unsafe, just call me."

I nodded glumly. "Okay. At least we'll see each other if or when you guys need me to bait one of those online daters."

"I'm counting on it." He leaned over and kissed my cheek. "Goodbye, Clarity."

CHAPTER 27

Tuesday morning had me scrambling to get everything done. With too much to do, I didn't even have time for lunch.

By two o'clock, I was so hungry and frazzled, I could barely see straight.

Unfortunately, I had a meeting to attend, so I couldn't even grab a cup of coffee from our office barista to keep me going.

Paul called the meeting to order.

"Jonah, you first. How are the graphics coming for all products soon to be launched?"

Jonah cleared his throat. "Everything but the graphics for The Womanizer are finished and are in QA for proofing."

"What's the hold up on The Womanizer graphics?" Paul asked.

Jonah paused a moment. "We're having a hard time making the product look appealing enough. We've decided to change the message to one of empowerment. So, we're working on putting together a new photoshoot. We're angling for a superhero vibe."

Paul glared at me. "This was supposed to be launching tomorrow. Clarity, why isn't this up and running already?"

I raised my eyebrows. "I just got the directive on this last week. This was a tougher sell than our other products."

"The whole idea of repurposing an older product was to fast-track this one. You know—so we could make more money with minimal effort?" He narrowed his eyes.

I could hear the venom in his words. When Paul was in one of these moods, we all knew to tread carefully. "Sir, with all due respect, because of the name of this product, we have to be very careful with how we market it. The term 'womanizer' is pretty loaded. We could be opening ourselves up for public ridicule and embarrassment. I thought if we could turn this around and twist the meaning of the word to illustrate female empowerment, we could avoid the negative press."

Paul looked a little less angry. But he was still on the warpath. "All press is good press. Even if it's negative. You should know that by now, Clarity."

I fought the urge to roll my eyes. "Would you rather we go back to the original plan, then?"

He growled. "No. Since you've already spent the money to book the shoot, go with your new plan. I'm warning you, don't ever do that again. Understand?"

I nodded, still feeling like I wanted to punch him.

"How is The Bathroom Buddy doing in sales?" he asked Greg, the head of the sales department.

"Terrible." Greg pushed his glasses back up the bridge of his nose. "These are by far the lowest numbers we've seen in product sales thus far."

Russell paled and shuffled the papers in front of him. He avoided making eye contact with Greg.

Paul turned to glare at me again. "Care to explain this?"

How would I explain that the product was stupid without pissing off Russell? This was his brainchild, not mine. I finally settled on, "You can't make a silk purse out of a sow's ear."

Now it was Russell who was glaring at me.

"Clarity," Paul said. "It doesn't matter how good or bad a product is—your job is to make it irresistible to the buying public. That's what I hired you for."

"I'm doing the best I can with what I have." I returned his glare.

"That's not good enough. Fix it." He looked down at his list. "Next up, Brandi, how are the financials looking?"

The meeting lasted an hour. My eyes glazed over by the end. I really needed some caffeine.

"Clarity?"

I jumped.

Paul gave me another one of his withering glances. "I'm assuming the details are all sown up for GadgetCon?"

I blinked. "The contracts are done. I still have to arrange for set-up, though."

"Again," Paul said. "That should've been done already. We can't afford to do a half-ass job at this convention."

"Wait a minute," Greg said. "Why is Clarity handling the event? Didn't you hire someone to fill Janice's position?"

"No. I did not hire someone to fill Janice's position. Clarity can handle the details."

Greg shook his head. "Seriously? That's a huge job."

Paul raised his eyebrows. "How would you know, Greg? I said Clarity can do it and that's that. Stay in your lane, Greg."

Greg looked down at his hands.

After the meeting adjourned, I walked back to my office with Brandi.

"What in the world has gotten into him?" Brandi brushed past me and sat the chair opposite my desk.

"I have no idea. One minute, I think he's happy with me, the next, he's ready to hang me from a rafter."

"And the worst part is, you're working your butt off for him. No one else works as hard as you do." Brandi puckered her lips. "I don't get it."

"Me neither." I opened my laptop and pulled up the spreadsheet for GadgetCon.

"And did you see that weasel, Russell?" Brandi continued. "He didn't take even a sliver of credit for his stupid product ideas. Paul raked you over the coals, and Russell was the one who came up with The Bathroom Buddy and The Womanizer. God, what a cluster."

I shrugged. "I know. But I don't have time to be mad. I've got to get this done or Paul will fire me."

Brandi got up. "Sorry to keep you from your work. When you're done, you want to meet Jonah and me for drinks?"

"I wish." I pointed to my screen. "I'm going to be working on this until it's done. I can't risk getting the same tongue-lashing I got during the meeting."

"Okay. But if you finish early, we'll be at the Grizzled Wizard." She waved and shut the door behind her.

***

At six o'clock, I packed up and went home. I still had hours of work ahead of me, but I needed to be home with Pumpkin. He punished me with a sour attitude if I stayed at work too long.

As soon as I'd eaten and was settled on the couch with my laptop and cat, my phone buzzed. It was Zen.

"Hello?"

"Sis, I have one more lead for you. We're down to the last guy on our list. His alibi looked solid, but on further investigation, we discovered it was fake."

"What? How can that be?"

"He'd said he was at a Mariners game. But after combing through ticket sales records, we couldn't pull anything up under his name."

"Could he have paid in cash?" I asked.

"Possibly. We couldn't reach him when we called the number he'd listed on his Pursuit dating profile. It was disconnected and the address on the profile led us to an empty lot in Kirkland," Zen said.

A chill ran down my spine. "Whoa. That's really creepy. So, you think this is the guy?"

"We don't know for sure. My gut says yes. His name is Chris Smith."

"What are you going to do?" I snuggled closer to Pumpkin and stroked his soft fur.

"We were hoping that we could get you to bait him on the Pursuit site."

I froze and the hairs on the back of my neck stood straight up. "For real?"

"Yep. I hate to ask you, but the case is getting cold and there are no female operatives available," said Zen. "Here's what I want you to do."

He spent the next fifteen minutes briefing me on my role. The police would be monitoring any correspondence through the dating site and email. I was to send the man a message asking for a date. If he responded, I would set one up at a local café. The police would wire me and be there waiting for the man to arrive.

Once we were seated, I would engage him in conversation. If there was any real or perceived danger during the date, the police would immediately intervene. Under no circumstances would I leave with the man.

My heart beat faster the longer we talked. Was I really going to bait a serial killer?

I held my breath as I listened to Zen talk. My screensaver kicked in. The selfie that Janice and I took while we were river rafting flashed into view. My sweet friend. Seeing her face made me realize that I had to do this for her—and for the next potential victims of the monster who'd extinguished her bright light.

CHAPTER 28

I arrived at work the next morning before anyone else. Determined to keep my job, I completed every task Paul and Russell had flung at me.

The night before, I'd carefully crafted a message to Chris Smith on the Pursuit site. Before I left for work, I checked my messages. As of yet, there was no response from him.

As soon as my favorite barista set up the coffee cart in the main area, I was the first person in line. "Venti Americano, please."

He furrowed his brows. "Are you sure you want a Venti? You normally get a Grande."

I nodded. "I'm sure. I need all the help I can get to make it through the day."

"I've noticed you've been pulling some really long hours lately. I hope you get a break soon." He packed the coffee grounds in the little metal cup and pulled the lever on the steaming water.

"I'm not likely to get a break. I've been assigned Janice's job on top of mine… permanently."

"Whoa! That's nuts." He poured the hot coffee into the giant to-go cup. "Do you want cream?"

"Yes, please."

He handed me the coffee and I thanked him and put a tip in his jar.

Back in my office, I started my double list of tasks for both GadgetCon and the monitoring and adjustments to the social media ads for Russell's harebrained product. The Bathroom Buddy was doing terrible in sales. I read a few of the online reviews and winced.

The first one read, "Whoever thought of this ridiculous product needs to be fired. If you want to listen to music while you're sitting on the toilet, all you need is your phone."

"I can't argue with that," I said out loud.

The next one said, "So glad someone invented The Bathroom Buddy. For years, I had no one to join me in the bathroom. Now, I have my buddy with me every time I take a dump. Life is good!"

I full on cackled while reading that one. The ad team was still reworking the advertisements for The Womanizer. I could only imagine what kind of reviews we'd get. I knew in my gut that it wouldn't sell. Any idiot could figure that out. Except Russell, of course.

My desk phone rang. "Clarity Bloom, how can I help you?"

It was Russell's secretary. "Russell would like to see you in his office."

"Okay. I'll be right there." I picked up my coffee and laptop and closed the door behind me.

My old office door was open. I knocked on the frame.

"Come in, Clarity." Russell sat like a toad in the usual place behind his desk.

"Hi, Russell." I sat down and perched my laptop on the end of his desk. I took a huge gulp of coffee in preparation for what he had in store for me.

"As you heard in the meeting, the sales numbers aren't good for The Bathroom Buddy. Can you explain to me why that is?"

I opened my mouth, but no sound came out. What I really wanted to say was, "Because it's a stupid product." But I knew better.

Instead, I carefully explained, "Well, because the function of that product can be fulfilled using a smart phone. Especially if you have Bluetooth speaker devices as well. Then you can listen to music in any room—bathroom included."

Russell grunted. "Do not lecture me on the topic of smartphones, Clarity. I understand how they work. The Bathroom Buddy is for people who don't know how to use smartphones—it's a totally different audience."

"So, it's for people over eighty years old, then?"

"Maybe. And for people who aren't sucked into technology," he said.

I couldn't explain to him how flawed his logic was. I'd get fired. The people who aren't sucked into technology wouldn't be buying frivolous gadgets either.

"Okay," I said. "I'm open to listen to your ideas on where to market. Social media won't work because if our audience isn't tech-savvy, they won't be on Facebook, Instagram, or Twitter."

He sighed. "I don't know, Clarity. That's your job to figure out. I expect to see these numbers change for the better in the next few days."

I grabbed my laptop and coffee and stood up. "I'll do my best." I went back to my office and closed the door. What a complete moron. Why was he even employed here? It seemed that he could do no wrong in Paul's eyes. And all of his stupid mistakes got blamed on me.

I plugged the laptop back into the docking station and stared at the external monitor. My fingers flew over the keyboard as I researched places to market to the elderly.

For the rest of the day, I worked on setting up distribution channels in mail order catalogs, drugstore chains, and stores like Walmart. This wasn't my job, but I realized that Russell wasn't doing his work at all. I was doing it. I had no idea what he did all day, besides stare out the window and think of dumb products we couldn't sell. The last thing I did before I went home was apply for a spot on QVC. They were excellent at selling all sorts of things. Maybe they'd even be able to sell The Bathroom Buddy.

I packed in as much work as I possibly could. Six o'clock came and went. I knew I had to get home to feed Pumpkin. He was not the typical independent cat. He was social and hated being alone for too long.

When I arrived at my house, he was waiting by the door, meowing.

"Sorry, kitty."

I hurried to get him fed and watered.

Once I heated up some leftovers for me and sat down to eat, I felt the loneliness settle in. My thoughts drifted to Hunter and what we could've had.

I pushed the food around on my plate. I wasn't hungry anymore.

My phone buzzed. It was Zen. "Any word from our suspect?" he texted.

I'd forgotten all about checking my Pursuit profile for messages. "I'll check my email," I texted back.

I put my plate on the floor for Pumpkin. Normally, I wouldn't do such a thing. Feeding a cat from the table was just as bad as feeding a dog from the table. And once you started indulging your furry child in this way, they thought it should be a regular occurrence. However, I was feeling extremely guilty for working so many hours. I had to spoil him a little to make up for it.

The laptop was sitting on the coffee table. I powered it up and navigated to the Pursuit website.

There was a message waiting for me.

I held my breath and clicked on it.

"Pursuit member: Chris Smith

Message: Hi Ashley. I'd love to meet you for coffee. The café on Occidental sounds great. My work days are usually completely booked with meetings, but I think I can grab a half hour tomorrow at around eleven. Sound good to you?"

I texted Zen the details.

He texted back. "Great. Hunter and I are coming right over to your place to brief you."

My heart sank. Hunter? I was trying to get over a relationship that had barely even started. How could I do that if I had to keep seeing him during the investigation?

"Okay," I texted. "See you soon."

I paced, holding Pumpkin tightly while I waited for them to arrive. My nerves were making my stomach feel queasy. If Zen's hunch was correct, then I would be coming face-to-face with a cold-blooded killer. The monster who had murdered my best friend. My second thoughts were having second thoughts.

The doorbell rang. I put the cat down and opened the door to find Zen and Hunter standing on my front porch. Both men were wearing their police windbreakers. I glanced up to see heavy clouds blanketing the dark sky. The air smelled of rain.

Hunter's eyes softened when he saw me.

I looked away. "Come in."

The men situated themselves in the living room. Zen had a hard plastic case with him. He opened it, revealing a device with wires and tiny microphones, plus tape and batteries. "I just wanted to show you what to expect tomorrow morning." He took out the tiny listening device. "Our team will wire you up before you meet the suspect."

I sat down next to the case and picked up the earpiece. "He won't see this?"

"No. Your wig will cover that up. We can feed you questions to ask him this way. You'll have to improvise and make it seem like it's just a regular conversation."

I nodded. "I hope I can do that. Where will you be?"

"In a white construction van parked at the side of the café. We won't be visible through the windows of the coffee shop. But we've already placed hidden cameras inside and outside the building. You have a code word that you'll use if you feel threatened in any way. Once we hear that word, we'll send an undercover police officer in. She'll pretend that you are friends and strike up a conversation. If she perceives a threat, we'll bust in and arrest him. Got it?"

I swallowed. "Okay. This is scary."

"You don't have to do this." Hunter gave Zen a stern look.

"He's right. I've thought all along that we should have a female undercover cop bait him."

"No." I jutted out my chin. "I'm doing this for Janice. And for any woman who is next on his list." My gut hardened in resolve. "I'd never forgive myself if I backed out and someone else died as a result."

"All right, then." Zen pointed to my laptop. "You'll need to confirm your date with him. Here's what you'll say."

***

Two hours later, Zen and Hunter had gone. I wanted desperately to get some sleep, but I couldn't stop thinking about what they'd told me. How was I supposed to remember everything without having a practice run? What if I did or said something wrong during tomorrow's date with a killer?

I had looked at Chris Smith's Pursuit profile. I'd memorized his face, though it was pretty non-descript. He was kind of handsome but had no discerning features. Nothing that would make him stand out in a crowd. No indication of malice in his brown eyes. He didn't fit the stereotypical look of the murderer we'd seen on late-night TV true crime shows. He didn't resemble John Wayne Gacy or any other creepy serial murderers we'd all seen mugshots of. He just looked like a regular guy.

Tomorrow morning, I'd go to work early. I'd get a bunch of work done, then slip downstairs to get into my disguise. I was to exit the building, where a plain-clothed police woman would be waiting outside for me. She would lead me to the white van parked near the café. I would be wired and technicians would test the equipment. Then, ten minutes before the "date," I would enter the coffee shop and wait for the killer to arrive.

I tossed and turned most of the night, only sleeping for minutes at a time. When I finally fell into a deep sleep, Pumpkin was laying on my chest, kneading my arm with his front paws. My furry alarm clock was hungry.

CHAPTER 29

Instead of butterflies in my stomach, I had giant condors flying around in there.

It was time to put on my disguise. I wasn't ready. No. I had to be ready.

I was in the bathroom on the first floor, away from my coworkers. Except Brandi, who was helping me with my makeup.

"You really should think about dyeing your hair this color," she said. "It suits you."

"Been there, done that." I adjusted the wig with my fingers. "It's too hard to maintain the roots. I prefer my natural dark color."

"Yeah, I hear you." Brandi blended the blush on my cheeks with a brush. "It's a real pain to get your roots done every few weeks."

My stomach made a loud growling noise.

"Didn't you eat breakfast?" She put the makeup back in my bag.

"I forgot. Too nervous to eat, anyway." I tried to take in a calming breath, but it ended up sounding like a weird hiccup.

"Here." She pulled a protein bar out of her pocket. "Eat this. You need energy."

"Thank you." I took the bar and unwrapped it.

"I'll leave first and head back up on the elevator. Wait five minutes before you leave the bathroom—just like we talked about."

"Okay." I was shaking when she closed the door softly behind her. I stared at myself in the mirror. The red hair looked authentic, as did the green contact lenses covering my blue eyes. I could almost pass for Janice's sister.

My stomach growled again. I choked down half the protein bar, wishing that Brandi had brought a bottle of water as well.

"Breathe," I told myself. "You can do this."

Maybe if I pretended that I was an actress playing a role, I wouldn't be as nervous. That might work. Let's see, who was an actress with red hair? Julianne Moore. Yes. I would be Julianne Moore in a thriller—an FBI agent who's trying to catch a killer. Perfect. FBI agents were savvy and smart. They went undercover all the time to catch the bad guys.

I took in a deep breath and shook out my hands. "I'm ready." I slung my purse over my shoulder and stepped out of the bathroom.

The elevator dinged.

Holy crap! I dodged back into the bathroom and stepped into a stall. The door open and a woman came in.

She went into the stall next to me. I flushed the toilet quickly, washed my hands, and was out the door before she could catch a glimpse of me.

When I stepped out into the sunshine, I walked a few feet before a woman in her mid-thirties fell into step alongside me.

"Hi, Ashley," the police officer said, using my fake name. "I'm Sarah. Take a right here and stay with me."

So much for my disguise. She recognized me right away.

"Okay." I tried to act casual.

We reached a white van parked on the stub of a side street. I looked over my shoulder to see if anyone on the street was watching. No one was. That was a relief. I couldn't imagine what people would think if they saw two women get into a construction van.

The side door opened and we both climbed inside.

The van was filled with electronic equipment. Two male officers, dressed as construction workers, greeted me.

A fresh-faced young man introduced himself. "I'm Garrett. Have a seat." He pointed toward the bench seat in the middle.

The guy at the wheel turned and nodded at me. "I'm Brian. Nice to meet you."

"Clarity, but my undercover name is Ashley." My throat was dry, and it came out as a croak.

"Good code name. Everyone knows an Ashley," Brian said.

Garrett chuckled. "Sarah and I are going to get you wired up."

The police woman sat next to me and smiled. "Don't worry. You'll be fine. We have people inside the café already. And the building is completely surrounded with undercover officers." She reached into her bag and brought out a bottle of water. "Have a sip. You don't want to appear too nervous."

I nodded, feeling a little better after tipping the bottle to my lips. I drank another sip before giving it back to her.

A sudden thought popped into my head. "Where are Zen and Hunter? Aren't they supposed to be here, watching?"

"There in the pub next to the café," Sarah said. "They'll be right there if anything happens, as will an entire team of undercover officers located in the café and in the general vicinity."

"That's a relief," I said.

Garrett handed Sarah a tiny round device and some tape.

"Can you undo a couple of buttons for me?" She pointed to my blouse.

I did as she instructed, and she taped the tiny device into place, just under my collarbone. "Let's do another one in case this one dies."

Garrett handed her another one, which she adhered on the opposite side. He got out another little device and Sarah pushed my wig hair away from my ear. She fitted a little earbud inside and taped it to my ear. Then, she arranged the hair back in place, covering my ear completely.

I buttoned my shirt up and made sure the devices couldn't be seen by anyone.

"We just need to test both mics and then we're good to go." He turned on the recording device located in a panel on the side of the van. "Say something."

Sarah said, "Testing, one, two, three. Clarity, can you repeat that?"

"Testing, one, two, three."

The lights on the panel lit up as I spoke.

"Perfect," Garrett said. "When you head toward the café, I want you to keep talking. We'll let you know if the mic is working before you go into the café."

As we walked, Sarah chatted about the weather, as if it was just another day in sunny Seattle.

"Clarity?" A voice sounded in my ear. That was weird. It felt like Garrett was inside my head. "Can you hear me?"

"Yes," I answered.

Sarah gave me a thumbs-up. "Here we go."

We stood in front of the café. It was time to do this.

I opened the door and went inside. My eyes scanned the café, looking for the man I was supposed to meet.

"If you're wondering if Chris Smith is there," Garrett said in my ear, "he hasn't arrived yet. Sarah is going to get a table."

I started to answer, but he stopped me. "Don't say a word. You don't want people to see you talking to yourself." His voice was calm yet commanding. "Go ahead and order your coffee. When you've got it, sit at the table with Sarah. She'll get up, so Mr. Smith can find you alone."

I did exactly as I was told.

When I sat down at Sarah's table, she stood up. "I'm so sorry. I've got to get back to work." She exited the café, and I was left alone.

Between the wig covering my head and my jittery nerves, I started to sweat. What if the microphones slid off my skin? I fervently hoped they'd used moisture-proof tape.

I had to get a grip. I took a sip of my hot coffee. Why hadn't I ordered an iced coffee? That might've cooled me down.

My phone buzzed. It was a text from Jonah. "Office people left for a donut break."

Shoot. This was not good.

"There's a group of people coming your way," Garrett said in my ear.

I looked out the window. Crap. I watched a group of familiar faces heading straight toward the coffee shop. What if they recognized me?

Placing my coffee in front of my lips, I said as quietly as possible, "They're from work. What if they figure out it's me?"

Garrett was quiet a moment. "Get out your phone and keep your head down—like you're immersed in reading a text or something."

I already had my phone out, so I did as I was told.

The café door opened, and my coworkers got in line. I caught bits and pieces of their conversation.

"Our numbers aren't so good," George said. "I guess that means no bonus this year."

"Probably not." Bernard got his coffee. "Want me to grab a table?"

There was an empty table near me. I prayed they wouldn't sit there. They did.

I quickly turned my head and looked out the window again. Maybe if I kept my face hidden from them, they wouldn't realize who I was. Plus, I was wearing a wig and green contact lenses. Hopefully, it was enough to fool them.

When I glanced out the window again, my heart stopped. Russell and Paul were heading toward the café. Good lord! This was turning into a nightmare. Especially because Russell had a bad habit of staring at any woman he encountered. If he stared at my face long enough, he would definitely know it was me.

I looked down at my phone. It was one minute to eleven—the time I was supposed to meet the killer. My coworkers were about to ruin this entire setup. I took another sip of coffee to hide my lips, and whispered urgently, "My bosses are on the sidewalk. I'm sure they'll recognize me."

"Don't panic," Garrett said. "Let's see what happens."

He sounded calm, but I had a feeling he was ready to pull the plug on this whole thing.

Paul and Russell came closer. Paul glanced into the shop. His eyes lingered on George and Bernard, then toward me. Did he see me? Then, an annoyed look crossed his face. He pulled the phone out of his pocket and answered it. He said a few words and frowned as he spoke. He pointed back toward our office building.

Russell looked longingly at the café but nodded and followed Paul back to work.

I breathed in a deep breath and let it out slowly. Bullet dodged.

"It's four minutes after eleven," Garrett's voice said in my ear.

The killer was late. Was he already in the café somewhere? I held my phone up and pretended I was immersed in reading a text, while my eyes slid from side to side. There was a guy in a baseball cap sitting near the door. Was that him?

A woman entered the café and he stood up to greet her. Not him.

George and Bernard were here. They were talking animatedly about The Bathroom Buddy and how dumb it was. Neither one was here to meet a woman.

A few more tense minutes went by. No one fitting the description of Chris Smith entered the café. By this time, my nerves were officially shot.

"Five more minutes, Clarity," Garrett's said in my ear. "Then, we'll call it off."

"Okay," I whispered.

Turned out that five minutes can feel like two hours, if given the right circumstances. Every time the café door opened, my heart jumped.

"I'm calling it," Garrett said. "Sarah will be right there to get you."

Even though I'd been terrified the killer would come in and sit down across from me, now that he hadn't, I somehow felt disappointed. Why hadn't he shown up? Did something or someone tip him off?

The door opened, and Sarah entered. I stood up and tossed my coffee cup in the bin.

"Headed back to the office?" Sarah asked. "I'll walk with you."

I looked back to see if George or Bernard had noticed me. They were still immersed in conversation.

Sarah and I went back to the van, where I took off the mics and earpiece, then headed to the downstairs bathroom in my office building. I shed my wig, contact lenses, and outfit I'd been wearing and got back into the clothes I'd had on when I'd arrived this morning.

Back in the office, it took me at least an hour to get back into the groove of working.

A knock at the door startled me.

Brandi came in and sat down across from me. "I've been dying to find out what happened."

Two seconds later, Jonah came in and sat down next to Brandi.

"He didn't show up." I looked down at my hands.

"What?" Brandi's eyebrows rose. "After all that?"

"I know." I sighed. "I'm so disappointed in myself. Something must've scared him off."

"Could've been the massive police presence. Sometimes, when cops are undercover, they think they don't look like cops. They still do, in my humble opinion. I can spot them a mile away." Jonah leaned back in his chair.

"Oh, really?" Brandi grinned. "It sounds like you're speaking from experience. Do tell."

He frowned. "Let's just say that in college, I hung out with a wild crowd."

A giggle escaped my lips. With the way Jonah stuck to the rules and his perfectionist tendencies, I had a really hard time believing he'd been a badass. Ever. "Thanks, you guys."

"For what?" Jonah asked.

"For being such good friends."

***

The rest of the day, I poured my heart and soul into the job I now loathed. But I had a job to do. I was determined to make a big batch of lemonade from all the lemons I'd been dealt.

Russell called me into his office several times, piling more work on top of the pile that I'd already been toiling over.

Seven o'clock rolled around before I even knew it. "Pumpkin is going to be so mad." I packed up my laptop, grabbed my jacket, and headed for home.

CHAPTER 30

The next morning, I arrived in my office at six o'clock. No one else was there. I'd tossed and turned all night, and I felt like I'd been hit by a truck. Nevertheless, there were a ton of tasks that needed to get done.

I rolled up my sleeves and worked non-stop until my favorite person on the planet arrived.

"Venti Triple Americano with cream, please." I waited patiently, while Mr. Awesome made me the elixir of life.

"Here you go. Enjoy." He handed me the giant cup.

"You, sir, know how to make a girl happy. Thank you."

At nine o'clock, Brandi texted me. "Don't forget we have our employee evaluations today."

"Damn," I said out loud. I'd forgotten all about that. Every year, we went through a rigorous evaluation process. Last year, I'd gotten an excellent rating plus a raise.

I'd been working so much harder this year. But with all the weird stuff happening lately, I wondered if I'd get a raise at all.

I checked my schedule. My evaluation wasn't scheduled until three o'clock. Good. That meant I had time to finish booking all the details for GadgetCon, plus all the other stuff I needed to finish for marketing and automating the social media posts for each and every product we had on the market.

My phone buzzed. It was Hunter.

"You did a really good job yesterday," he texted.

"Yeah, right," I responded.

"No, you did! Sometimes the bad guys get a step ahead of us. This one is smart."

"Have you found out any more about him?" I texted.

"We have specialists working on tracing his online and email activity."

"Good. Let me know if you want me to message him to ask if we could reschedule the date," I texted.

"We already did. A specialist has taken over your Pursuit account and is trying to lure him."

"What? I should've done that." I was hurt. Didn't they hire me to do this?

"No. We've put you in too much danger already. If he goes for the date, we'll let you know."

I didn't respond. What the hell? I was the one who set this all in motion? Why wasn't Hunter letting me finish it?

Shaking off my irritation, I dove back into my work.

My timer went off a few minutes before my evaluation was to begin. I gathered up my completed pile of work and took it to Paul's office.

Paul's door was locked. That was odd. I rechecked the calendar on my cell phone. The appointment was listed. Three o'clock, employee evaluation.

Maybe Paul was with Russell. It made sense that they would both go over my evaluation since Russell had only been my boss for a short time. I walked down the hall to my old office. Russell was there alone, staring out the window.

"Ah, Clarity. Have a seat." He motioned toward the chair opposite his desk.

"Where's Paul?" I sat down. "I thought my evaluation was with him?"

He shook his head. "Paul was called out of the office before lunch to meet with a potential client. He told me to go ahead with your evaluation."

It felt weird for Russell to be doing my eval. I was used to meeting with Paul each year. Since Russell was my new boss now, it seemed reasonable.

"Okay, that's fine. Here." I pushed the pile of completed work toward him. "Those are the confirmations of market placement and distribution channels we talked about. Also, I completed the paperwork for every conference and event Opulent will be attending for the next year. All booths are arranged, set-up is scheduled, and hotel rooms have been confirmed, booked, and paid for."

I was proud of all that I'd accomplished. Should I be asking for a raise? Paul seemed against it, even though I was doing two fulltime jobs, if not three. But maybe Russell would think differently.

"Impressive. Thank you." Russell slid the paperwork into a bin on the corner of his desk. He opened a folder in front of him.

"Let's see here. You've done a nice job with scheduling and tracking details. That's fine. You got an average score for punctuality and work ethic. Though, I noticed you took an extra-long coffee break this morning."

I swallowed hard. Had he recognized me in the café?

"Uh, sorry. I've been working sixteen hours or more every day. I guess I needed the extra caffeine."

"That's why we have a barista here at the office. So employees don't have to leave." His bulgy eyes bored a hole through me.

Then why had half the office, plus he and Paul, wandered over to the café? Was I the only person being called out for this?

He looked back down at the paper in his folder. "You've had average marks across the board, mostly. But here's the part that concerns me. While you had above average sales on the BFF Bangle, the sales on both The Bathroom Buddy and The Womanizer have been absolutely dismal. Paul and I are very disappointed in your results."

My results? Maybe if Russell hadn't come with the worst product ideas ever, the numbers would be better. I couldn't just let him blame me for his mistakes.

"Perhaps it's the products themselves? Not to say that they aren't, uh, interesting products. But maybe if we had a few more cutting-edge products to sell, instead of ones with slightly outdated technology, we could sell more."

His eyes bulged more than normal. "Are you saying my product ideas are bad?"

"No. I shifted in my chair. "Not at all. I'm just saying that for the next products, I hope we try for newer and more current ideas and higher-tech designs."

Russell laughed, but it wasn't the amused kind of laugh. It was tinged with sarcasm. "So, your poor performance isn't to blame? Clarity, if I've told you once, I've told you a hundred times, a good salesperson should be able to sell just about anything."

My temper was rising, and I needed to get a handle on it. But he was being an ass. "I pulled out all the stops for those two products. I had the ad team delivering three different versions of ads, which we tested in every targeted market out there. I even set up a focus group to make sure we were hitting the mark. And you know what they said? They said they were ridiculous products, and not even their clutter-loving grandmothers would buy them."

Oops. I may have gone too far, but it was all true.

"How dare you!" Russell's face was beet red.

"I gave you the results of that market research. You knew this would be a hard sell." I jutted my chin out. "How can I be responsible for poor sales? I gave you all the information you needed. Those products should never have been released to the public. They were doomed to fail."

Russell leaned forward. "You know what else is doomed to fail?"

I gritted my teeth.

"Your career, Clarity. You are fired."

Fired? Now I'd done it. Why couldn't I have kept my mouth shut? Dread crept into the pit of my stomach. I was too angry to grovel and beg for forgiveness. I needed to collect my thoughts. I needed to talk to Paul instead of this idiot.

I got up to leave.

"And before you think of contacting Paul," Russel said, "he's already given me permission to let you go."

"What?" I narrowed my eyes. "You mean to tell me that you two planned this all along? You gave me triple the work responsibility, giving me my job, Janice's job, and your job. And when I can't sell the two worst product ideas in the history of all product ideas—you fire me? That's a set-up. Tell you what. You can discuss this with my lawyer. Because I'm filing a lawsuit against you, Paul, and Opulent."

Russell waved me away, like some kind of annoying insect buzzing in his ear.

Two big men I'd never seen before appeared in Russell's doorway. They were wearing dark uniforms with the word "Security" printed across their chests.

"These gentlemen will escort you back to your office, where you will pack up your belongings, and then you will exit the building. Goodbye, Clarity."

CHAPTER 31

On the walk of shame back to my office, my heart sank. What had I done? How did I go from busting my butt for this company to getting fired? It was like going from zero to sixty in a heartbeat.

Jonah entered the hall just as the goons and I approached my office door.

"Clarity, what's going on?" Jonah stood frozen, like a possum on his way across a busy road at night.

"Russell fired me."

"What?"

"You heard me." I opened my office door. "Could you grab a few boxes out of the copy room for me?"

"Uh, sure. Yeah." Jonah disappeared for a few minutes and came back with three good-sized boxes.

"Thanks." I began loading the boxes with my personal effects. Pictures of Janice and me, a coffee cup, the new rug I'd just purchased, and more.

When I reached for the laptop, the guards, or whatever they were, shook their heads. "That's company property," the bald one said. "You can't take that home."

"But I have a few personal things I need to get off of there."

The other guy grinned. "How personal?"

"Ew, yuck. Not that personal." What a pervert. "I have some photos of friends and family plus a few notes to myself that I'd like to keep."

The bald guy shrugged. "Okay. As long as you aren't taking any proprietary company documents or anything that belongs to the company at all, that should be fine."

Jonah distracted the goons with small talk, while I popped in a flash drive and transferred over my photos. My eyes flicked up to the guards. Technically, my email was mine, right? I quickly clicked "Export" on my email and saved the entire shebang to the flash drive. I needed these to prove to my lawyer—once I hired a lawyer—that I'd worked more than just about anyone at Opulent.

I pulled the flash drive out and put it in my purse.

The walk to the elevator was sheer humiliation. Everyone in the main room stopped what they were doing to watch me struggle to carry my boxes, with the guards flanking my sides.

Jonah carried the heaviest box for me, which was very nice of him. Brandi was across the room, her mouth hanging open. She rushed over and grabbed another box off the stack I precariously held in my arms.

"My God! What happened?" Her face wrinkled in concern.

One of the guards pushed the down button and the doors slid open. I hurried inside, trying not to catch anyone else's eye.

I breathed a sigh of relief when the doors closed. "Russell fired me," I said to her.

"What? How is that possible? You put in more hours than anyone else. This is insane." Brandi's face was turning red. Her temper was flaring—something that rarely happened.

The elevator pinged, and we headed into the parking garage to load up my Prius.

The guards stood and watched as I climbed into my car. I rolled down the window. "Will you guys keep me posted on the fallout?"

"Of course," Jonah said. "Can we take you out for dinner after we get off work tonight? To celebrate your—freedom?"

"That would be nice. Thank you." It was now that my emotions overtook me. "I'll talk to you later," I croaked. A sob escaped my lips, and I covered my mouth with my hand.

"Oh, Clarity." Brandi's look of sympathy nearly broke me.

I took a breath and said in the strongest voice I could muster, "I'll be all right."

"You will." Jonah patted my shoulder through the open window. "I know you will."

I gave them a little wave and drove out of the garage, tears streaking down my face. "Oh, Janice," I sobbed. "Life has been miserable since you left us."

✳✳✳

When I got home, I piled my boxes in the living room. I was so glad to be in my own home. My relief at being somewhere safe and private was palpable. I could put on my pajamas, eat ice cream, and watch sad movies until the cows came home.

And I could snuggle with my cat. Speaking of cats, where was my little guy? I needed him right now.

"Pumpkin!" I called out. "I'm home!"

I waited for a moment, but no orange feline came to greet me. Was he still mad that I'd gotten home so late last night?

"Pumpkin!" I went into the kitchen and opened the treat cupboard. Just hearing the creak of treat cupboard opening would bring him running. Worked every time.

Except this time.

I grabbed a box of his favorite snacks and rattled it. "Pumpkin!"

Nothing.

What on earth? I walked briskly to my bedroom and checked under the bed and in the closet. No cat. I looked in the adjoining bathroom. He wasn't there.

I ran upstairs to check the other bedrooms and bathroom.

Then, I remembered the deck. He was probably outside sunning himself on the deck and hadn't heard me come home.

When I got to the French doors that led to the deck, the hairs on my arm stuck straight up. I opened the door and stepped outside.

I'd had the part of the deck separate for Pumpkin fenced from the bottom to about seven feet high. The metal fencing also covered the top of that area, so that predators couldn't get to Pumpkin and so Pumpkin couldn't get out of the enclosed area. There was a gate for me to traverse between the people side of the deck and the kitty side of the deck.

My eyes searched first. No sign of him. The blood pounded in my ears. Where was Pumpkin?

I opened the gate to his deck. Maybe he was behind the big flowerpot in the corner. Peeking behind it, my heart sank. No Pumpkin.

Where could he be? He definitely wasn't inside the house. And he wasn't outside either. Could he have escaped the deck somehow? That seemed impossible. My eyes scanned the metal fencing. The top and sides looked fine.

When my eyes reached the section where the fencing met the floor of the deck, I noticed a break in the pattern. I got down on my hands and knees. The fencing had been cut away, making an opening the size of a bread box... or a cat.

The blood pounded in my ears. I sank to the deck on weak knees.

Someone had stolen Pumpkin.

CHAPTER 32

I only allowed myself a second to recover from the shock before I acted. Racing back through the gate and inside the house, I grabbed my cell phone off the counter where I'd left it. I had to call Zen to ask for help.

I let the phone ring until it kicked over to voice mail. Damn it! I tried Hunter's number next. Same deal. I didn't have time to leave voice mail. I was about to try Brandi when a text message arrived from a number I didn't recognize.

"Missing something?" it read.

Icy fear chilled my veins. What was happening?

"Who is this?" My fingers shook as I texted.

"If you want to see your cat alive, don't call the police or anybody else. I will know if you do. Your cat will die."

I swallowed hard, and texted, "Who are you? What do you mean you'll know if I do?"

"Stop asking questions. All you need to know is that I'm tracking you. I know where you are, and I know who you call."

Fighting the urge to ask how, I took a breath and texted, "What do you want me to do?"

"Head toward Northgate Mall. Your cat will be dead if you don't show up."

"Where in Northgate Mall?" I texted, my heart pounding so loud I thought the neighbor might hear it. I couldn't comprehend who this person was and why he wanted me to go to a mall.

"Parking lot. More information coming in fifteen minutes. Remember, do not call or text anyone or I'll know. Go now."

Oh my God. This couldn't be happening. Chris Smith had Pumpkin, and he was luring me to my death with my very own sweet cat. If I didn't do what he said, he'd kill Pumpkin for sure. Maybe he already had. I had to think this through, but there was no time.

I ran to my bedroom and changed into jeans and a t-shirt. I pulled a hoodie over my head and ran to the kitchen. What kind of weapon should I take with me? Something that wasn't obvious. No baseball bats or golf clubs. I cursed Zen for discouraging me from getting a gun.

My eyes scanned the kitchen. A knife? Maybe two. A grabbed a small butcher knife from the drawer and wrapped the blade in a hand towel. I shoved it into the front pouch of my hooded sweatshirt. Then, I pulled a smaller paring knife out of the wooden block on the counter top and put it in my back pocket. I sure hoped it wouldn't poke me in the butt while I drove. I'd worry about that later. Pumpkin's life was in danger.

I grabbed my purse and flew out the door.

***

Fifteen minutes later, I sat in the Northgate Mall parking lot. Sweat dripped down the back of my neck as I stared at my phone, waiting for the next text.

My cell buzzed. It was Brandi. "Where are you? Jonah and I are here to pick you up. I thought we were going out to dinner and drinks."

I wasn't supposed to call or text anyone. I couldn't respond or else Pumpkin would die.

The phone buzzed again. "Drive to Everett Mall. I'll text you in thirty minutes," the killer texted. "And if you tell your friends or anyone else about this, I'll know."

Thirty minutes.

Could I even get there in thirty minutes? Rush hour was in full swing. I opened my traffic app and let it pick the fastest route to Everett Mall. The app said it would take twenty-eight minutes. I hoped it was right.

Back on the freeway, my mind raced. Where was this guy leading me? Why would he take Pumpkin to Everett? How did he find out who I was? Had he been in the coffee shop this morning and followed me?

A chill ran down my spine. I desperately wanted to call my brother or Hunter. They would know what to do. But if I did, the killer would end Pumpkin's life.

The phone lit up several times with text messages from both Brandi and Jonah. They seemed annoyed. I hoped they would figure out something was wrong and call my brother.

Tears ran down my cheeks as I changed lanes and haphazardly dodged traffic, which wasn't easy in a Prius. The kidnapper said he'd know if I sent texts. Could he also see my incoming messages? How was he tracking my phone?

Another text from Brandi came through. "We figured you might be out for shopping therapy. Take your time. We'll be at Bizarro's."

My heart sank. If they weren't expecting me until later, they wouldn't be calling Zen or Hunter.

One more text from Brandi appeared. "Oh, and guess what? I poked around in Russell's expense reports from July. I found something odd. Russell sent Janice flowers in July— just a week before she was killed. I sent Zen a text. Let's talk about it when you get here."

My heart banged like a drum. Russell sent Janice flowers? Why hadn't she told me?

Finally, I arrived at Everett Mall, just in the nick of time. As soon as I found a parking spot, my phone buzzed.

"Ready for more instructions?"

"Yes," I texted.

"Drive to Burlington Mall," the killer texted.

What in the world? That was at least forty-five minutes to an hour away. Why was he stringing me along like this? I clenched my jaw and texted, "Okay."

By this time, my phone had buzzed with texts from both Brandi and Jonah. I was much later than they thought I'd be, and now they were concerned. Hunter and Zen had both texted as well, since they'd received alarming texts and a phone call from Brandi.

Then, a thought struck me. Was this really the killer who was texting me, or was it some weird cat kidnapper? If that was the case, why hadn't he asked for a ransom? No, that was an irrational thought. It had to be the man who'd killed Janice and those other women he'd murdered and deposited in dumpsters.

I slogged through traffic, my mind racing to figure a way out of this. Would he be waiting for me in the Burlington Mall parking lot? Or would he make me drive to Canada? Joke's on him if he did. My passport had just expired. But then, I guess the joke would be on Pumpkin if I couldn't get to him.

My poor baby! Had that monster already killed him?

Tears threatened to spill down my cheeks, but I refused to cry. I had to be strong to get through this. And I had to have a clear head.

"Janice, if you can hear me up in heaven, please help me and Pumpkin."

As I thought of her untimely and violent death, the anger inside me began to take root. It focused my attention and gave me purpose. I rolled down the window to feel the air on my face. Since my concentration was better now, I wanted to keep it that way.

The scent of warm earth and evergreen trees rushing through the window honed my senses. I could do this.

I arrived at the Burlington Mall and found a parking spot in the last row, closest to the freeway. Staring at my phone, I waited for the anonymous text to come through. I got out of the car and stretched. I patted the knife in my front hoodie pocket and the one in my back jeans pocket. They were right where they were supposed to be.

A few minutes later, my phone buzzed.

"You're in Burlington," he texted.

"Yes."

"Go to this address. 5512 Juniper Road."

I stared at the screen. 5512 Juniper Road. Oh, dear lord.

That was my parents' address.

CHAPTER 33

I jumped into the car and started it up.

Oh my God. He had my cat. He had my parents.

Anger and fear boiled inside me. He had killed my best friend. Now, he wanted to kill me and everyone I loved.

I tore out of the parking lot and headed for my parents' house.

By now, the sun was a little lower in the sky. Dusk was fast approaching. I wanted to get out there before darkness enveloped the landscape. I wanted to meet this man head on and see him for what he was in broad daylight—a stone cold killer. I would not let him kill my family. I would get him before he got us.

My traffic app said I'd get there in twenty minutes.

I made it in fifteen.

The sky was still somewhat light when I turned onto Juniper Road. I parked away from the house. I didn't want Chris Smith to see me drive up. I wanted to catch him by surprise.

The lights were on in the new addition of Mom and Dad's place, but the main house was dark. I was sure they were in the bed and breakfast wing.

Making as little sound as possible, I snuck up the dirt road and hunkered down in the bushes close to the house. A mosquito buzzed in my ear. I swatted it away, hoping it would leave me alone. I couldn't afford distraction.

Before I got anywhere near their house, I turned my phone to silent and placed a call to my brother.

"Clarity? Are you okay?"

"Shhh," I whispered. "I'm at Mom and Dad's. He's here, Zen. And he's got our parents and Pumpkin."

"What do you mean?" Zen's voice was charged with alarm.

"He's going to kill them. He lured me here by stealing Pumpkin from my house."

There was a long pause, then he said, "Clarity, we're already on our way. Brandi shared your location from her phone with us. Get away from there as fast as you can."

"I can't. He said he'd kill Mom and Dad if I didn't come to him."

He started to argue.

"Hush. I can't talk, but I'm leaving my phone on." I slipped my phone, still connected to Zen, in my other back pocket—the one without the paring knife.

I snuck closer to the house and carefully rose up enough to peek through the window. Mom and Dad were tied up and bound to chairs. Pumpkin paced back and forth between their legs, clearly upset.

But where was Chris Smith? I had to get him in my sight, so he couldn't sneak up on me. I creeped along the edge of the house, my knees low as I crouched down below the window's edge. My heart threatened to explode with my growing panic.

A twig snapped somewhere to my right. I froze.

I didn't dare to breathe, unwilling to make even the tiniest of noise.

Expecting to see a man come out from behind the rhododendron bush to my right, my hand automatically reached for the knife in my hoodie pocket.

Suddenly, a squirrel emerged from under the bush, carrying a nut in his tiny teeth.

I let out a whoosh of air, relieved that I wouldn't have to face the killer for at least a few more minutes.

I got back to the business of locating Chris Smith. I needed to see him in the room with my parents and Pumpkin, so I could catch him by surprise or lure him out, and then face him on my terms.

Peeking into the side window, my mom caught sight of me. Her eyes grew wide, and she shook her head furiously.

"Mom?" I whispered hoarsely.

My phone buzzed. I glanced at the screen.

"Welcome home," it read.

The blow to the back of my head made my eyes flutter for a second before everything went black.

✳✳✳

The sharp pain radiating in my head woke me up.

My eyelids practically groaned with effort as they opened.

I was tied with my hands behind my back, on one of the new wooden dining chairs in Mom and Dad's bed and breakfast wing. I struggled to free my hands to no avail.

The large kitchen knife I'd stowed in the front pocket of my hoodie lay on the table in the middle of the room.

Mom and Dad were bound and strapped to chairs too. They had duct tape strapped across their mouths, so they couldn't speak or scream. Their faces were bruised and bloodied.

Dad had tears streaming down his ruddy cheeks, and in his eyes I saw an apology.

For what? I wondered. I should be the one who was sorry.

Pumpkin was at my feet, meowing pitifully.

A man's voice coming from behind me jolted me completely awake. "Your cat is a pathetic and annoying creature. I should've killed it at your house. But then, I wouldn't have been able to lure you here. You seem to care more about that thing than you do your parents."

The voice was familiar. Where had I heard it before?

He stepped out into my view.

My eyes widened in shock. "Paul?"

Paul Walker, my former boss, stood relaxed as he gave me a cold grin. "The one and only."

"I… I don't understand. Why are you doing this?" I knew I must've sounded ridiculous. Why does any psychopath kill innocent people?

"Because I can," he answered without haste. "I'm always the smartest person in the room, Clarity. I enjoy fooling the police. Their ignorance and stupidity never ceases to amaze me."

"You're killing women because you like fooling the police?"

He chuckled. "Well, that's only part of it. I kill certain people because they are doing harm to our society."

"What are you talking about?" Anger bloomed in my chest. "You think Janice was doing harm to society? She was a good person, and you know it!"

"Janice?" He flicked his hand, as if she were an insignificant insect buzzing around his ears. "No. But she was doing harm to me. She discovered my secret by uncovering a little evidence I'd left behind at the office. Of course, I didn't know this until she set up a date with me on Pursuit. I was quite surprised to see her. I had to kill her before she exposed me. Unfortunately, there was no time to properly dispose of her body. I normally like to, shall we say, spread the evidence around?" He laughed. "I have to admit, she was a clever little thing. She caught me off guard."

"What evidence did she find?" I said, trying to stall. Maybe the police would show up soon.

He shook his head with disdain. "I'd forgotten to lock my screen while I left for the bathroom one night. She came in to ask me a question and saw the Pursuit website. Apparently, she also found my bloody shirt peeking out of the garbage can next to my desk. It was careless of me, I know. I'd planned on taking that garbage with me on my way out of the office to dispose of it somewhere. I didn't think anyone else was at the office that late at night. And I didn't even know what she'd seen—until she confronted me on our 'date.'"

"That's why she joined Pursuit? Because she thought she could stop you? Why didn't she tell the police?" I couldn't believe Janice had been more reckless than I'd been.

He smirked. "She said she had to be sure. She'd heard about a murder the day she'd discovered the shirt in my garbage. A body I'd left in the SeaTac area. Just another one of those whores on the SeaTac strip. It was all just practice for the real murders to come."

My stomach dropped, and my mind raced to work out a way to stall him. I needed to keep him talking. I brought the conversation back to what he'd said earlier. "You said you targeted people who did harm to society. What did you mean by that?"

Pumpkin plastered himself against my legs and let out a pitiful meow.

Paul sneered in disdain. "Women. Women who think they have to have a career—and children."

I frowned. "I don't understand."

My hands, which were tied behind my back with zip ties, just happened to be in the right position for me to reach the paring knife in my back pocket. I said a silent prayer of gratitude that Paul hadn't discovered it when he'd bound my hands behind my back.

"Whores—just like my mother." He let out a half hysterical bark of laughter. "Oh, she thought she wanted it all. Except when it came to raising me. She discovered that having it all wasn't really what she wanted. She left me when I was eight years old. Eight!"

Not knowing how to respond, I just said, "I'm sorry."

With the dexterity of a surgeon, I slowly but steadily pulled the paring knife out and clutched it tightly. If I dropped it, I would lose my last chance to get out of this alive.

"You're sorry that my mom left me with a dad who never once told me he loved me? Are you sorry that he left me alone for hours and hours while he went to the bar with his buddies? Are you sorry that Daddy Dear blamed me for

Mommy Dearest leaving and beat me every single day thereafter?"

He began pacing around the room, raking his fingers through his hair. "She left so she could go back to the career she loved. An executive in a major Fortune 500 company— all the way across the country. Do you know how many times she called to check on me?"

I shook my head.

"How about never? She never called to see if I was okay. She knew my dad was a drunk. She left me with a cold-hearted, abusive excuse of a man."

I began sawing through the zip tie gently, trying not to make a sound.

"That's awful." I tried my best to convey sympathy without being over the top. I didn't want him to think I was trying to trick him with false empathy. I needed to keep him talking.

"Is that why you married Audrey?" I asked. "Because she's the opposite of women like your mom?"

He straightened his shoulders. "Exactly. She's only ever wanted to be a mother. And she takes excellent care of our children."

Mom was watching us talk. Her eyes darted to my back. She must've seen what I was doing with the knife. She blinked in acknowledgment of my mission.

I kept talking. "So, if you're eliminating career women who also want to have children, why did you kill the 'whore,' as you call her, at SeaTac?"

He rolled his eyes, as if I was stupid for asking such a childish question. "Obviously, because those kinds of women are also a scourge to society. And by killing them, I have the added bonus of throwing the police off. I don't want cops alarming the public if too many career-driven women go missing."

"Smart," I said. The zip tie was severed. I held onto it and the small knife, so he wouldn't suspect I was free. "Is Russell somehow involved with this?"

Paul made a raspberry noise. "Russell. Russell's an idiot. But he knows just enough about me and my online dating habit that I had to give him that raise. Plus, he threatened to tell my wife."

"And you gave him my office," I added.

He laughed. "Ah, that was payback. It felt so good to take that office away from you."

A twinge of anger and sadness seethed inside me. "Why? What did I do to deserve that?"

"Come on, Clarity. Your brother, the homicide detective, just couldn't leave well enough alone. He interviewed me one time too many. I couldn't have the police breathing down my neck while trying to run a business. Someone had to pay for that. That someone was you. Besides, you fit the type of woman I can't stand. The kind who values her career over family."

None of what he was saying was making sense to me. It occurred to me how flawed and twisted his reasoning had become.

"You had me fired because of my brother?"

"Well, in part. Russell can't stand you either. He sensed your disdain for his stupid product ideas."

"You have to admit—his ideas are ridiculous."

He nodded. "Maybe so. But the last straw was that set-up you pulled at the café. My senses were alerted when I noticed how many people were trying to look casual on the sidewalk. Then, when I looked inside, I saw you in that preposterous disguise."

"I thought it was pretty good." I tried to remain calm and sound conversational. Then, if I saw a chance to rush him, I might be able to catch him completely off guard.

"You know what gave you away?" Paul smirked. "It was your pink phone case. I've never seen anyone else with that pink case."

I cursed my habit of shopping on Etsy. Buying from artists who created unique products was my downfall.

"And of course, I knew your phone from earlier." The corner of his mouth twitched. "Remember when you left it in the conference room? I took the opportunity to install an invisible tracking app I could link to my phone before I gave it back to you."

I cursed under my breath. That devious creeper.

Pumpkin stalked over to where my parents were tied up.

Paul took his eyes off me for a moment, following Pumpkin's motion.

Now was my chance.

I jumped forward, knife in hand.

Paul turned his head, but too late. I was on him. Before he realized what was happening, I jabbed the paring knife into the side of his neck.

He shrieked and floundered backward, pulling the knife out of his flesh. Blood spurted out in a steady stream and dripped between his fingers.

The pain ignited his anger, turning his face purple with rage. "I'll kill you!"

He lunged toward me.

Suddenly, Pumpkin leaped out of nowhere and flew at Paul, biting his leg. Paul kicked out, sending my cat flying.

Anger burned inside me. How dare he hurt my baby!

Mom and Dad squirmed in their chairs, trying to free themselves.

My eyes landed on the table where my large kitchen knife sat, wrapped partially in a towel.

Paul's gaze followed mine.

He took one look back at me and then lunged toward the big knife.

I catapulted myself at the table, reaching for the weapon.

He reached the knife before I could. I screamed with rage as he grabbed me with his other hand and held my back tightly to his chest.

Sirens wailed in the distance.

Paul dragged me past my parents, who struggled and rocked their chairs, trying to get loose.

He kicked the door open and lifted me off my feet while he stumbled toward the dense brush. Blood trickled down the back of my neck, where his wound was still gushing.

The sirens grew louder.

Remembering that my phone was still on and connected to Zen's line, I screamed as loud as I could. "Help! He's taking me into the bushes past the chicken coop!"

"You've got your phone on," he growled. His hands groped my body, searching for it. He found it in my back pocket, turned it off, and threw it into the bushes. Then, he put his bloody hand over my mouth and tightened his hold on me.

I couldn't let him pull me into the brush.

Though I knew time was zipping by at lightning speed, suddenly everything seemed as though it were happening in slow motion. My senses were heightened, and my brain cleared. My thoughts went straight to Hunter's self-defense course.

Paul held me from behind, dragging me into the heavy brush. The line of trees behind the bushes would soon camouflage me from the police. The time for me to act was now.

Paul's hand was covering my mouth. I bit down hard on the top edge of his palm, while kicking my foot backward into his shin.

He loosened his hold as he screamed in pain. Reflexively, he used his other hand to grab my throat.

I choked but managed to wrench myself free of his grip and face him.

He was slightly bent over, but not so much that I couldn't get him where it hurt. I grabbed him by the shoulders and brought my knee up hard into his groin.

Paul doubled over and cried out in pain.

Using my elbow, I brought it down like a hammer to his back, sending him sprawling on the ground.

"Freeze!" a man shouted.

My eyes caught the glare of a police cruiser's headlights. Several more vehicles pulled in next to it, sirens wailing.

I stood stock still, my hands raised.

Paul groaned. The ground beneath his head was stained with the blood of his neck wound. His fingers twitched.

"It's the guy on the ground! Paul Walker!" I shouted into the bright lights. "He's the killer—and he's injured. Call an ambulance!"

"Are you Clarity?" the cop asked.

"Yes."

"Okay, ma'am, stay right there."

Two uniformed officers silhouetted in glare of the headlights made their way toward me. One of them gently touched my elbow and led me away from Paul, while the other trained his gun on the injured killer.

"My parents," I croaked.

"Where are they?" the officer asked. "Are they hurt?"

I pointed toward the house. "I don't know. They're tied up. Can you check on them? And my cat?"

As more police cars and an ambulance littered the driveway, I pulled the officer with me to the bed and breakfast side of the house. "They're in there. I'll show you."

"Wait." He turned to block me. "You need medical attention. That's quite the bump on your head. And you're bleeding."

I glanced back at the medics putting Paul on a stretcher. "I think it's mostly his blood. I kind of stabbed him in the neck with a paring knife."

His eyebrows rose. "Wow. Tough lady. Okay, we'll go in together, but if I sense that you're not doing well, I'm taking you straight to the ambulance."

I nodded. My head ached, but I had to see if my parents were all right.

When we entered the house, Mom and Dad were still tied up, their eyes red from crying.

I rushed over to my mom and gently peeled the duct tape away from her mouth.

"Clarity!" Mom sobbed. "We thought he'd killed you."

I kneeled beside her and laid a hand on her knee. "I'm okay, Mom. I got him before he got me."

The officer peeled the tape from my dad's mouth.

"That's my girl!" Dad could hardly contain his pride. "Did you kill him?"

I shook my head. "I don't think so. But I hurt him pretty bad."

Pumpkin appeared from behind the couch facing the fireplace. He purred loudly and hopped into my arms. His eye was swollen shut where Paul had kicked him.

"Oh, my poor kitty." I kissed the top of his head. "We need to get you to the vet."

I stood up with him in my arms, and my vision blurred. "Oh!" I stumbled a few steps, dizziness throwing me off balance.

Strong arms caught me as I pitched forward. The scent of bergamot and sandalwood lingered as darkness enveloped me once again.

***

"Clarity?"

My eyes fluttered open.

A gorgeous, dark-eyed man looked down at me. Was I dead? If so, this was what heaven must look like.

My vision went from blurry to clear after a heartbeat, and I recognized the handsome man peering anxiously at my face.

"Hunter?" I tried to sit up.

"Oh, no you don't." He gently pushed my head and shoulders down on one of the pillows from the couch. "The EMTs will be here in just a second. We had to get another ambulance for you. Paul's on his way to the hospital."

"What about my parents?" I tried lifting my head again, but the sharp pain throbbing at the back of my neck got the better of me.

"They're fine." He patted my shoulder. "Zen took them to the hospital. Both of them have cuts and bruises. Your dad was having slight chest pains—probably from all the stress. He just wanted them to get checked out to be sure they're both all right."

I sighed in relief. "Okay." Then I remembered my cat. "Pumpkin!"

Hunter held my hand and squeezed. "One of the officers took him to the local vet. Don't worry. I'm sure he'll be all right."

I let myself relax just a bit. "I hope so."

Hunter cleared his throat. "Clarity, you were amazing. You took down an extremely dangerous serial killer. We suspect there at least three more women he may have killed, and possibly more. There may be more body parts in dumpsters all around the Seattle area."

An involuntary shudder ran down my spine. "And to think, I worked for him for over two years and had no idea what kind of person he really is."

"How could you know? He's smart and determined to kill." Hunter clenched his jaw. "You got his confession on your phone. Did you know that? That alone should put him away for the rest of his life."

"Did you suspect it was Paul?" I asked.

I paused for a moment. "We knew there was something off about him. Last week, we interviewed Bill quite extensively."

"The janitor?" I tried lifting my head again. "So that's who you had in the conference room for so long! We were trying to figure out who you were talking to. Was he a part of Paul's killing spree?"

Hunter shook his head. "No. But when he emptied the garbage in Paul's office, he saw a man's shirt stained with blood."

"And he didn't call the police?"

"He just figured that Paul had accidentally cut himself or something. He didn't have any reason to believe his boss was a serial killer."

"But—the shirt. The blood must've matched one of the victims. Why didn't you arrest Paul after you were told about the shirt?" I rubbed my forehead, where a headache had been steadily building since I woke up.

"Bill didn't keep the shirt. It went out with all the other office garbage that day. There was nothing to test. Paul was getting cocky—and sloppy. In his position of power, he didn't think anyone would question him."

I let that sink in. "And Russell? Did he have a part in this?"

"Russell knew just enough to blackmail Paul, according to his confession to us just an hour after he fired you. Then, because we heard your conversation with Paul when you left your cell open for us to hear, we discovered he knew about Paul's online dating. He thought his boss was having an affair, but he didn't know about the murders."

I barked out a laugh. "He knew enough to get a promotion, take my office, and then fire me. I hope you can convict Russell of something."

"You can't put someone in jail for being an a-hole."

I shifted on the couch trying to get more comfortable. "I guess you're right."

"And one other thing," Hunter said. "On the way over here, we got a report from our investigative team. The FCC reported that someone was selling off shares of Opulent's stock. We think it was Paul, and he was preparing to run right after he sewed up some loose ends." He pointed at me.

I gritted my teeth. "I'm glad you nailed him before he killed me, Mom and Dad, and Pumpkin." It was horrifying to think what could've happened. Would he have gone after Jonah and Brandi too?

Two EMTs rushed through the door with a stretcher. "Let's get you to the hospital," the stocky one said.

Hunter stepped back to let the men do their job. Once I was strapped onto the stretcher, he held my hand and climbed into the ambulance with me.

"Are you sure Zen would approve of this?" I glanced at his hand in mine.

"Zen ordered me to make sure you were taken care of." He winked at me.

For the first time all day, I smiled.

CHAPTER 34

"Grab that goat!" I ran for the fence, where a dip in the ground had left just enough room for a small goat to squeeze through.

In a swift and agile motion, Zen grabbed the brown and white spotted animal and tucked it under his arm. "Dad, we need another board over here."

Dad took a board from the stack behind the chicken coop and kneeled next to the dip in the ground. He lined up the plank and nailed it into place. "There." He got up and brushed the dirt off his jeans. "That ought to do it."

Zen set the little goat down and it ran off to join the others.

My eyes skimmed my parents' property, where all eight of my brothers and sisters were working on building a patio with brick pavers.

"Hey, Wanda!" Dad shouted. "Can you bring the lavender lemonade out? It's getting hot out here."

"In a minute," Mom called from somewhere inside the house. "I have to get these chickens out of the kitchen."

I laughed and went to join my siblings. "Need a hand?"

"Sure," my sister, Karma, said. "Can you wheel over that bag of sand?"

I pushed the wheelbarrow over to where she was working.

"Just dump it here." She pointed to the bare ground, which had already been leveled and smoothed, ready for the sand to be put down.

My younger brother, Birch, was laying the pavers down in a neat pattern in the sand and tamping them down as we went. "This is going to look great when it's all done."

I nodded. "Thanks for coming to help. It's been a while since we've all been together."

"Way too long." Karma spread the sand out with a shovel. "I guess it takes almost losing our parents and you for us to have some family time. That's a very sad commentary."

"It really is. I feel so guilty for not making more of an effort." I grabbed another shovel and helped spread the sand over the even ground.

"We're all guilty of it—not just you." Birch finished a row of pavers and started on the next.

Deep down I knew that how we grew up had affected all of us. Our childhood had been good in some ways. We'd never been lonely and had always had some sort of project to work on together, depending on our parents' whims. There'd been laughter, love, and plenty of fun. But with such a large family to take care of, we'd also had an enormous burden to shoulder at a young age.

For me, it meant I had to work menial jobs during my teen years just to help put food on the table. And we were homeschooled for most of my elementary and middle school years, making it difficult to make or keep friendships outside our family.

I knew that my siblings and I often resented the way we were raised, but now, as I looked around at the fellowship and teamwork between my siblings, I realized that maybe we didn't have it so bad after all.

✳✳✳

The sun was shining brightly as I opened the hatch to my Prius. "I can't believe you couldn't fit all your stuff in your cars." I glanced across the parking lot at the other employees packing up their vehicles.

Brandi leaned up against her car and shrugged. "Well, we thought we'd be at Opulent for a long time. We practically lived there. But now that everyone knows our CEO is a serial killer, there's no way the company can continue—even if new leadership takes over."

"Yeah." Jonah lifted a box and placed it in the back of my car. "But now we have to cart all this stuff back to our homes. And speaking of homes, how are we even going to pay our mortgage now that the company is closed?"

"Maybe we can refinance our loans," Brandi offered. She frowned. "That's not easy when you don't have a job."

I couldn't wait to get their reaction after I told them what I'd discovered on the way over. "This morning, I noticed that a cute little shop on the corner of my street has a 'For Lease' sign on it..."

Brandi furrowed her brows. "And?"

"Remember how you told me once that you've always wanted to open your own little business?" I asked.

Brandi smiled. "Yeah," she said dreamily. "I'd do bookkeeping and taxes for small businesses. I could work at my own pace and provide excellent customer service to my clients."

I grinned. "Jonah, what did you tell me about wanting to do freelance design work?"

"I said I wanted to have a boutique design studio." He cocked his head to one side. "Where are you going with this?"

"Personally, I think it would be great to open up my own private investigation business—and be a social media consultant on the side." I picked up another box and loaded it into my car. "Wouldn't it be fun to share an office? Say, the one near my house in Wallingford? We all live close by, and our commute time would be nearly non-existent."

I watched as both Brandi's and Jonah's expressions went from confusion to understanding, and then to excitement.

Brandi's hand flew to her mouth. "Oh my God! Do you really think we can do that?"

Jonah's wide smile lit up his face. "Why not? What have we got to lose?"

"Just all of our savings if we don't make money." Brandi's practical nature always seemed to make an appearance when ideas were flowing.

"I checked with the property owner, and he's willing to let us sign a six-month lease. We'd be splitting the rent three ways. And the rent isn't as high as I thought it would be."

A few moments of silence ticked by. I looked from one friend to the other. "Well, what do you think?"

They both threw their arms around me in an awkward group hug.

"We're in!" Brandi giggled.

"Jonah?" I lifted my head and waited for his answer.

"It's a no-brainer." He broke our huddle and stepped back with a grin. "Let's do it."

ABOUT THE AUTHOR

Martina Dalton writes young adult fiction and lives in the Pacific Northwest with her family. Born and raised in Alaska, she can nimbly catch a fish, dress for rain, and know what to do when encountering a grizzly bear. Now living in the Seattle area, she uses those same skills to navigate through rush-hour traffic.

If you liked this book, please consider leaving a review!

Visit the website at **www.martinadalton.com** to join my mailing list and get the latest news on upcoming books, giveaways, and more!

I love connecting with readers, so please don't hesitate to follow me on Instagram at martinadaltonauthor or Facebook at AuthorMartinaDalton/!

Other books by Martina Dalton
The Third Eye of Jenny Crumb
The Sixth Sense of Jenny Crumb
The Nine Lives of Jenny Crumb
The Witching Hour: Jenny Crumb
Night Collector: Jenny Crumb
Jenny Crumb and the Twelve Days of Christmas (novella)

If you liked Killer Bait, stay tuned for the next books in the series coming soon!

ACKNOWLEDGMENTS

As always, I'd like to give special thanks to my writing critique partners, Brenda Beem, Dennis Robertson, Fabio Bueno, Suma Subramaniam, Maren Higbee, and Eileen Riccio. They are simply the best! I'd also like to thank my wonderful editor, Alyssa Palmer. Last but not least, I'd like to give a shout out to my sweet family. They are always there for me when I need them.

Thanks for reading! Please add a short review on Amazon and let me know what you thought!

Visit the website at **www.martinadalton.com** to join my mailing list and get the latest news on upcoming books, giveaways, and more!